For Hazard as ~
~ of old times ~

~ Ralph

Rue the Day

A Novel

by Ralph Freedman

Twilight Times Books
Kingsport Tennessee

Rue the Day

Twilight Times Books
P O Box 3340
Kingsport, TN 37664
www.twilighttimesbooks.com/

First Edition: April 2009

Library of Congress Cataloging-in-Publication Data

Freedman, Ralph
Pending

Cover design by Ardy M. Scott

Photo credit: Canwell Committee protestors outside Armory, July 20, 1948. Courtesy of Seattle Post-Intelligencer Collection, Museum of History & Industry. [PI 21683]

Printed in the United States of America

For Ruth, my daughter
Who had just begun

Acknowledgments

Throughout the years I have worked on this book, I have been indebted to my friend of half a century, Florence Byham Weinberg, a family member indeed, who steadfastly believed in my work and what I sought to achieve. She contributed decisively to its conception and led me to the discovery of a new sense for the language of fiction designed to make my characters and scenes more believable and real. Her critiques—of both criticism and approval—were a constant support. Nothing can fully express my gratitude for her decisive help.

My warmest thanks go also to Lesly Fredman, a fine editor, who helped perceptively and with great skill throughout the text. She showed an uncanny sense for just the right phrase, for just the right moment to reveal a character or scene, particularly in the resolution of this book. Her expertise was as invaluable as her friendship.

Gerald Oppenheimer shared with me his intimate knowledge of the place and history of Seattle and the Pacific Northwest. I owe him my appreciation for providing details of the arena in which the Canwell Committee could operate at the time, which would have been long and arduous to acquire, and which formed the foundation of my research. Thanks, Gerry, for putting me again in touch with the world of my generation.

Anca Vlasopolis, always a stalwart supporter, stuck with my project throughout times of questioning and doubt, and her poetic sensibility helped guide my style. My thanks to her and her husband Anthony Ambrogio for their many patient readings.

Juliet Popkin—my former agent and friend of a near-lifetime—was extremely helpful in the early stages of my work with constant encouragement and many perceptive suggestions. But beyond my work, she and her late husband, the philosopher Richard Popkin, are part of one generation that left its mark on my book. I thank her especially for the link with my past which she brought into my life.

In recent years, I benefited especially from two sound judgments. Ann Mahoney read an early version with a sharp eye to details of language and dialogue, from which *Rue the Day* benefited until the end. She conceived a love and affection for my characters, which made her comments extraordinarily helpful. Similarly, Edna McCown's careful reading of the manuscript suggested several scenes, which turned out to be vital to the development of my story.

To them and many others who read and often helped in the book, I express my deepest thanks.

Prologue

Wars, all wars, create winds of chaos that blow long after the last shot is fired. World War II was no exception. Jacob and Francesca, like Dante's Paolo and Francesca, are caught up in those winds. Jacob, haunted by overwhelming fear caused by persecution in his past, damages himself and those he loves. Francesca, hardened by the war, finds it impossible to forgive.

Part One

Jacob's Trial

The chairman rapped his gavel. "Jacob Becher, state your name for the record. Clearly, please."

An eerie silence reigned.

The road that began on a snowy mountain was nearing its disastrous end.

A Time of Becoming
(1945-1947)

Chapter 1
Fiery Encounter

Jacob Becher pushed the tent flap aside and exhaled a lungful of the stale air he'd endured for hours. The snores of the three men behind him in their sleeping bags blended with the whistle of the sharp wind blowing from the mountains. The chill of icy fresh air took his breath away, and a tear threatened to freeze on his cheek. It must be somewhere around zero. His first step proved that; he slipped and almost fell on the frozen footpath. Last night's snow had melted, and the slush had turned into ugly jagged ice. He looked northward at the Apennines across the valley. This damned hostile wind came from those mountains on the other side, where the Germans were entrenched.

He was afraid. He had fled Germany with his parents in February 1939 when he was still twenty-three, propelled by fear of further persecution as a dissident Jew. The entire family immigrated together to the United States. Never since his flight had he felt such intense dread of the enemy. Still, he had to do his duty.

Colonel Riggs had called him into his trailer last night.

"Yes, sir?"

The old man grinned. "At ease, Becher. I've got a new assignment for you. A snap. All you have to do is take your jeep close to those mountains and meet an Italian partisan—a *partigiana*, actually. They tell me she's been working with the Resistance. She'll pass you some documents from where she worked undercover—in German headquarters, yet! She refuses to cross the lines and bring them to us—afraid she'll be caught, I expect."

Close to the German lines? My nightmares have entangled me in an assignment like this for months. I got away from them once, but, by God I won't make it a second time. He felt his body, his face, turning to granite. It was not his most dangerous assignment. He had risked more in the past, but this one was so damned personal: stolen enemy documents! He'd be shot without question if he was caught. His stony mouth could still form a few terse words.

"I understand, sir."

Riggs elaborated. "That woman knows German, of course, so you can work together. Those documents are indispensable for our next offensive. The *partigiana* will give you all the info you need to read them. Verbally. So it had to be you."

"I see." Jacob's throat closed and cut off any protest.

"We've got to maintain absolute secrecy, Lieutenant, so you'll not take a driver."

ဆာၺ

Jacob stooped, swung his gear to his shoulder, and began crunching his way to the motor pool, where the jeep awaited.

"Lieutenant Becher!"

Colonel Riggs stood outside his trailer as he passed by. He was holding out his hand.

"Good luck, Becher!"

Jacob pretended not to see, his chest tight with foreboding. "Thank you, sir. I'll do what I can." His hand rose in an automatic salute, and he continued toward the motor pool.

During his last dangerous engagement, February 1943 in Tunisia's Kasserine Pass, he had proven he was no longer a victim but capable of decisive, aggressive action.

The sky had been alive with skeins of stars against a steel gray background. No one was able to sleep, since word had come down that they must be ready to leave their bivouac at any second. Jacob was taking down the pup tent with his buddy, Sergeant Ehlers, when he heard a shot. His friend abruptly collapsed beside him. One glance told Jacob he was dead, transformed into an inanimate object.

A raging fury seized him; he glared in all directions. There, on the nearby ridge, silhouetted in the eerie light of the stars, he saw a German soldier and a machine gun. Without thinking, he plunged forward. He would never know why the machine gun did not fire, but its failure saved his and many other lives. He pounced on the gunner, frustrating his attempt to escape, and wrestled him down. Other American soldiers rushed to help and pinned the man to the ground. Jacob stood confused, panting, when another shot rang out—no prisoners, not that night.

The word came to evacuate. They lined up in single file to move in absolute silence so as not to alert the surrounding enemy. Patrols had discovered that an Italian unit had moved out, breaking the cordon the German command had drawn tight around them. Step by step, each man touching the back of the man in front, they moved through the gap, stealthily, quietly.

Jacob had eliminated a machine-gun nest before it was set up. Later, he received a bronze star and later still was offered a battlefield commission, which he accepted. Thanks to his knowledge of German and French, he received a favored assignment as intelligence officer in Italy. September 1943 found him in Caserta, ready to go on the long trek up the Italian peninsula to Verona.

He'd been afraid back then, but not like now. Why? The answer became clear as he climbed into the jeep. He was so much closer to the nearest concentration camp, only a few kilometers away.

ഇറ

Hadn't he been driving for hours? His watch told him otherwise, but rough conditions stretched the time. The icy road, winding ever higher between smothering stands of black pines, became increasingly perilous. Fear, more than the penetrating cold, froze his hands to the wheel, as bright bursts of artillery closed in on both sides. The jeep skidded and bucked over a new snowfall blanketing the rutted sheet of ice, and as he neared the forward lines, the tight switchbacks grew steeper and narrower.

At last! A human shape crouched under a dwarf pine. He slowed to a stop, and the tall figure rose from the roadside and without hesitation clambered into the jeep. Was this the *partigiana*? He drove on, glancing sideways. Yes, a woman, surprisingly young, dressed in faded fatigues, short brown hair, a graceful profile. She sat next to him, silent and erect, her arms locked around a worn briefcase on her lap. He could not see her eyes, fixed on the road ahead.

He should be the first to speak, but it was she, turning to glance at him, who broke the silence, and in German. The hair on his nape prickled.

"Mein Name ist Olga. Sie sind Tenente Becher?"

"Si." He emphasized his scant Italian. *"Jacopo Becher."*

He drove on in limbo, in no-man's-land. Icicles hung like glittering knives from shrubs and low pine branches. The sky was gun-metal blue. Despite heavy gloves, his fingers began to ache. Her quiet presence increased his discomfort.

His orders told him to hide the jeep where she would indicate, then to follow her on foot to a "safe house." There she would deliver the documents and explain their contents.

He spoke thoughtlessly in English. "Where is the house?"

She seemed puzzled, but must have caught the word 'house.' *"Presto."* Her voice sounded light and pleasant.

A heavy jolt. The jeep hit a pothole. Their bodies collided, and Jacob's flash of anxiety briefly overwhelmed his fear of shells and land mines. The stubborn silence continued as he drove ever higher. Cocooned by the shared sense of danger and by the metal but vulnerable shell of the jeep, they stared at the road, ears tuned to the rumbling of guns as they skirted the northernmost edge of the American lines.

So far, the artillery exchanges had sounded muted, but suddenly, hostile mortar shells exploded all around them. A sorcerer had surely conjured up these sharp whistles, these growling thuds. Shells came ever closer. When one—thank God a dud—landed just yards away, he knew they'd been spotted. They must have crossed the fluid, almost invisible border into enemy territory.

"Get out!" His voice cracked. She'd understood him, but he screamed again in German. *"Raus!"*

In a blur of movement, they scrambled from the jeep. Yes, the partisan till clutched her battered briefcase. They ran for cover among snow-draped pines and heavy underbrush. They cowered in sudden terror at a sharp whistle and ear-splitting explosion. Behind them, the jeep burst into flames. They stood transfixed, mouths agape, aware of the hairbreadth escape, then dropped to the ground for cover. *"Danke,"* she muttered in the enemy's language.

For a brief moment, the guns were silent. Then, abruptly, a hideous mechanical scream sliced the air. A mere two hundred yards away a thunderous crash flared into blinding light. The earth shuddered. Their bodies shot up. In a frantic embrace they clutched each other, falling to earth, hands gripping rough cloth warmed by pulsing life underneath. Jacob found himself looking down into dark eyes wild with terror and the fear of death.

It had lasted only a moment. Now they lay still and separate. The forest lay quiet around them.

ಖುಣ

The safe house was now out of reach. They must spend the freezing night in the underbrush, pinned down by enemy fire. They dared not stir. They remained tense and alert for enemy patrols, for soldiers crashing through the underbrush, searching, seeking, groping for them. Each slight rustle in the woods—the wind? A nocturnal animal?—brought their guard up, eyes and ears straining in the dark. Fearful, they huddled in their nests of pine needles amid patches of icy snow under the looming pines and tangled shrubs. The enemy commander must have decided they'd died in the jeep or in that final round of fire, for nobody came to hunt them. They could only wait in fear and discomfort for the dawn.

Sleep would not come. He began to talk to her in short bursts, and her replies were likewise staccato. "Are you comfortable?" "Are you cold?" "Let's get under that clump of trees." "What time is it?" "How are your feet?" He fretted about frostbite and wondered, too, how he and the documents would ever find their way back without the jeep.

Dawn began to turn the sky gray. Surely artillery and mortar fire would resume in full force, yet the silence continued. Rising cautiously, brushing off iced-over twigs and dead leaves, they crunched through the snow. They followed the road but hugged the line of trees for protection. A steep, rocky path branched away from the road to climb yet another mountain. She led him and he followed, both bending low. At last, a clearing opened ahead.

Olga pointed at the half-hidden villa in the woods. "*Hier sind wir.*" We're here.

Before them rose a modern palazzo the partisans had taken over when the owners fled. They climbed a majestic driveway and slipped through the back door. He stared, disoriented by the sudden luxury of white fixtures in the sumptuous kitchen, still impressive despite the grime left by recent occupants. Olga broke the spell. She placed the old briefcase on a kitchen chair and passed a hand over her hair. Her eyes, anxious, measuring him. He held her gaze, straining to break the silence with a personal word. She spoke first.

"*Tenente Becher, an die Arbeit!*" To work!

୫୦୧୫

Later that day, Lieutenant Becher closed the rear door behind him and plunged into the forest below, the old leather briefcase gripped under his arm. A strange young man in blue overalls led the way, wearing a ragged red armband. Jacob did not turn, for Olga had already gone. No word of farewell.

Chapter 2
A Proposal

Olga, Jacob pictured her shadowy figure huddled beside the road, then sitting beside him, tense, clutching a scuffed briefcase. Olga, her pure, refined profile indelibly engraved in his memory, a silhouette against the snow outside. Most of all, Olga, momentarily under him, frantic with fear—like him—as the exploding shell lit them in a solar flare.

Although he had not seen her after she left him at the safe house on that cold winter day, he'd begun to search for her after the war ended four months ago in May. He finally tracked her down through Army Intelligence channels. She had allowed herself to be found, but she still wore her partisan mask in their brief telephonic exchange. He hoped fervently that this would change.

His hands gripped the railing of what had once been Florence's Ponte Santa Trinità, now a temporary Army replacement, and he leaned toward the river. His eyes seemed focused on the brown waters of the Arno, but they saw only Olga. In a few minutes he would meet her again, see her in broad daylight, get to know her. His heart hammered, and his face felt oddly warm, though the breeze was chilly.

He began to pace, jerky steps back and forth, refusing to look at the jumbled chaos on the southern side of the Arno, those collapsing roofs and partially demolished walls, loose bricks and gaping holes where windows had been, a grim reminder that peace was only a few months old. The retreating Germans had blown up the old bridge, too. He faced the row of unscathed rooming houses where he knew she lived. The heavy traffic was mostly military, rumbling olive drab trucks with white stars, surrounded by packs of civilian bicycles. His eyes flicked over them, dismissed them. Only she mattered. The cool September day penetrated his Army raincoat, and he shivered.

Another truck passed and she stood before him as if she'd stepped from behind a curtain. Her face and figure were unchanged, although her worn fatigues had been replaced by a blue blouse and navy slacks, with a beige woolen cape thrown around her shoulders. Her dark eyes gazed at him with the same quiet concentration.

"Where to?" She spoke in German and took his arm casually, with the ease of an old friend.

"There's an officers' club not far from here. The food should be good."

Over a large American steak served with Italian pasta, they drank a pleasant Chianti to each other's health and laughed with an air of solemnity. Was this a beginning or an end? He couldn't be sure. They didn't speak of that moment when the exploding shell lit up their faces. Their bodies no longer touched.

He did not want to pry but had to know more.

"Olga, ah ... that's your code name, I know. But the war's over now. Can we be ourselves or?—"

Her smile and raised hand interrupted him. Her eyes glowed, startling in their intensity. "Gladly, Lieutenant Becher. My real name is Francesca. Francesca Mancini, and I was a student in Turin before the war."

"What were you studying?"

"The law. I still want to become a lawyer."

The conversation continued, but he learned little more.

They met two weeks later, and he ached with expectation. As they walked randomly together, he asked, "Can you tell me about your home? Your parents?"

"Some other time. Where shall we eat this evening?"

He didn't press her, more interested in the present moment than the past. Like last time, their exchanges never penetrated beneath the surface. Francesca happily walked with him and shared a meal, but an unbridgeable gap opened between them. Unsure of himself, he took her arm, but he felt only an ephemeral pressure in return. Instead of growing more familiar with further acquaintance, Francesca moved away. The momentary union in that blinding blast, to Jacob something like a marriage, dwindled into a looser, more distant connection.

As they crossed the Arno on one of their rambles, he found the courage to ask, "Do you have a lover? A fiancé?"

She laughed. "I had no time for such things. I was a serious student, then an activist and a partisan." Her clear voice speaking crisp, idiomatic

German betrayed barely a trace of an accent. The answer told him little. Was the door open to him or shut?

"You say you were a serious student. Surely, you didn't have your nose in the books all the time. What else did you do in those years?"

"I hated Mussolini's regime, so I joined a clandestine student organization and got involved in radical left-wing politics. That could have been lethal in a fascist state like our pre-war Italy, especially after Mussolini was more and more taken over by Hitler.

"But you got away with it?"

"I was lucky. When the war broke out, I joined the Resistance. After a year in the field, I landed a job, a secret job in important German headquarters, where I was one of very few Italians still trusted with handling sensitive material. Though I was, of course, a low-level civilian secretary, I occasionally had to handle secret documents. As an undercover Resistance fighter, I was amazingly successful." Her voice was filled with satisfaction.

"That must have been tricky."

"Yes, a living hell—always dissembling, completely alone, knowing I couldn't count on the least support from the Movement. I had nightmares, when I slept at all, about exposure. I was relieved when I was done with that assignment and could go back into the field again."

Jacob heard her words but did not take them in, his mind busy in search of greater intimacy. Had he really listened, she might have shared confidences about her girlhood in Turin as the protected daughter of a distinguished attorney, how she and her two very proper sisters had grown up in their suburban villa where abundant hedges overflowed the black iron fence, and how she had fled this comfort and beauty by deciding to study law and eventually to take up arms. She might also have confided how she had learned about the cruelty of the system in which her own parents had played such a significant role. But, blinded by his need, he paid little attention to her confidences about the gravity of her choices and the pain of loneliness that followed. Perceiving his absence, she turned the conversation from her life to his.

"And you," she asked, "Where have you served?"

Jacob ducked his head with a slight smile. "Before Italy, I was assigned to the 34th Infantry Division in North Africa. We fought in Tunisia, in the Kasserine Pass. Thanks to my service there, I was granted a battle commission and sent here. You saw what sort of predicament I could get myself into—you were there."

She laughed.

The terror they had shared obsessed him. Repeatedly, her face, her frightened eyes possessed him once again, the feel of her body beneath him amid the soaring pine trees in a world lit by the exploding shell. Those eyes could mock him, too, that much he knew.

One of her friends joined them for lunch once, a pale young woman in a blue Italian uniform that he could not identify.

"This is Tenente Becher. He's the young officer I told you about. We shared a stormy night."

The three sat in a tiny sidewalk café, wedged between a building north of the Palazzo Vecchio and a narrow street. Tables were packed together and chairs tiny, but the food was savory. They chatted in the usual pleasant, desultory way. Jacob remained tongue-tied despite his improved Italian. He could only admire Francesca's poise and witty ripostes in silence.

ৡぴ৸

He recalled their last weeks together. He saw himself mounting the paneled staircase to the third floor of the grand old building. Francesca climbed ahead of him, her tan beret and moss green blouse providing spots of color in the stairway's gloom. The door opened to a babble of voices and to the figure of a slight man, who, Jacob sensed at once, was a rival for her esteem. The ascot and graying hair combed *en brosse* gave him an air both nonchalant and distinguished.

The man greeted her with enthusiasm. "Olga! What a pleasure!"

A crowd milled about in the hall and living room, pointing and chatting as they strolled past pictures of many styles and genres: mostly watercolors, prints, a few oils. Had he heard right, unused as he still was to rapid Italian? Gregor Matthäus, that fabled painter everyone talked about? At first, he wasn't sure, but Francesca confirmed his suspicion, taking his arm and walking him from picture to picture, explaining. He felt out of place and awkward in his uniform, among well-dressed civilians. The woman at his side was no longer the partisan in the jeep.

"The war is over," declared Olga-Francesca. "I can be myself now."

ৡぴ৸

His last meeting with Francesca brought him no solace. They lunched in another sidewalk café, this time in the Piazza della Repubblica, not far from the Duomo. Her face, glowing in the October sun, seemed closed only to him. Francesca seemed unwilling to explain herself. Had she given up any thought of being understood? Instead, she encouraged Jacob to talk about himself.

"Tell me your plans and your hopes. You said you were a professor of history?"

"Well, yes, an Instructor. I was far enough advanced in my graduate studies in Germany to be a lycée teacher there for two years, before the infamous Crystal Night of November 9-10, 1938, when all Jewish men were arrested and temporarily imprisoned in concentration camps. We were released after a few weeks. Luckily, our family had been in line to immigrate to America, and we did. We arrived safely with great relief as early as three months later. My luck held: I found a teaching post at a private high school. Then the University of Washington in Seattle needed an instructor of Central European history—my specialty—so they hired me with my German *Doktorat* that I earned while I was teaching. I'll be going back to Seattle to continue my teaching career."

"Seattle? Where's that?"

"It's as far away from Italy as you can get in the USA. It's where my family settled, on the Pacific coast, the northernmost state."

"Ah! I only have the vaguest idea of your geography. I'd better find an atlas."

Their talks taught them much about geography, distances, and different mores but not much essential about themselves. They defined the shallow limits of their friendship.

                                         ଏଓଃ

The orders to return home for demobilization forced Jacob's decision. He wrote her a long letter proposing marriage. Arrogant and innocent, he counted on immediate acceptance. He assumed that his offer to make her a war bride would be a welcome rescue from an uncertain future. He expected gratitude. But instead, his proposal altered everything. When they met again at their favorite café near the Duomo, she seemed stiff and awkward for the first time since he'd known her. Her first words made it clear that his offer was by no means welcome. She spoke in German, though they often tried to speak Italian by then.

"Jakob, you wrote a beautiful letter. But, *mein Lieber,* we hardly know each other."

For a long time he did not respond. He sat in his neatly pressed uniform, his gray eyes looking both startled and confused. He drew in his lips, as if he had allowed them to be too forward, leaned back in his chair and rocked imperceptibly. He played with the stem of his glass while the silence grew heavier.

"What makes you think that?"

"Don't you see?" She stopped, unsure how to go on, then tried again. "Don't you see, we were together on the threshold of death ... *auf der Schwelle des Todes* ... how could we be anything but *Geschwister*—brother and sister—bound together by unspilled blood and by an arbitrary *Vorsehung*—no, certainly not Providence, nothing religious. It was sheer chance, a fluke ..." She trailed off.

He still didn't answer, and she went on with difficulty, "How can I make a choice for a lifetime based on such whimsy? Don't you see: *The whole thing was coincidence!* The idea that I, a woman who speaks next to no English, should be asked to explain those stolen documents to some American officer who might not understand me—"

He broke in at last in a rough voice. "But why were *you* chosen?" Now, too late, he wanted to know.

Her voice quavered and she paused to clear her throat before continuing. "An old and dear friend was picked up by the Fascists and shot, just as he was preparing to meet one of your people. He was a splendid worker and spoke English like an American." She took a deep breath. "The Germans were just getting rid of us Italians because we were too 'unreliable,' but there was a lot of confusion when we left. They're usually so security-minded, but in this instance, one of the officers left the door of the safe unlocked and slightly ajar. I noticed it, and since I had a good idea what those papers and maps contained from typing and handling them while I was still trusted, I knew their value and simply stole them ... and got away with it. I just slipped them into my big handbag. Later, I took my friend's place and met you."

She stopped, flushed with pride, and her voice took on a wistful tone. "I really was the best person anyway. I knew enough to help you interpret them, didn't I? And it worked." She lifted her chin. "A quirk of fate."

"Yes, I see what you're saying." He squirmed a bit and grimaced, suddenly aware of their surroundings: distant laughter, a teasing male voice.

When he spoke again, he reminded her. "Let's not forget our biggest 'fluke.' Three miracles: one dud and two extremely close calls."

She was not deflected. "Jacopo, *please!* You've never stopped to ask me my feelings; you never seemed to listen. You never heard that yes, the flukes brought us together, yes, I like you very much, but, no ... not in that way."

He peered at the glass in front of him as into a mirror, seeing his distorted reflection in the dark vermouth. Even now, he couldn't accept where she stood. "Tell me again. Why did my letter disappoint you? It was meant as a great compliment."

"I know what you meant... only too well." She looked up, seeking his eyes. "You never understood me, and you don't now. I could love you as a brother. I want and need one. Why is that inconceivable to a man?" The words rang like crystal. And, after another long pause, "What do you know about me really, my upbringing, my work, my dead comrade, my politics?"

She didn't need to continue. He now knew. With a blindness he no longer understood, he had seen her only through his desire. And there was no way back.

She raised her glass, repeating a phrase he had heard not too long ago, "The war is over. I can be myself."

The iron chairs scraped on the pavement as they rose. Bending toward him, she kissed him lightly on the lips.

❧❦

November 1945. Jacob Becher stood at the ship's railing, staring at the turbulent water below. He had no sense of the life that would await him on the other shore; even he, the most reluctant of soldiers, could not imagine a life without soldiering.

The liberty ship filled with weary men glided westward, the waves glistening in the night. Jacob recalled a famous title: *The Long Voyage Home.*

Chapter 3
Expulsion

Yes, Jacob saw, felt, and heard it all: Boston, where he first landed, the views from the train windows on the long ride back to Seattle to be demobilized, his arrival on the platform, where his parents embraced him and his mother wet his cheeks with her tears. Yet only Francesca— her voice, her touch, and her light kiss—remained truly present, while the rest faded in sepia tones. Nonetheless, he rediscovered his adopted hometown, walking through the city from the port to the lakes, roaming through parks and the university campus with its shadowy green. He applied for his old position at the University of Washington, and the history department rehired him as an Assistant Professor. He plunged into his work.

But austere Olga, the woman in the jeep, never left his thoughts, nor did laughing Francesca, the companion of those days in Florence. He remained a man possessed.

ഇരുന്നു

Francesca stared out the window, where the overcast sky reflected her mood. Her world had transformed itself with frightening speed from at least partial sun to continual gloom. She had indeed become her "own person," but misery had seized her in a way she had not foreseen.

She missed the uplift of the more relaxed Allied presence. Equally depressing, Gregor Matthäus had vanished from her circle of friends. She missed him, too. No more parties at artists' studios, no one to take his place. She sank onto the armchair, resting her chin in her hand as she thought about him. Something had gone very wrong.

For the past year, maybe more, he had lived clandestinely in Florence, a deserter, a former German officer, serving with the army of occupation. A year before the official end of hostilities in Florence, he had put on civilian clothes and disappeared among the people. Italy was like a second home to him, since he had studied art there as a young student, and he spoke fluent Italian. He was a homosexual, a grave criminal offense in Germany, enforced with particular cruelty by the

Nazis wherever they went, including all occupied countries. He feared discovery.

Francesca shifted her hand to her forehead. She mourned him. She and other like-minded young Italians, especially his fellow artists, had protected his hideout from the Germans during that first year. After the Allies liberated Florence, he began giving parties; he nurtured friendships. None of them could ever understand where he found the money to entertain them while he lived and worked among them. Yet his studio became a rallying point for those who believed in art and freedom, a world not run by greed, free of totalitarianism.

And then it was over. Strange stories began to spring up around him. He was seen in the company of so-and-so, a former bigwig during the German occupation, or of Signora X, the wife of a financier. As Gregor disappeared from their circle, his paintings appeared in all the established galleries in town. Had he, too, been bought? Her disillusionment lodged in her throat, in her chest, like a physical ache.

The loss of Gregor was the beginning of the decline. A dreary pall settled over her life. She endured month after month, barely earning enough for room and board, unable to resume her law studies. Her parents rejected her appeals for financial help and had seen her briefly only once. They probably still pictured her in some subversive uniform. Now, acquaintances scorned her as a former partisan—suspecting her of loose morals because she, a woman, had chosen to fight.

Her dismal walk-up flat seemed continents removed from the cheerful room that had been her first post-war home during that hopeful summer of 1945. Nostalgic, she recalled the small *pensione* and the diminutive, white-haired landlady, her admiring eyes welcoming Francesca-Olga, still in her combat fatigues, when she asked about lodgings. She'd traveled a long way down since those early days and that other place with its open view of the Arno. Even the cragged remains of demolished buildings on the other side of the river had seemed to promise a new life growing out of the ruins, a new time.

But the new time never came. Her savings almost gone, she had been forced to give up that fine room for this more affordable place bordering on a slum. Poverty threatened. Feeling trapped, claustrophobic, she rose and opened the window but found no comfort there. The dark, narrow and noisy street had nothing in common with her former flat, with its view of the river. It lay far from the Duomo and the square where she had teased and clinked glasses with her friends. Below, she saw only a butcher shop, a dingy *trattoria*, a rusty bicycle leaning against a lamppost. Noise assaulted her as a gray-haired man in a faded business suit raced a moped without a muffler past a shrill chorus of scolding voices.

Her back to the window, she surveyed the cluttered room. Half-read newspapers littered the table along with a stocking tossed there for mending and a haphazard stack of torn envelopes. Among them, the many long, slim envelopes from America reminded her insistently of Jacob Becher. He sent her unrelenting invitations, and his display of longing made her nervous. She preferred to think of him as a brother, but long months had passed since their last meeting, and she was no longer sure of her feelings. It was a relief not to have heard from him for a while, yet the long gap made her uneasy, too.

Today she would have welcomed one of his long, closely scribbled letters. She was about to meet her mother, daring to hope they might rediscover some common ground. It did seem possible. Two days ago, her mother's letter announced her arrival in Florence to visit Leona Tommasini, a family friend Francesca had known since childhood. She felt hurt not to have been asked to the old lady's house, even though she'd made a point of avoiding family connections. But she was pleased that her mother invited her to lunch "for some good talk" at a restaurant in the Centro. They would meet, her mother wrote, on the steps of the Duomo.

Her face darkened as she recalled their one meeting months ago—a disaster. She'd given in to her parents' pressure to visit them in her old home in Turin. The three of them sat around the familiar dining-room table without her married sisters. She was glad of the intimacy; she hoped to reach her mother, at least, for the slightest renewal of their old close bond. But with her father present, the gap had proved impossible to bridge. He had shut her out, reminding her, his face a mask of censure, that she had broken with her family when she joined the partisans "to fight for the *enemy.*"

He was tall and spare, with a high, bald forehead, a sharp nose, and penetrating brown eyes. He spoke in a loud voice like the lawyer he was as they sat down to dinner.

"Francesca! Think of what you've done. The tragic consequences ...
your own country!"

She had been his most promising child.

Her father avoided her eyes throughout the meal, and she felt even
more wounded by that rejection than by his words. They touched on
nothing personal or important again, but as Francesca said good-bye
with the taste of the custard dessert turned sour in her mouth, her
mother put a hand on her arm. They agreed to meet the next time she
was in Florence. That meeting was today.

Francesca dressed simply in a cotton skirt and a light blouse to avoid
any reminder of that "subversive uniform." She wheeled her bicycle out
of the dim vestibule and pedaled toward the Centro, filled with angry,
self-pitying thoughts. Foreboding increased as she crossed the Piazza
della Repubblica, where she'd sat with Jacopo many months ago. She
locked her bicycle in a rack, then sat on the steps of the great church.
She expected her mother to get off the bus with the forced smile she
had come to recognize and distrust, the outward sign of the wall of
hostility that had grown up between them, leaving no trace of their
intimacy. But when she saw the familiar figure, with flowing brown hair
and a smart military raincoat, she could not help but admire her. *She
could pass for my age!*

Her mother, brisk and determined, chose an elegant restaurant, too
pricey for the average tourist, its black-and-white art deco interior
echoed by white tablecloths and black chairs. They followed the
headwaiter to a table in a comfortable nook and ordered. As they sat
facing each other over a glass of wine, her mother focused solemn eyes
upon her. Her tone matched her grave face.

"Francesca, come home."

Francesca stiffened. "Come home" meant capitulation to her parents'
way of thinking. She hadn't expected this assault.

"How could I come home, even if I wanted to? Can't you accept me
as I am?" Dismayed at her own pleading tone, she fell silent. Had the
cold, judgmental family gathering two months ago taught them nothing?
On either side?

Under an inner compulsion, she changed the subject. "I fought because
I believed and still believe in a free Italy, a true democracy, governed by
just laws, not by a dictator. I was not a Communist, Mother, I've told

you that before. Hitler and Mussolini were an evil pair, and I joined the Allies to rid the earth of them."

"My dear, you merely opened the door to the Stalinists. Better to accept a native son, however autocratic, as our ruler. At least there was order, discipline, and clarity under Benito Mussolini. Look at the chaos you—you people—have brought to us!"

"Too many people believe what you're saying, Mama." Francesca changed the subject again. "I've failed to find a job that pays me more than just enough to live from hand to mouth, and I have no hope of continuing my legal studies. I need help." In her intensity, her concentration, she'd hardly lifted a fork. The place began to empty, and the impatient waiter hovered just outside the nook. All at once she became conscious of the voices around them—other lives—strains of music. She ignored the waiter. Ashamed of her need, she spoke with bowed head.

"You and Papa could help me. I would be so grateful. My law studies. I must get back to them."

Signora Camilla Mancini raised her eyes to her daughter. They were clear, with a touch of anger, and yet not without warmth. "You know there would be a price. I asked you to come home."

Francesca felt her face stiffen. "You heard Papa the other evening. How could I live with that?"

"By understanding us, admitting you were wrong. We brought you up to love your country, not help destroy it. Don't you understand? You fought on the other side! You helped bring us down. You and your free-loving, socialist comrades!"

Francesca sat up straight, her chin jutting out. "Mama! All those letters I managed to smuggle out to you! Didn't you read them? If you had, you'd know I was with a wing of the movement that fought the Germans but tried to stay clear of Communists."

Signora Mancini turned her face away. A door had closed.

Her daughter tried to continue. "The Yugoslavs—"

"Let's not go on with this. You know perfectly well what I mean. I never used the word "communist." I only meant the way you people lived. Free love and no patriotism! Fighting against your own country, your own people. You were traitors!"

Even their slender connection had shattered. Her voice came out tense, her throat clogged. "Italy was in great danger. We weren't free. The Germans took us over. Even your Duce became a puppet." She looked down on her plate. "I was, I am, a *partigiana*. I believe I served my country well."

"Endangering us! And yet—you are our child—we protected you."

There was nothing more to say. Her mother raised her glass, which she had barely touched. It had been a long and difficult hour. Her voice shook slightly with her affection. "My dear, do what you must. I think I know what you're telling me. For us, *cara*, it's beyond understanding. Your father finds it unacceptable."

"And you?"

Camilla Mancini, on the brink of emotion, reached for her military raincoat. "It's time, Francesca. I must go." They were silent, eyes averted. "*Arrividerla.*"

Her mother's formal good-bye stung like a slap. They stood at the door. Early-winter dusk cast shadows outside the circle of light where they stood.

"*Ciao*, Mama, I'll walk you to the bus."

She watched as the tall figure in her severe tan coat bent to pay the driver, her face concealed by a curtain of brown hair. Despite the barriers, Francesca still loved her mother for her wisdom and continual support when she was young. Would she see her again?

Francesca pedaled mechanically back to her squalid flat. The gloom of failure surrounded and trailed behind her like shadows of giant bat wings. She had become an orphan. She kicked off her shoes and flung herself on the bed. Where would it end? For a moment she thought of Jacopo as she first saw him, the shy young officer bent over the steering wheel, peering into the frost-hung night. His letters repeated that he wanted her for life. What could he give her? Would she be less lonely with him over there than alone here? What should her role be? Daughter or lover? Her only desire, her lifelong ambition, was to be a lawyer, an attorney-at-law who would support and rescue men and women in need. Meanwhile, she earned a bare living as a flunky, typing through gray, wearisome hours.

ಇೂಲ

September 1946. Little of her old life remained. She filled her time away from work meeting occasionally with friends who had shared the last war years. Occasionally she wrote. Journalism preserved some meaning in her life, and she pursued it by writing an article now and then for minor magazines and journals, where she attacked postwar corruption. Her severe disappointment in Gregor Matthäus led to an angry article about him, which she managed somehow to place in *Il Tempo*. That, she hoped, would have an impact.

Another long envelope. From Jacopo, of course. She opened it with some reluctance. It was, as she expected, an intense letter, pages long, written mostly in German, their personal *lingua franca*. For the first time, she noticed with pleasure that he included a carefully worded paragraph in simple English—an instant response. She had confided that she'd taken up English as a new door to the inner workings of any profession, notably the law. *"My dear Francesca,"* she read. *"Why didn't you say so before? I'd be happy to help you with your English or any language or skill I may be able to put at your disposal."* He added in less stilted German, *"If you need me, I'd even be your brother."* She was moved; such a response had never come to her before, nor had he ever offered so much.

He had at last transcended mere desire. He had come to understand her. She was moved by his acceptance.

ജ&ß

November, 1946. The sky hung leaden over Florence. The cluttered office, dank and dreary in the late afternoon, depressed her. She felt used and yawned wearily. After months of futile searching, she had finally landed a small job in a questionable one-man business, trading in the surplus clothing left by several armies. It was a living at least. No one had wanted her, not the city or national government, or anyone in private business. No one would hire a used-up *partigiana*. For months, she had lived from hand to mouth, from one short-term job to another, mostly typing and filing. At last, she had a steady job that provided enough money to eat and to live in that grimy flat without fear of being unable to pay the rent. But as she opened the thick notebook, its pages filled with shorthand letters waiting to be converted into typescript, she could not suppress a wave of despair.

She was not alone. Her friends, too, were caught in this same grayness, this lack of purpose—a lack of the very thing that had held them together. Their vision had become increasingly blurred, a dim present and dubious future muddying the clarity that had given them so much strength during the war. In a way, her parents were right. Who won the war? Who lost it? It was hard to tell in these times. All that was left was a world of empty, self-serving men and women. And she'd dreamt of becoming an attorney!

She rose to feel the radiator, stone cold under her hands, then heard a sharp rap on the door. Two men walked in without a word of greeting, a tall man in a shiny blue business suit followed by another who wore the all-too-familiar uniform of a policeman.

The tall one spoke first. "Where's Signor Silvaggio?"

She turned to face them. Her first thought was of Silvaggio. She was not surprised. His business was supported by all kinds of questionable deals: American, British, German, Italian uniform pieces had found their way from warehouses emptied in both official and unofficial ways after the armies had left or surrendered, and Silvaggio sold them mostly, she supposed, on the black market. Although he seemed likeable enough, he represented the postwar climate she abhorred.

"I expect Signor Silvaggio later this afternoon."

The policeman's probing gaze scanned the reams of loose papers piled on her desk and her employer's, the filing cabinet spilling over with its partly opened drawers, disgorging a multitude of folders, and rested tentatively on the old Olivetti typewriter next to her purse.

Concerned for her boss, she asked, "May I take a message?"

The tall man in the blue suit wheeled, eyes hard and cold on her. "Listen, Signora, we don't give a damn about Signor Silvaggio. *It's you we want to know about.* You're Francesca Mancini, right?" And when she didn't answer at once, "Also known as 'Olga'?"

Fear knifed through her, and shock. 'Olga'! Her war name! But wouldn't it be more likely for them to know 'Olga' rather than her real name? She waited. The uniformed man repeated the question his partner had just asked, scanning a formal document, then looking fixedly at her.

"Mancini?" And even more sharply, "You *were* 'Olga'?"

She was stunned. Where did they get her war name? Someone had betrayed her, someone high enough in her movement to have given in under pressure.

"Why? What do you want with 'Olga'?"

The next statement struck her like a fist in the stomach. "You were a translator and interpreter with a logistical command at the headquarters of the German Tenth Army from September 1944 until you vanished in February."

They seemed to know everything.

She answered through stiff lips. "Yes, of course! I was doing my patriotic duty. The German Army command 'purified' itself, meaning that all Italians were about to be dismissed. My own partisan command ordered me to disappear anyway. What am I accused of?"

"Theft, and…"

She exhaled a long breath. "Oh, that! I can explain."

"Yes, we'd like to hear that, your explanation." The tone was sarcastic. "What did you do with the missing twenty thousand lire? They vanished with you. We've finally tracked you down."

Twenty thousand lire? What did they mean? They might not believe the truth. She locked eyes with the tall man, her voice quavering slightly with indignation and anxiety. It was obvious he would be deaf to anything but his own conviction.

Her chin came up and her voice became hard and proud. "I did steal. I stole for my country. I stole maps and papers, highly secret papers I discovered and took to the Americans south of the German command. I was lucky to secure such protected documents in a secret vault that somebody had momentarily left open—lucky, too, that I was still trusted by my immediate superior whom I had to betray. I did it for our cause, and received praise from my partisan command. *I did not steal money.*"

For a moment, the man seemed off balance. Then he rallied. "Twenty thousand lire are missing. The Germans were furious! Many were arrested."

"They may have said 'money,' but they meant those maps."

The policemen studied their papers. "No word here of maps, only money… money you never turned in to us. If you didn't steal it, then where is it now, 'patriot'?"

Before she could protest, she heard handcuffs jingling in his hands. He never dropped his gaze.

She would try one last thing before submitting to those cuffs. Once she was behind bars, she could be held indefinitely. "I need to make a telephone call. Do I have your permission?"

"I suppose so," the policeman said in a reluctant tone, "One."

She called 'Luigi,' a highly placed friend and comrade in the Resistance who was now an elected deputy. To her relief, she reached him in his office and after a moment, she handed the receiver to the plainclothes man.

"Signor, my friend, the deputy, wants to talk to you."

She heard emphatic words from the receiver. Her would-be captor flushed with anger and slammed down the phone. "REDS!" he muttered under his breath. Then, turning to Francesca, he commanded, "Don't go too far. We'll drop this for the moment, but your Red comrades can't shield you forever."

The door closed behind them and she collapsed on her chair with a gusty sigh of relief. Thank God, the matter had been resolved, before her employer reappeared.

☙ℭ

But while 'Luigi' had rescued her for the moment, he was unable to squelch the trumped-up charge altogether. The sordid episode typified the tensions of that second year of peace. Communism became a target of suspicion and fear to some, an opportunity for others, as everyone from left to right fought over the legacy of Fascism.

Now she sent an urgent letter to her friend Jacopo in Seattle and he answered by return mail. Hers had not yet been a love letter. She simply pleaded for help, with as much dignity as she could muster, now that her life had become too precarious.

"Together, my friend, we underwent a trial of fire. We had barely met when death almost took us." Recalling his last letter with its unquestioning acceptance, she set down words she thought she would never write. "Together, we were on trial for death. Should we now attempt a trial for life?"

Jacob Becher acted at once, telephoning her at great expense to reassure her. "We'll work it out, my darling," words he couldn't have imagined saying only a short time ago. "Colonel Riggs, who ordered our mission, is a top lawyer now. I'll get his help. This whole thing is preposterous."

Filled with gratitude, she felt insecure as well. Even though her "theft" was revealed for what it was—purloining maps and papers that had been of material help in the Allied offensive—her accusers were never satisfied. Still, in the end, they were obliged to drop the matter.

Three times she'd experienced exile in the country to which she had offered her life. When Gregor Matthäus left her and her friends, he had stolen away their spiritual home. When she asked her parents for help, she was rebuffed. And for risking her life in support of her country, she was threatened with arrest and imprisonment. Rejected and expelled, she cast her eyes across the sea.

&OCß

Jacob no longer needed to implore her; he wanted to build a new life with her at his side—he'd told her so. To such acceptance, there could be no resistance, only regret and a backward glance.

Chapter 4
Precarious Immigration

Is it politics? Jacob asked himself as he peered through the window of his taxi at the cold, rain-drenched New York landscape. Heading west on Forty-second Street through dense traffic, they moved amid a flood of cars, cabs, and belching trucks. By the time they crossed Ninth Avenue, there were no pedestrians left, only grimy brick walls and garish advertising posters obscured by dirt and rain. A huge red and white Coca-Cola sign dominated a scene orchestrated by the ear-shattering sound of steam hammers tearing up the pavement, by insistently blowing horns, by raucous shouts of workers in slickers.

The cab rattled along on the cobblestones of Twelfth Avenue to the pier, and worry jolted Jacob's mind. Had Francesca *actually* arrived to become his bride? Had she *really* accepted his proposal? Had she *truly* come to love him, or was she merely determined to marry him to escape impossible conditions at home? Because of *politics?* With the distrustfulness of an anxious man, he continued to question her sincerity. The taxi slowed. He had reached the berth where the ship was moored. The small freighter, with its two thin funnels thrusting into the rainy sky, reminded him of the liberty ship of not too long ago. He asked the driver to wait. Finding another taxi in this weather on this deserted pier was improbable. Still, his impatience would not let him rest. He scrambled out of the cab, but when he felt needles of icy late-winter rain pelting his face, he drew back.

"I'm leaving my bags in your cab."

The cabby nodded, took out a newspaper, and began to read. Jacob paced nervously, wondering when and how he would ever find Francesca.

Several people were clustered on the pier at the foot of the gangplank from the rain-soaked ship. His eyes strained to see what was happening on board. Nothing—just eerie quiet. The weather had driven everyone below decks. A station wagon stood nearby, rain streaking its wooden sides. A tiny American flag hung limp and wet on the right fender, suggesting that an official had gone aboard.

This sight doubled Jacob's worry. Didn't immigration officers usually board before a ship entered the harbor? Perhaps Francesca was caught in a special interrogation? He imagined disaster. The rain became stronger. For a moment, Jacob sought shelter in the cab, but within minutes, he paced outside again.

A few passengers appeared at last. They waved wildly as they emerged. "*Caro!*" A young woman rushed down the gangplank into the arms of her lover who leaped toward her, colliding with her as she touched the pier. The woman was not Francesca Mancini.

Again, more movement on board: three men and four women, all of them elderly, toting bundles and shabby leather valises. They stumbled down the shaky gangplank to welcoming shouts of a small crowd that had gathered quickly out of nowhere to receive them. Then again nobody.

Rainwater ran down Jacob's cheeks and soaked through his raincoat. Was it the wrong boat? He had received her wire from aboard ship before he left Seattle. This was the boat. Again, he climbed into the cab. Again, he got out a few minutes later.

It was political, he knew. Was it really over? Did they pursue her—even here?

At last, he saw her tall figure emerge from a cabin, looking down in her regal way at the small crowd as she prepared to descend. A man in tweeds appeared behind her, struggling into his raincoat. At first glance, Jacob feared she had been detained. But, to his relief, the man politely signaled that she might walk down ahead of him.

She saw Jacob. She waved. The bride came slowly down the gangplank to meet the bridegroom, fighting gusts of rain. When she arrived, they kissed for the first time in earnest, but it was comically difficult with the rain running down their cheeks and noses.

He opened his raincoat to envelop her in his welcome. "You look so different," she said with wonderment, and he realized she'd never seen him in civilian clothes. But at once, they were caught by practicalities. Her luggage. She had left it on the boat. Together they walked back up the gangplank. On deck, they all but stumbled over her large valise and her bag of books. She'd left them during her trying session with the immigration officer. Worried and nervous, Francesca had walked past her baggage.

Once in the taxi, drenched, there was no time to celebrate. He took her hand.

"Where are we going?" asked Francesca. They were riding along Eighth Avenue past shops and restaurants.

"To the hotel." Jacob saw at once it was a mistake. He tried to mend it. "It's a nice place. The Barbizon Plaza, near Central Park."

"A hotel?" she echoed in disbelief. "But Jacopo, we aren't married yet."

"Nobody asks." He ducked his head, sheepish.

They had started in Italian. Now she switched into German to be completely clear: "*Auf keinen Fall.* Under no circumstances. *Kommt nicht in Frage.* Out of the question."

He glanced at her profile. Her face looked taut and pained. For a moment, he thought of calling the hotel to ask for separate rooms. But when he heard her low voice again, he abandoned the idea.

"My dear, I can't risk it. Just something more to pin on me when the time comes: 'Suspect Red immigrant in bed with a man not her husband.'"

"Red immigrant?" he repeated mechanically.

"Yes. That's how it felt aboard ship for the past hour. If you hadn't been a former officer, who knows where I'd be."

"But ..."

She raised her hand. "No, Jacopo. I'm afraid I know how it'll play. Please, let's not be seen together in that hotel. Let's go on to Seattle. *Now!*"

He told the driver to head for Grand Central.

೫೦ಲೞ

They made love for the first time west of Bismarck as they rolled through the endless North Dakota plain. It was past midnight, and brilliant skeins of stars hung above the moving train. They shivered in the unheated car, sitting side-by-side on the lower berth of their sleeping compartment. Francesca spread her winter coat over them both, her face shadowy in the dark.

They talked about mundane matters in quiet, intimate voices, about Jacob's small apartment, about the elder Bechers, who, they hoped, would not prove difficult. They did not touch on the past, on the distant horror they shared, or on her more recent brush with the post-fascist police and an American immigration officer. On impulse, Jacob took her hand and was startled to feel her tremble. Delighted, he saw her turn toward him in the glimmering light of the stars flying by the window. A surge of feeling took them both by surprise.

Their hands sought each other's bodies. They lay back in the berth kissing. A sudden release in the dark, moonlit train, a suppressed shout of joy defying their impossible, ludicrous situation.

For a moment, they froze as the heavy steps of the conductor approached, hesitated, then went past the door of their compartment. When they heard the metallic click of the door between the carriages—a signal he had entered the next car—they reached for each other again. Once more touching, exploring each other's contours beneath their heavy clothes, they revived the intimacy of a common death that had delayed its coming.

"*Mio sposo!*" she whispered. "My stubborn, ridiculous man."

And after a long pause, anxiously: "Where do we go from here?"

ജോവ

Francesca looked about her. The airy Meeting Room of the Friends Center near the University of Washington campus was unlike any church she knew. On this bright late-winter day, a cold sun cast surreal patterns on the white walls and freshly painted doors and on chairs arranged in a semi-circle. Knowing no one except the man she was about to marry—and not enough about him—she smiled nervously at a small party of cheerful people she had yet to meet. They were mostly students and junior faculty, youngish men in gray or brown suits, their white shirts enlivened by wine red or blue ties. Many were balding, some scarred by war. She liked Jacob's friends, their serious intensity, especially the young women, bright and open in their long skirts and colorful blouses. Still, her unease persisted, anxiety about the step she was about to take.

A broad-shouldered man stepped forward to greet her, a sheaf of notes in his hand. Elmo Jackson, one of Jacob Becher's old friends, a young Unitarian minister. Since Jacob preferred the informal ambience of the Quakers, the Friends had generously offered their meeting house for this ecumenical gathering, combining a Unitarian service, a vaguely Catholic bride, and an indifferently Jewish groom. Francesca exchanged some polite words with Jackson but was not sure how to take him, for he seemed stiff and detached.

She realized that Elmo was merely awkward, relieved at being 'rescued' by a pleasant-looking woman in her late twenties, her brown hair in a bun, who did not wait for an introduction. "*Benvenuta* Francesca!" She held out her hand, and added in acceptable Italian how pleased she and Jacob's friends were that she had come to join them. "I'm Katherine Rombeck. *Katya* to my friends. We'll need you on our side when the protests start. You'll be our inspiration." And she added, "For all this we thank our friend Jacob, who worked so hard for this moment."

Puzzled, Francesca thanked her, while her eyes shifted to the flowers decorating the simple podium. Elmo now rose, signaling that the ceremony was about to begin. Relief swept over her. The man facing them with his black string tie and gray corduroy jacket seemed so out of tune with any idea of a wedding that, paradoxically, she was reassured. The white doorframes and cornices around panels of flowery wallpaper suggested openness, the possibility of escape.

Jacopo stood beside her, looking strained by his long effort to bring her here. His face reflected exhaustion, not joy. But now he turned to her, sweeping her with an approving glance, taking in her elegant blue silk dress—a special luxury acquired for this occasion—along with the orchid his father had given her, which he had deftly pinned on her shoulder. Suddenly Jacopo's face glowed with a beatific expression she couldn't resist. Her lips parted in an answering smile.

Dr. Otto Becher, now a pharmacist, retained the rigid posture of a onetime German doctor of medicine forced to settle for less following his immigration and diminished funds. She felt instinctively drawn to him. As she and Jacob stepped forward to exchange vows, she thought she heard his mother's quick intake of breath behind her. Yet, while detecting discomfort and worry in Martha Becher, in Otto she perceived only reluctance, a waiting.

She stared fixedly ahead. She had stepped through a transparent barrier into a new state, seemingly identical but totally new. Except for their moment on the train, treasured despite herself, her resolution had remained firm, and she had visited her fiancé's apartment only briefly. Partly out of fear, but also from some inexplicable reluctance, she had insisted on staying at the nearby Meany Hotel, graciously paid for by the elder Becher. Having once seen Jacopo as a brother, she found it difficult to change that image. She remembered her heartfelt words on their last evening in Florence: "We were together on the threshold of death, how could we be anything but *Geschwister*, bound together by a purely arbitrary *Vorsehung*?" The fervent formality of these words, tossed off casually between sips of vermouth on a sunny piazza, still startled her. One doesn't talk that way, she concluded, except in a foreign language. Nor does one marry one's 'brother' in an awkward ceremony in an alien land, when marriage itself seemed foreign to everything she believed. Yet, much had happened since their first day. Now she stood with Jacopo at her side, his face still aglow with his extraordinary smile, holding out his arm to take her with him into that unknowable state. Abruptly, she was filled with quiet joy.

ഇൗരു

Their brief honeymoon began in the modest living room of Jacob's apartment, where they listened to Vivaldi while drinking hot chocolate. Through the courtesy of Otto Becher, there had been a small reception in the Meany Hotel, where Francesca became better acquainted with Jacob's friends. Perhaps she would have much in common with many of them, especially with that impressive young woman called Katya. Her passable Italian, which Katya had learned during a year's study in Lugano before the war, could be a further bond.

Most remarkable, however, was the change she discerned in Otto Becher. When the toasts had been drunk and the cake consumed, as the newly married couple was saying good-byes and thanks, Martha merely mumbled, "You're welcome. Least we could do." But Otto had smiled. "It was a good beginning," he said, and he'd embraced his new daughter.

Now it was over, and the two sat with their cocoa on the worn sofa, discussing this beginning. She was not yet accustomed to the trappings of her husband's culture—the brick-and-board shelves stuffed with a motley collection of books, the worn easy chairs, the cheap prints and unframed posters on the wall. She rose. Still in the spirit of the ceremony, she hung her own contribution: a small watercolor by Gregor Matthäus, named *War and Peace*, which she'd had framed and brought with her as her offering. And to confirm her intimate new state, she took off her one good silk dress and put on a dressing gown. Jacopo smiled his pleasure at the gesture that signaled she felt at home.

She remembered a remark Katya had made just before the ceremony. She spoke up abruptly in German. "Jakob, what did Katya mean when she said I'd inspire them all in their 'protest groups'? What's this all about?"

"It's nothing. Just politics."

She insisted, suddenly alert, turning her new ring on her finger. "You owe me an explanation."

"It's nothing," he reiterated. "Some clown of a state legislator has been making a big noise about all kinds of institutions in the state, and there are rumors he wants to go after the university. We're too Left."

She was not satisfied. "And what were all those hymns of praise about? What did you tell your friends about me?"

"I just told them what you were when we met."

"So—?" She filled in the rest with silence.

Jacopo's eyes darted away from her clear, direct gaze. She heard his breath quicken, saw his hands tighten on the arms of the chair. "None of that will affect us," he said, still not quite looking at her. "Small fry like us won't interest them."

She knew he was lying, and her fear was aroused. Their first night in a shared bed was disturbed by nagging anxieties that haunted her. His restlessness told her he was haunted, too. Still, the barriers came down in the end, and Francesca basked in the sweetness of their bonding. Several days later, she called Katya to assess the danger. When she hung up, she knew. She turned to her new husband. "Why do you keep me from knowing the truth? Ever since my disillusionment with Gregor Matthäus, I've worried about not knowing the truth, especially from the man I married."

Jacob didn't respond directly. "What about Matthäus?" He raised his eyebrows.

"He's a fine artist and gave wonderful parties, but he used us all. He changed and began to lick the boots of Fascists. I'm tired of people who say they're one thing and end up being something else." She fixed him with angry eyes.

If there was an innuendo in her words, Jacopo refused to hear it. "You needn't be afraid on my score. I just worry about worrying *you*."

"And that's exactly what worries *me*," she answered emphatically. "If I see danger, I want to know all of it all the time."

Cloudy Weather
(1947-1948)

Chapter 5
A Fateful Error

"You know, Katya, everything's so different from what I expected, but life often outstrips imagination."

The two women sat together near a window, coffee cups in hand. Outside, a haze of drizzling rain enveloped the wet street—East Forty-second Street not far from Seattle's university district. Francesca felt relieved and comforted to be able to confide in her friend in her own Italian, leaning far back in her rocking chair and stretching her legs.

"It's frightening. Everything's calm on the surface, and Jacopo and I manage OK, but I can't trust this calm—not since that first night. He was so damned evasive about important things that I had to call you to get at least some of it straight." She blushed, then hurried on with a light laugh, "Some wedding night." Her tone became serious. "I shouldn't talk this way; it makes even the good things seem bad. If only there weren't those closed-off corners in his mind. If only I could trust him more. It would be so easy to love him."

Katya smiled but made no reply, and Francesca wondered if she should have revealed her marital worries. The silence lengthened as gray shadows blurred Katya's pleasant, round face in the fading light of the dreary afternoon. She did not turn on the lamp to dispel the growing dark.

Francesca burst out suddenly. "I'm just not ready for politics again. You see, America was to be my refuge. I was *so* hoping. I was tired. I *am* tired. I want to find a *home*. But instead, things here are getting to be like Italy, too close to all that fascist rigmarole about Communism and Reds and all that. I thought I could find myself again—career, marriage, you know be normal, start over after the war."

She looked up, saw her friend biting her lip and was suddenly apologetic.

"Oh no, Katya! I wasn't questioning what *you* do. I admired you the other day running that meeting of the... AYD—American Youth for Democracy, is that it? It's frankly Communist, you say? You manage it well, steering it around the roadblocks, the hostility and misunderstandings. The university is lucky to have you. It's just me, *cara*, and Jacopo not being open."

Katya's voice was low, almost dispirited. "All this is so much more dangerous than it used to be, especially for people like you. Now, since that McCarran-Walters Act passed, you can even be *deported*. I'd been on the point of asking if you felt like joining us in a People's March to Olympia. Now I have to warn you against it."

Francesca frowned in puzzlement. "Thanks for warning me, but what's the march about?"

"We're protesting these creepy investigations. It seems they suspect our Washington State Pension Union of communist infiltration, and the university won't be far behind on the same charge!" Katya's eyes blazed with anger. "So, now you know, Francesca. That's why some of us will join the protest march to Olympia. All the way to the capitol, if we get that far."

"Who's going from the university?"

"At least three faculty, including, we hope, your husband, and a number of students. We don't know how many. We hope it'll be a good turnout. You mustn't walk with us though."

Francesca clenched her hands together. "I'm not sure what I'll do ..." She continued in an angry voice. "Why didn't he write me about this mess back in Italy when I still had a choice?"

Katya ignored the remark, concentrating on her concern for Francesca. "There isn't much they can do to us. But you ... I should have foreseen all this from the moment I met you. I won't let you come."

Francesca countered, a shade more sharply than she'd intended. "Thanks, I'm angry at Jacob for holding out on me, but I'm used to making my own decisions—and that's what I have to do now."

Abruptly, she put down her cup and looked at her watch. "God, I'm late!" She turned to Katya, her lips widening in a shy smile, hoping to make amends. "I must go meet Jacopo. You're a true friend, Katya. I thank you. You're very kind." A quick kiss on her forehead. "But, you see, I've got to work this out for myself. *Ciao!*"

Running down the creaking stairs of the old building, ignoring voices from the rooms she passed, she still felt the warmth of friendship, even as it was tempered by the chill of apprehension. As she walked briskly through the rain toward University Way, she again felt threatened, feared any hope for a normal life was eluding her once more.

Jacopo was waiting on the library steps, in the rain, bareheaded, his Army raincoat drenched dark. Seeing him standing there, almost lost in the gathering dusk, some of her anger evaporated, and she felt a wave of tenderness practically against her will. There he stood, faintly visible in the light of the massive amber lanterns reflected on the slick concrete. For a moment, she again saw him in his uniform in that sunny Florentine piazza, the same lostness, the same intensity, the same boyish look.

"Hey, beauty! Where've you been?"

"Jacopo! I'm so sorry to keep you waiting in this weather. I was with Katya, and we lost track of time."

His expression showed no irritation.

"Jacopo. I must talk to you. Dinner can wait." Despite the rain and his hatless head, she drew him down the steps and led him along the sidewalk to the footpath she had already begun to think of as her own. It led past beds of roses, flowerless, their stalks long and leggy, needing to be pruned, the soil still unturned, waiting for warmer weather.

"Please, let's walk a bit," she urged him.

Jacob looked at the brown earth as he allowed his new wife to lead him toward a grove of pines at the end of the path. He glanced at her sidewise, as if puzzled by her determined stride. She stopped and faced him, starting slowly in German. "I've been here over six weeks now, Jakob, and I've been your wife for almost that long, yet you're still hiding from me." She struggled to suppress another wave of anger, something she knew she had inherited from her father. "You've always known I was a target back in Italy for my politics. You've always known knew why I came here. I thought I'd be able to leave all that behind, at least once I got past that gatekeeper on the boat. I thought I'd finally escaped to live with you and build a career. But you've left me in the dark about the real political situation over here—constantly telling me that it's not real for people like us, just newspaper verbiage and radio chatter—and now there's no escaping it."

He stopped at the pond near the fountain and drew her close to him without answering. He kissed her, and after a moment, she responded. They stood beside the bed where roses would bloom again in time, the rain pouring over them, like lovers at their first encounter, as though their kiss would never end. She recalled their first embrace on the train, how that single moment had transformed a hesitant bride into a lover. That moment came back to her now with lively pleasure.

Nevertheless, Jacopo, her lover, had not answered her question.

Her deep disappointment at his lack of candor came back despite the kiss, seizing her once more before she allowed her sense of tenderness to return to the surface. "*Was willst Du sagen?*" she asked when she finally broke away. "What are you trying to say?"

His voice was tight. "Let's walk some more."

They followed the muddy path farther into the still uncultivated rose garden. Finally, he began, almost inaudibly. "What can I say that you don't already know? Most of my friends are political, some members of this party, some of that. But as a group we aren't affiliated with anything except ... that we all want something better."

"Jacopo!" she cried. "Why didn't you tell me?"

He remained silent. They plodded with mud-caked shoes over the wet earth, through the puddles. The rain sluiced down as the dark closed around them.

At last, he answered. "When I was discharged and resigned my commission, I just wanted to be free to marry you and lead my own life. Then I met my friends here in Seattle and was caught by their earnestness, their commitment. But I loved you, and I was afraid to lose you. So I kept mum about it all."

Some love, she thought, still angry, but his gentle voice caught her once more. She relented. Hadn't she also kept quiet about her struggle as a partisan to be recognized and respected despite her sex and patrician origin? About her militant, sporadic journalism? Why hadn't she made her history clear to her husband and lover?

She took his hand. "Let's go eat. We have decisions to make."

&OCR&

Albert Canwell, a former sheriff from Spokane, hated Communists. His hatred had crystallized during the waterfront strikes of the 1930s.

He was sitting pretty now as a newly-elected legislator, swept in with a large majority of conservatives in the 1946 elections. Now, the legislature prepared to pounce upon and expose communist influence in all state institutions, and Canwell was in line to head the committee to root out subversion. He'd already investigated and was about to "purge" the Washington Pension Union and was poised to launch an assault on the university that he considered a hot-bed of Reds. Canwell's appointment came promptly in March at the end of the 1947 legislative session.

The march on Olympia, including Katya, Elmo, Jacob, and their friends, took place just before Canwell took office. The atmosphere was already tense.

Francesca reluctantly gave in and did not march. "How can I not march, now that I live with you people?" But finally, fear of another expulsion won out. Francesca remained behind in the apartment, watching them pile into two cars on their way to Olympia. She brewed pots of coffee for their return, anxious for their safety.

They came back safely, but they were silent. On their faces, she saw a deep and discouraged fatigue. Elmo pulled his sweater over his head, his voice momentarily muffled. "Why do they do all this? Why do we have to respond? It's all about the past, what people once were, isn't it? There's nothing in it about the future."

Katya spoke with staunch conviction. "*We* are the future. They don't believe it. Nobody does. But they'll see."

છ૭ભ

Francesca's bonds with Jacob grew stronger during the following months of relative quiet. She opened herself to his love without reserve, for he had convinced her of his support. She also befriended the elder Bechers, whose well-scrubbed home they visited regularly. As she had from the beginning, she felt particular affection for Jacob's father, and saw it reciprocated. Undaunted by his Prussian mannerisms, she was able to see through and beyond them.

"I'm amazed at your success with my father," said Jacob. "I never thought it possible. He's such a conservative."

"But I'm one, too, you know, when you get down to it. I love his poise, his controlled manner. We can talk to each other." She could tell that by now, Otto could see her as the tough, honest fighter she continued to be.

She stopped by one day on her walk home from the university to give Otto the good news that she had been granted provisional admission to the Law School. He was delighted and shook her hand vigorously. "We need someone like you who knows about Fascism."

She smiled. "Jacob helped, of course. The war may be over, but his credentials as a former officer have made a difference—along with my Italian academic credentials."

Otto laid a hand on her arm and proposed a toast. "Let's drink to it before I drive you home. It's a great day."

Martha joined them and raised her glass as well. "Congratulations, Francesca!" She, too, was beginning to thaw.

Perhaps the new life she'd hoped for was finally becoming a reality.

ॐ⊙ଔ

In September 1947, Francesca applied for a part-time position at the university, teaching Italian, and was immediately accepted. The job was more than welcome, since Jacob's salary as a junior faculty member in the history department was barely enough to make ends meet. A good part of his income went to pay for her tuition at the Law School.

But despite Francesca's amazing fluency in English, the result of months of intensive study during the past year, she was still insecure about bureaucratic language and procedures, more attentive to details than strictly necessary. When the secretary handed her, among other documents, a form including a request for biographical information, she filled it in with care, listing her law courses in Turin, her various small jobs before and after the war, and, finally, with some pride, adding her contribution to the war as a partisan, as if it were just an ordinary form of military service. Though she was careful not to disclose any specific information, she felt a need to come forward with what had been her unique and honorable past. The departmental office was intolerably overheated on another wet, depressing day, and she was relieved to hand in all those bothersome papers at last and prepare to walk home.

The door banged behind her. "Jacopo, I'm sorry to be late, but I had to fill in a bunch of papers to qualify for the new job."

"What papers?"

"Among other things, there was a form asking for my background."

Jacob straightened, his eyes wide. "What did you write?"

"I told them about my law courses in Turin and the jobs I've had and that I'd been a *partigiana.*"

"*What? How can you be such a fool?* Why did you do it? What you did over there is nobody's business."

೩అಂ

She had months to mull over her incomprehensible blunder. Why, with her political savvy, had she been so naively unaware of the implications of her service as a partisan, especially at a time as intolerant of left-wing dissent at this period of Cold War tension? The wheels of authority ground slowly, but soon after Christmas, she received a formal letter signed by a Gerald Dougherty, special investigator retained by the Canwell Committee. In a few clipped sentences, he requested her presence at his private office on the following Tuesday at 2:00 P.M.

The Bechers were having coffee together on that winter day, opening the morning's mail. When she grasped the meaning of the letter, she instinctively closed the envelope. Silently, she handed it to her husband. This time, he was gentle.

"I'm so sorry. I'd hoped the grilling you got aboard ship would be the end. What more could they possibly want?"

But she knew, and surely he did, too.

She arrived punctually at the investigator's office, prepared for the worst but was pleasantly surprised. Gerald Dougherty presented a most agreeable façade, with benevolent eyes and a perpetual smile. Short and heavyset, his build suggested impressive hidden strength, At first, they talked about her Italian citizenship, her immigration and marriage. Sitting in his spacious office in the Dexter Horton Building in downtown Seattle, with busy secretaries flitting past the open door, Francesca felt reassured, as if such goings on made the place as normal as these activities suggested.

She knew, of course, that this man was about to examine the very innards of her political life. But having spent her decisive years as a dissenter in a fascist country where each move might have had lethal consequences, she was, oddly, lulled into complacency by this more relaxed American interrogation. However, an abrupt new tone broke into their courteous talk, reminding her sharply why she'd been summoned.

"You were a partisan, I understand. What communist unit did you answer to?"

Francesca was now wary. "None where I was."

Dougherty leaned back in his desk chair. "Tell me then, do you believe in the communist conspiracy?"

Francesca stiffened, totally alert: "I'm not sure what you mean, sir. I'm for democracy."

The man bowed his head, "Of course, we all are." His face darkened. "These are difficult times, Mrs. Becher, very dangerous. We must keep our eyes open. You admit you were a partisan, yet you stated in writing that you weren't a Communist. How so? Can you swear to that?"

She felt pained at having to explain. "Yes, of course. There were different groups of partisans; some, like the cadres I worked with, weren't Communists. I just said so. But, sir, those were hard times for us, too—wartime, more or less occupied by the Germans."

To her surprise, she found herself becoming voluble. "Communist forces were gaining strength in the northeastern part of my country. But then," she went on, increasingly uncertain that she was understood, "everything is different over there. Many cities now have communist mayors... a large communist percentage of legislators. The situation," she repeated, stressing her words, "is very different over there."

The investigator seemed not to hear her. It was as if she'd never spoken. Unperturbed, he completed his question, "...or that you've never been a Communist?"

Her pause grew uncomfortably long. Then came her impatient, emphatic reply.

"No, never!"

Moments later, she spoke again, her voice ringing sharply. "I worked with non-communist groups in my movement." This was the truth and had been the truth through most of the war. But not in her distant past, her student days. She'd sidestepped the question.

"I don't doubt it," said Mr. Dougherty, relenting. "But I do understand you correctly, don't I, that you're prepared to swear you were never a Communist—never part of the Movement, the big Conspiracy?"

"Yes, I said so."

Her interrogator rose and held out his hand. "We may need to get together again," he said conversationally. "I'll give you a call."

Outside, Francesca breathed more lightly. Although the man had left no doubt that this interview had been merely an opening skirmish in an as-yet-undisclosed campaign, she felt she had done tolerably well. All she would have to do in the future, she decided, was to reiterate what was indisputably true: that her wing of the Resistance had remained aloof from the Communists.

She called Jacob at his office from a public telephone, and they agreed to meet for a quick beer before going home. It was three in the afternoon, and a brilliant winter sun was shining in Seattle.

ಐಲ

Jacob saw her hat first, an old-fashioned, wide-brimmed affair she'd proudly picked up in a second-hand clothing store on First Avenue. She sat in the bar by the large window, the hat framing her face. Waves of pleasure warmed him; she looked extraordinarily beautiful.

He sat down across from her, eager to hear the news. "How did it go?"

She had ordered for both of them and pushed his glass toward him. She shrugged. "I'm not really sure. Hard to tell. I really don't know what this was all about—except, of course, he knew I was a partisan. Part of my history now."

"We have to learn about police being everywhere, knowing everything. True, it wasn't some gremlin that whispered in his ear. You can't even fill out a form honestly."

She sighed. "You were right. So right."

He was moved by the admission. "Listen, the situation is different over here. But Communism—it's become a real bugaboo in people's minds. Who knows what Canwell will do?"

It now came to her, as a belated insight. Her admission was bound to implicate her in charges of Communism, and she had also endangered others. Her careless entry on an unimportant form could affect everyone she knew whose life and livelihood depended on a politically aseptic reputation: all their friends as well as this husband of hers, now reaching over to take her hand. Though her war service had been no secret to the immigration officer who had questioned her on the boat, knowledge of it had not yet come to the attention of powerful local watchdogs. Now she'd revealed too much and created waves that might reach far beyond her.

She took his hand across the table. "*Scusi, caro.* I'm so sorry."

They got up slowly, and, arm-in-arm, walked out into an indifferent street.

ഇരൻ

That night she telephoned Katya. When she told about the delayed consequences of her senseless error on the employment form, her voice was so tight her friend could hardly hear her.

"Katya, how could I?" she whispered in Italian. And in a slightly louder voice, "It seemed so routine to fill out a form. How could I be so stupid to reveal something so dangerous, something so open to misunderstanding?"

"Especially when you talk Communism," Katya said, audibly striking a match to light a cigarette.

"I know."

The phone went silent for a moment.

Like Jacob, Katya perceived the real danger. With her denial of *any* ties with Communism, even of the most ephemeral and distant kind, Francesca would inevitably be caught in an apparent lie. Her answer might turn into a potential trap. Having come to love her, Katya feared that when Francesca married Jacob, she had become an unwitting target of their adversaries' campaign for political purity. But she was also anxious to protect her friend from debilitating fears.

Katya spoke at last. "Don't worry; it probably wasn't even all your doing. He may have heard from the immigration people back East. And your candor may actually help you."

"Help me? I sabotaged myself! At the very least, I alerted them."

"You're still one of us. Think of all the things you did while we did nothing at home."

For a moment, Francesca saw herself and Jacob lit by that blinding flash. But that was long ago. It was no help, no consolation.

"Oh, Katya!" she moaned. "Oh Katya! What have I done?"

Chapter 6
Escalating Danger

Francesca pressed her shoulders hard against the ornate mantelpiece in the common room of the New Life Cooperative. "Nonsense!" Her decisive tone bordered on anger. Katya, sitting on the sofa in front of her, raised a hand in warning, but her friend ignored her, continuing in Italian. "I want to hear Goddard! I've heard so much about him, and what I've heard doesn't make him a Communist. You know that. You people are obsessed with Communism—on both sides." Outside, a gentle rain streaked the window.

"It isn't what *you* think that matters. It's what *they* think: the Canwell Committee and its spies. From the Pension Union to the university—for them, it's all one crusade. What makes you think they'll ease off?"

Francesca shook her head. The whole issue seemed ludicrous. What was dangerous about a mere lecture by a left-leaning liberal, a well-known historian? Her old fighting spirit flared up. "I'm going. I don't give a damn *what* they think."

"I don't either. But they have the power."

Francesca put on her hat and raincoat. She stood tall, her eyes bright and combative. "Let them come and ask me. I'm studying to be a lawyer, an *American* lawyer." She picked up her shoulder bag. "So I must know American history, and, from what they tell me, Goddard delivers it."

Katya's eyebrows drew together in concern. "You still don't know? Goddard's been cited for being 'subversive,' and you'll be contaminated if they see you at his lecture. You already had one close call. You don't need this."

Francesca met her eyes with a level gaze. "I'm a student, Katya, and I need to learn. I didn't come here to pour at a ladies' afternoon tea."

"Francesca, listen! I've failed you, failed to make clear how the danger has grown and deepened and spread ..."

But Francesca was gone. The outside door shut with a bang. She enjoyed the drizzle on her face, triumphant at having reconfirmed her decision to live her own life. She remembered the heady early days of peace: "The war is over. I can be myself now."

৪০৫৪

Jacob lounged in his threadbare easy chair, reading, pencil in hand. The soft light of the table lamp warmed his head and shoulders. He looked up. "Hi, beauty," he greeted his wife, smiling. "Are we going tonight?"

"Of course. What do *you* think?"

"I can't figure this one at all." Jacob put down his book with a slow, unconscious movement. "It's not as clear-cut as the march. But then Katya is more up on these things."

Francesca gave an impatient shrug and walked into the small kitchen, pulling off her wet raincoat. He heard a loud rattle of pots and pans, then running water. "Pasta tonight, Jacopo!"

But his mind was far removed from their evening meal as he mulled over their decision. "He's a Marxist historian, known for that."

"Garbage!" The bang on the stovetop told him she'd put on a pot of water. "If so, what does that make him? A professor, right? A man with things to say. What about Katya's Marxist discussion group? And you? Have you all turned into blubber?"

For a moment, he was silent, then he spoke with slow emphasis. "Francesca darling, it's not about us. It's about you."

Her voice was hard, and she spoke in Italian. "Let me be. The war was over three years ago. I've been myself for some time now."

৪০৫৪

Meany Hall was unusually crowded. As Jacob and Francesca entered the building from the tree-lined walk, she wondered why so many people were drawn to a lecture by a distinguished but not widely popular speaker. Clearly, word had spread that he and his topic of slavery would be controversial. But looking at the mix of staid professional types, veterans in blue jeans and serious young women, all busy talking, she felt safe after all. She had held her breath against a surge of anxiety on entering the hall, but now she sighed and her stomach muscles unclenched.

Also reassuring was Harold Goddard himself, his modest appearance contrasting sharply with his vivid speaking style. They sat close to the podium and Francesca could observe how this pale blond figure came alive as he warmed to his topic. She knew next to nothing about it, having formed her image of the American South from a childhood reading of *Uncle Tom's Cabin* in Italian translation and a recent discovery of Faulkner and *The Sound and the Fury*.

But that was enough to allow her to follow Goddard with intense interest, intrigued by the contrast between his sober economic analysis and the intense passion of his delivery. His Marxist approach was evident, but she was puzzled, for in the political scene she'd left behind after the fall of Fascism, his reading of history would have seemed far from radical.

Electricity crackled in the hall at the first question by a young man with sandy hair and round glasses. His left hand in his pocket, he gesticulated with his right arm, the forefinger stabbing at the speaker, his deceptively gentle voice a striking contrast. "Professor Goddard, my name is Ed Arnold, and I'm majoring in Speech. But don't worry; I'm not questioning your forensic skills." He smirked.

The audience gasped. The presiding young professor stepped forward anxiously, but Goddard waved him off.

Ed Arnold resumed after a dramatic pause. "May I ask, sir, where you got your so-called facts, basing everything on money and power?"

The chairman placed himself next to the speaker as if to protect him. "Your point, please, be more specific." A slight tremor crept into his voice.

Arnold's tone struck Francesca as all too familiar from a recent past. The faltering chairman annoyed and chilled her. Her attention returned to the student, whose pose was belligerent, his grin smug.

"OK, my question. How do you explain the religious fervor, the piety? All those magnificent spirituals and all that banjo playing? The bond between master and slave, slave and master?"

Francesca scowled. *What nonsense!*

If Goddard thought it was nonsense, he did not let on. He spoke clearly, patiently, at some length. The questioner finally sat down. But she felt a changed atmosphere in the vast hall. Although substantial questions followed, lucidly answered, the tone remained depressed. The early excitement about learning she'd shared with the audience was never restored. When the chairman signaled the end of the lecture, people around her rose in haste and made for the doors, speaking in subdued voices.

Jacob and Francesca were about to reach the fresh air outside when they heard Elmo Jackson's rasping voice.

"You're not going to the reception, are you? If you do, you're out of your minds." His jacket, flung over his turtleneck in haste, slipped off one shoulder as he stretched out his hand in warning.

"You better believe it." Francesca relished the new expression while Jacob said nothing. She added, relenting, "We won't stay long."

"It doesn't matter how long. Stick your head in there, and the FBI will know it. They'll list everyone at the party in no time."

Francesca's militancy reasserted itself, and she swept past Elmo, peremptorily urging Jacob to join her. But their friend, apparently believing his mere presence would protect them, invited himself along. Slightly annoyed, she agreed. Together they piled into the Bechers' old Plymouth and headed for the party.

80C3

Gretta Dalton, their hostess, proudly introduced her to the guest of honor. "This is Francesca Mancini. She came to us from Italy, a war bride who fought on our side."

Francesca knew her hostess as a widow who thought it her duty to take care of promising young women, now seemingly delighted to take Francesca under her wing to present her to Professor Goddard. Mrs. Dalton struck her as imposing. Braids of generous graying hair towered on her head like a crown as she extended her arm in a welcoming gesture. Her hazel eyes, barricaded behind thick glasses, darted back and forth between her two guests. She took a sip from her glass of bourbon. "Both of you are rare birds, with courage and conviction at the lectern and in battle."

Francesca's face reddened at this compliment, and Goddard looked at his feet with a sheepish grin. But their hostess did not elaborate and soon left them to themselves, bustling off to tend to her other guests.

Francesca hurried to fill the awkward silence. "Thank you so much for your lecture, Professor Goddard. Being from abroad, I still know far too little about America, especially the South and such issues as slavery. But you made it all clear."

Goddard's reply was cautious, tentative. "I don't know what your convictions are. Mine are very simple. I see the entire slave culture as a model of what society will do if unchecked."

"That was behind the young man's anger, wasn't it?" She glanced around them. They were isolated, no one nearby. On the other side of the room, Mrs. Dalton was passing canapés of crackers laden with dainty portions of pâté or fish.

"I suppose so, but that student's anger signaled his denial of the obvious. As I said, our society, today's society, reflects the same structure as the old slave culture. It's still the powerless exploited by the powerful." He shrugged. "Arnold doesn't like that view of the world. He wants some kind of sentimental harmony instead. One can't really discuss ideas like mine without running into all kinds of problems. Especially these days." He stopped and for the moment they were silent, finding themselves on an imaginary island amid party noise and clinking glasses.

He smiled at her. "Mrs. Dalton said you fought on our side in the war. What did you do?"

For a moment she hesitated, then, encouraged by his open smile, she plunged ahead, once more needing to declare herself. She spoke distinctly, her words ringing bell-like in an unexpected lull in the background conversation.

"I was a *partigiana*."

Heads turned. She recognized none of them.

They talked a moment longer until Goddard was politely drawn away by another guest who claimed he'd waited all evening for a word with the guest of honor. Francesca moved away, the glass of wine in her hand. She felt unexpectedly exposed, adrift.

Two couples hurriedly left the room, the door clicking shut behind them. Elmo appeared beside her, urging her in his gravelly voice. "Let's go. Jacob will follow us."

"I can't."

Goddard was now standing in a far corner in animated talk. How could she leave just like that, without a word to him and their hostess?

"I must say goodbye to Mrs. Dalton. We were invited to a late supper. What makes you think ...?"

"Partisan means Communist in most people's minds. *Andiamo!*"

"Not yet ..." She rebelled against leaving so abruptly, as if in panic. Then she felt a warm hand on her shoulder, and, turning, she met Mrs. Dalton's grave eyes. "Don't worry, dear. There'll be other times. Your friend may be right." She opened her arms as if to embrace her, caught herself and, as if stirred by unexpected emotion, walked quickly away. The expression in Mrs. Dalton's hazel eyes lingered in Francesca's mind as the three of them left the room.

As they drove through the night-cloaked city, Francesca felt an oppressive weight bearing down upon her, stifling her breathing. She rubbed her forehead with the fingers of one hand. A headache was coming on.

৪০৫৪

The consequences were not long in coming. Only one week later, Francesca received a phone call from Investigator Gerald Dougherty, whose mellifluous voice filled her ear and brain with anxiety. The proximity of the hearings must have brought on this quick and unwelcome attention.

His tone was conversational. "I'd like to get together with you again." He made it sound almost like a date, but there was steel in his voice, as he set up another round of questioning for the following Tuesday. "Is 4:00 P.M. convenient? All right, I'll see you then."

She arrived precisely on time on a sunny afternoon, and he greeted her with a broad smile. "Mrs. Becher! Good to see you." The man in banker's gray walked around his desk to shake her hand. "Please sit down."

He returned to his seat, still smiling benignly, as she settled herself across from him.

For a moment, neither of them spoke, but Francesca was unwilling to wait for his opening. She smiled in turn. "What can I do for you?"

Dougherty at once launched into his own line of questioning, proving to be amazingly well informed. He confronted her bluntly, "Mrs. Becher, you've been here such a short time, and yet I'm wondering about the direction of your social life, your associations. With and without your husband."

Francesca's eyebrows rose, but she remained silent.

"For example, we know you've been a constant visitor at that Red commune on Forty-second Street. You're there often by yourself."

She blanched inwardly, realizing how closely she was being observed and wondering why she required so much attention. She froze her face in a neutral expression. "I'm not sure what you mean, sir. It's just a student co-operative. I have friends there. They don't all have the same politics—or religion."

The man looked skeptical but changed the subject. "The university hosts lots of interesting lectures on campus. Hard to choose among them. Do you pick a certain kind?"

She shrugged. "I don't have much time, so I choose what interests me most."

"Slavery, for instance? Delivered by a known fellow traveler?"

She made no reply.

Her interrogator again changed the subject. Among a number of further, well-placed questions, he jolted her by revealing some knowledge of the painter Gregor Matthäus far away in Italy. He hinted he knew there had been a certain article attacking the painter, a piece published in *Il* Tempo in September 1946. What had been his role in the fight against Communism? Which side was he on—for or against the Conspiracy?

Stunned, Francesca was unable to deny that she was the author. Before she could give a reasoned answer, Dougherty suggested he already knew. "We hear this painter was harassed by the Communists over there." He looked at her, no trace of his former joviality in his face. "You say you're not a Communist yourself, and I try to believe you, but what about that article, Mrs. Becher? It sounds like you joined the pack."

Francesca held the man's gaze. "I talked about Nazis and Fascists, Mr. Dougherty. Not one word about Communism."

To her relief, he left her response unanswered and surprised her by signaling their interview was at an end. Coming around the desk, he put his hand on her shoulder.

"Will that be all?" she asked, angry at herself for accepting his familiarity and for the hint of anxiety in her voice.

"I'll let you know."

Deep in thought, Francesca walked down the steps and into the darkening day.

Chapter 7
The Decisive Moment

Jacob shifted on the ancient straight chair, causing a medley of creaks and hoping it wouldn't collapse. He'd chosen to sit there to remain inconspicuous rather than occupy one of the musty, dusty upholstered chairs and couches in the common room of the New World Cooperative. He didn't belong here at this special meeting of the AYD, but Francesca would speak today, and he was here to support her. The clock on the ornate mantelpiece struck five. Outside, the dreary Seattle day filtered its dying sunlight through a veil of misty rain. Inside, the room was still empty except for one tired young man in a plaid work shirt, dozing on an easy chair.

Where had Francesca gone? He had dropped her off and gone to find a parking space, and now she was nowhere to be seen. She must be upstairs with Katya, who had called the meeting. Francesca had agreed to talk about her life as a partisan during the recent war and to field questions. His brow wrinkled and his stomach rumbled. Why should it be less dangerous for his wife to meet with these radical students than to attend a public lecture by a Left-liberal professor?

He recalled the conversation with Katya. "I already had an earful from Elmo," she'd said. "All this makes me feel bad, since I've tried to protect her, but Francesca wanted to participate, and in the end she has to make up her own mind. It's a small, intimate group, after all."

"Are you sure there are no undercover—"

Katya had cut him off. "Of course I am. I know these people."

Two young women strolled in from opposite directions, wearing pieces of the usual student uniform, one in a brown corduroy jacket, the other in a black turtleneck sweater.

"Jean! Glad you could come after all!"

"Yeah. This speaker looked so interesting, I couldn't pass her up. A real live partisan! Do you know who she is, Beth?"

"Sort of." She pulled out a wrinkled memo. "Her name's Francesca Mancini. She used to be a partisan but now she's married to Becher in History."

Jean laughed. "I guess that's where those bourgeois militants end up. In some professor's bed!"

Jacob, on his rickety chair in the back, couldn't quite suppress a smile. No one noticed him.

Three men joined them. "Where were you, Jean? I was looking for you," one of them asked. Jean pulled out her notebook and looked for her pen, ignoring the man. "She'll have something to say. They won the war, after all."

"Don't be foolish," Beth admonished. "Foot soldiers don't win wars, especially not women soldiers."

Increasingly nervous, Jacob squirmed on the chair. Were these people hostile or welcoming? More students filed in, some by themselves, looking shy or assertive, others with wives, husbands, girlfriends, some quietly looking for a place to sit, others loud and aggressive.

Finally, Katya and Francesca strode to the front of the room and Jacob sat forward, watching. The two women stood side by side. The newcomer towered over Katya; her dark eyes swept the audience, her dark hair and regal stance lending her an air of mystery. Talk ceased altogether. The two sat down on folding chairs, facing the group.

Katya began with announcements: the time of their next meeting, that attendees who wished to do so could bring sandwiches. Then she came to the point. "We have a special meeting of our group today. I want you to meet Francesca. She was an Italian partisan during the war, and that made her a true revolutionary—a fighter for her beliefs."

"Aw, come on, cut it out." Beth in the front row challenged Katya again. "You know what Professor Pembroke thinks of empty, inflated rhetoric like that. Like posing as a revolutionary without knowing what the word means."

Even Jean was annoyed. "*You* cut it out! Let her talk!"

Francesca rose, but found it impossible to smile. This was not the audience of pliant students she had expected. Still, she spoke clearly and precisely. "I was a foot soldier to free my country from Nazis and Fascists, sometimes with a rifle, at other times in enemy headquarters, helping our side."

Now a man named Hal interrupted. "We know it was war, and we know you took risks. We appreciate that. Many Americans did that, too. Lots of our soldiers 'fought for their country' in Italy, France, or

Guadalcanal. But how did you line up in the class struggle?"

Katya's face flushed. "Let her *talk* for God's sake!"

"It's a *valid* question!" Hal was shouting now. "Francesca, I repeat, where did you stand? Were you 'just' a patriot, or what?"

Francesca's eyes blazed and she clasped her hands together in a tight grip. She had not expected suspicion and hostility along with such familiarity. Whatever made her accept this invitation to lecture to a Communist youth group? She hadn't been a Communist since her student days, and she refused to speak their jargon.

She began again. "I don't know what your Professor Pembroke would say to this, but my ideology and yours are not the same. Still, I can tell you what it's like, fighting in a civil war."

Taut, muscular, in her blue shirt and slacks, her short hair framing her pale face and dark eyes, Jacob saw her as the image of the classic militant they all wanted to meet. Yet she kept on insisting she was not a Communist. He could see how confusing that must be for this group.

Francesca continued. "Your thinking and mine have a lot in common." She was being more conciliatory. "I fought to liberate my country. Ho Chi Min fights that way against the French. He's Marxist but also…"

"Yeah!" Beth and Hal shouted almost in unison while the rest of the group looked uncomfortable. "That's how it is in colonized countries. Class struggle and national struggles come together. But remember, lady, Italy hasn't been colonized since the Goths!"

Francesca's tone became acid. "That's all theory. We put our lives on the line against the reality of Fascism, not for some theory." She felt defensive, not because of this continuing battle of words but because she felt it necessary to make the distinction—especially for this group—between being a militant and being a Communist.

Katya rescued her. "Tell us what it's like under fire when you're fighting your own people."

"Class enemies!" Even Jean shouted and two or three hands went up to say the same. "We've got to remember that when the Soviet Union gets into the act."

Beth took up the thread. "It's not national. It's world revolution! The line changes depending on the tactics, but what Marx said in the opining line of *The Communist Manifesto* is still true. 'A spectre is haunting Europe—the spectre of Communism!'" She intoned the words with feeling, unaware that they had long since become a cliché.

Francesca's stern 'Olga' voice cut through the confusion. "It's not that simple. Your enemy—class enemy, if you will, though a good number who were workers were also Fascists—that enemy hates you, not for what you are but for the horrors you represent to him. You challenge his life and his society, everything he holds dear, common language and all that be damned. And you understand him because that soldier was part of your life. He was your friend, your brother, or the baker down the street. Yet, when he aims a gun muzzle at you, you have to react. Even if you played on the same football team, it's that gun muzzle you have to deal with, not the enemy's place in the social structure."

Beth called out, "What *are* you driving at?"

Francesca, now 'Olga,' ignored Beth, because she now knew she had something important to say. "You are the Other on the opposite side of the firing line, on the rooftop, peering around the street corner. And for you, that soldier facing you must become the Other, too. It's always a tragedy."

For a moment, there was silence.

Beth spoke up. "That's sentimental trash! You fight the *power* on the other side. What the hell do you care what language they speak? They're *on the other side!*" She paused and glared belligerently through her wire-rimmed glasses. "We shouldn't even discuss this. Talking this way dissipates the strength of the militants. All our strengths!"

Francesca couldn't conceal her irritation. "This *is* all talk." She faced Beth squarely. "We just talked about that. There's theory, my friend, but there's also the reality of combat. Such talk as this is meaningless there. When you're in combat, you wipe out everything personal and certainly everything theoretical in your mind." She scanned the room. "You veterans know that in combat you're always at risk. Ideology be damned. I shot and was shot at, all the way from Palermo to Verona. There's always someone—another human being—behind the gun trained on you." She fell silent.

Beth persisted loftily. "People went to Spain and got themselves killed and killed their own, too, for what they believed. If you want to be effective, Francesca, you have to accept all these hesitations, but for chris-sake don't contaminate us with all that maudlin stuff."

Francesca felt an unexpected wave of hostility sweep the room.

Now Katya, who had stood by quietly until then, tried to end the discussion. "It's all a matter of ideology. But it's possible for militants, fighting the same enemies but with different ideologies, to try to understand each other. And remember, unlike you and me, this woman faced the enemy off and on for more than three years. That's what I wanted her to tell you about."

Francesca looked at her friend, relief visible on her face. "Thank you. What I wanted to say is outside politics. You can't get around this: In my situation, there was another human being and, for me, an Italian human being whom I had to kill. No ideology can save you from that stark reality, that ambivalence. Struggling with that ambivalence is part of the soldier's burden in any civil war. You don't need a big thing like 'world revolution' or some such ideology. Fighting an enemy like Mussolini's Black Shirts will do."

More people stirred as they heard a strong male voice, a new voice they hadn't heard before. "You said you were a *partigiana?*"

Francesca nodded and turned a quarter circle to face him. "Yes," she said quietly and added, in spite of her audience, "but not a Communist. As I said, ideology was not the main issue."

"Excuse me." Katya's voice was high and imperious. "Who are you?"

All eyes turned toward the stranger who was sitting cross-legged on the floor, against the wall near the doorway. He was a burly man wearing old-fashioned blue overalls and a checkered lumberman's shirt. A visored cap was turned around and pushed back on his head, yet he left the impression that the entire outfit, like his awkward position on the floor, was a kind of disguise. His eyes flashed sparks of indignation. "Is this a closed club? Elmo invited me. I didn't expect this to be only one kind of—"

Elmo, visiting the group as an outsider, spoke up with some heat, his voice betraying annoyance with Katya's challenge. "Pardon me for bringing a friend. He's new in town. This was announced as an open meeting. So it's his privilege to talk. Or am I mistaken, and it's closed today? In that case, I shouldn't be here either."

"OK," Katya agreed reluctantly, her authority undermined. She had not known everyone at the meeting after all. "Go ahead. Speak."

They all heard her undertone of anger touched by anxiety.

Francesca remained calm. "I said 'ideology be damned.' I served as a partisan, not as a Communist. I served as a fighting soldier in the field and I also attacked the enemy indirectly by working under cover in his command posts."

Jacob sat up, his spine stiff with foreboding. The man burst out angrily. "Garbage! You had to be a Communist. It's a known fact that the Resistance was dominated by them. All the rest is crap."

"You're wrong," Francesca explained patiently, her own anger rising in her throat. "We were not a Communist outfit. Others were, but not us. The party had no control over us."

"Francesca!" Beth called out, "Listen to that man! Is he right or wrong? And why weren't you a Communist if you fought on the same side?"

Francesca hesitated briefly then decided to ignore that question. But she did listen to 'that man.' For all his combativeness, he tried to reach out even as he attacked.

"I was in strategic intelligence in Italy," he explained. "We had to work with you people of all stripes. Again and again you betrayed us."

"Not us."

"Yes, you!"

The group of students stirred in discomfort; they were not sure where Francesca stood.

Jacob, on the sidelines, clenched his teeth. *What irony! These people are hostile because Francesca isn't a Communist and the government and this fellow are after her because they think she is. She loses on both fronts.* Elmo intervened, trying to moderate. "Please, Mike, say what you have to say and say it clearly."

"I said it," Mike responded. "You dewy-eyed romantics, you don't want to know what's happened all over Eastern Europe. A hungry tyranny ... "

"Not true!" shouted a tall man in the back. He was wearing Army fatigues and held an unlit cigarette in his hand.

"He was talking to me. Let me answer," Olga-Francesca said calmly, and speaking as precisely as she could in her adopted English, "Mike, we never met till now, but my friend Elmo knows you, and that's enough. Yes, you're right, there are people in Eastern Europe living under oppressive regimes. And there are people like us who still have a voice. You call us 'romantics.' But that doesn't invalidate what we do. We need to continue to fight against oppression. That's why I fought the Germans—and many of my own people along with them."

Beth had the last word. "We're AYD, you know. They don't like Commies out there. What are we going to do? Go underground? Stop being Communists or any kind of socialists? Or fight like the Italian partisans we've been hearing about? Or what?"

Katya left Beth's question hanging and concluded the official meeting. "We all have much to think about and we must thank Francesca for helping us see new questions and old ones in a new light this evening. We've got to prepare ourselves, people. Those hearings are not far off." She paused and cocked her head as if considering their implications and dangers. "Well, let's break up now and talk over coffee."

After some perfunctory applause, the group rose at once and crowded around the coffee urn, gesturing vehemently as they confronted Francesca. Most of them thought themselves to be Communists with various shades of opinion and levels of commitment, and Francesca had triggered a wide range of reactions to the role of Communists in the Italian war. They argued fiercely, as if compelled to persuade this knowledgeable and attractive woman of their various positions.

The core problem had become Communism—Communist power and wartime resistance. Looking at the intense faces around her, Francesca found it hard to respond in ways that would meet their different expectations. "I really don't know," she said honestly. "Each situation is different," she argued. "Each needs its own difficult solution."

"Did you guys support the Red Army... or turn your backs on them?" The man in the Army fatigues fixed her with a skeptical look as he spoke.

"Where *do* you stand?" Beth asked her directly.

The girl named Jean, who had remained quiet for the entire evening, looked Francesca squarely in the eye, asking, without any challenge in her voice, "If you people weren't Communists, what *were* you committed to? There had to be *something*."

Francesca felt hopeless. *I lose no matter what I do. Everybody wants me to be someone I'm not. How can I be myself?* How *can I find Olga again?"*

⟡⟢

The Green Pheasant, a small Chinese restaurant on University Way, was full, but Francesca, along with Jacob and Katya, took the large corner booth as its four diners rose to leave. Her companions' worried looks mirrored her own anxious face. The meeting had taken a strange turn, and the hearings were looming ever closer.

Katya spoke first. "You were magnificent! Calm, unflappable, direct, and yet you kept up such an easy, inviting attitude, listening to everyone's questions."

She knew Katya expected her to be pleased with the praise, but she felt sullen instead. "I know you're sincere, but what you say is just not true. How can I be 'magnificent' when I can't make clear to these bright young people that action in a civil war *requires* acceptance of an ambivalence those soldiers have to live with. I must have come across as a pompous ass with good words but no answers."

"It didn't show," Jacob interjected. "You asked an awful lot of them—that they see something as negative as 'ambivalence' in a positive light. And you did well. I was convinced myself."

"And remember," Katya added, "this is a Communist group. Unlike you, most of us are *actually* Communists. We can hardly be ambivalent. Still, it was great. Your talk showed the students what they're up against. And you did that brilliantly in ways they could really accept."

Francesca didn't answer. They ordered and sipped their tea.

Katya broke the silence with an admission. "I'm worried. I had no idea that fellow would be there. Great as you were, I shouldn't have had you speak." She gave Francesca a wan smile. "Oh, I know, I know, my loyalties are divided. I want to protect you at any price, but my obligations to the Party keep me from doing that. Today I wanted my AYD-ers to have a chance to meet you and learn from you. And after all my worries about your safety!"

Francesca laid a reassuring hand on Katya's arm. "But I wanted to meet them, too. I want to reach real people involved in what matters. Why am I not a Communist? Not just because it's dangerous. It's because I know what things are like over there. Mike's not wrong."

"I'm worried, too, Katya." Jacob stared at the table. "Terror is coming from all sides—left *and* right. You never know how things will go from one day to the next."

At that moment, Elmo walked in followed by Mike. They came straight to their booth, hesitating at the last minute. "May we join you, or is this a private gathering?"

"No, it's OK." Katya spoke quickly, scooting over.

Elmo continued with slight embarrassment as they both sat down. "I don't think you met Mike Simonetti before this evening. He's new here, just up from L.A. and already we've clashed over politics." The waitress brought their food and took orders for the two newcomers. Francesca could barely wait for her to leave. "I wish I could be clearer, Mike. You're not entirely wrong. You just go too far; your sweep is too broad."

A change came over Mike Simonetti. Keeping a steady eye on Francesca, he said without preliminaries, "Don't get me wrong either. I'm not on the side of the professional Red-baiters—the Canwell Committee, I mean." He poured his tea. "The other side of Communism—its lethal, repressive side—needs to be exposed, that's all. You've got to understand that."

Francesca bristled. "Who says I don't understand? I said so at the meeting." She gave him a hard stare over her plate of chow mein.

Mike was not deterred. "How could you stay clear of the Communists when you were doing what you did?"

Francesca shifted in discomfort, feeling that her armor had been pierced, revealing the vulnerable core, the painful tissue of uncertainty. She shrugged but began to feel seriously threatened as old, dormant fears returned. Obeying a sudden, irrational urge to escape from her simmering anxiety, she started to get up from her chair, when Mike gently put his hand on her arm.

"Wait a minute. Go ahead and eat while we talk some. I'm sorry if I was offensive, but I'm furious. You're all ignoring what's happening to millions of people. Please, let's talk."

She sat down again, and they talked. It was not a long conversation as such talks go, but it showed Mike Simonetti in a very different light. He sipped his tea and spoke earnestly, the cap pushed far back on his head, about 'the persistence of the Fascist spirit' in whatever form. "You did your best, I'm sure."

"I'm glad you struck a different note, Mike." Francesca was only partly appeased. "One has to be somewhere: with the hunters or the hunted. I'm with the hunted."

She was seized by ever-greater waves of anxiety. Her life seemed constricted; she saw herself in an alien world, surrounded by well-meaning, lovable people—but it was not hers. She got up impulsively and held out her hand to Mike. "I'm sorry, everyone, but I couldn't touch my dinner. Why don't you eat it? It's too good to waste." Filled with an inexplicable premonition, she turned and walked out. Jacob stood and put some money on the table as he and Katya followed Francesca outside.

"You can bring me the bill," Elmo told the worried waitress.

Now the three of them stood outside at the corner of Fortieth Street, shivering in the thin rain. Neither Jacob nor Katya questioned Francesca's impulsive exit. "Let's go back to the Co-op," Katya suggested. "Just sit in the Common Room and talk. And maybe you could still eat a bite, Francesca. There's plenty of food in the fridge."

"Thanks, Katya."

She bent down quickly and kissed her friend on the top of her head. "*Ciao, cara.*" And she disappeared down the avenue, heading toward their car. Jacob caught up and strode beside her, taking her arm as her support and anchor.

കൗഠ

They drove for a long time in rain that ebbed and flowed like alternating waves of an ocean falling from the sky. They reached the shore of Lake Washington and crossed the floating bridge enveloped by shapeless wads of wet mist, while the on-again, off-again rain chased a pale moon between jagged clouds. A wind had come up as they headed east on US 10, surrounded by woods that seemed impenetrable in the dark. They said nothing while Jacob drove on. Their old Plymouth became the jeep; the occasional flashes of lightning became gunfire, the inevitable connection plain to them both.

The impassive woman next to Jacob looked straight ahead.

He recognized her profile. The large handbag on her lap became the briefcase. They drove on.

She remained far away, even when he turned into a side road a few miles inland and drove on for a time before stopping at a slope from which they could look back at the city below, glittering through the watery film of the rain.

They sat and looked.

"We already looked death in the face," Jacob said in a low voice.

No answer.

He took her hand; it was cold and limp. A moment later, she withdrew it, still not speaking.

They sat for a long time, the motor running, the windshield wipers beating furiously.

"Let's go back," she said finally. "This is no escape."

It was a silent ride home. The rain began to let up as the city took them back, enveloping them with the dangers they had briefly left behind.

৪৩৫৪৪

A man awaited them in the dim foyer of their apartment house. He was plainly dressed in rain gear. His blank face revealed nothing. "Are you Jacob Becher, formerly Lieutenant Becher, Army of the United States?"

"Yes, sir." Jacob automatically gave a military response.

"By authority of the State of Washington and the Committee on Un-American Activities, Representative Albert F. Canwell, Chairman, I hereby serve this subpoena for you to appear before the committee on Monday, July 19, 1948, at 10:00 A.M., and at any time thereafter until released." He groped for a pen in his breast pocket. "Please sign here." He held out the pen and a clipboard with a form ready for Jacob to sign. With a trembling hand, Jacob signed as directed.

The man turned to Francesca, who stood aloof, tall and erect. His eyes narrowed. He pulled an identical sheet of paper out of his briefcase, but his manner now seemed peremptory. "Are you Mrs. Francesca Mancini Becher?" he demanded. Upon her nod, he repeated the identical phrases he had used in addressing her husband, but his voice now took on a less neutral quality.

"Sign here." And, with an unmistakable note of warning: "You know the date and time. The committee expects you."

Upstairs, Francesca disappeared into the bathroom. Jacob sat in his chair and lit a cigarette, wondering whether her sixth sense had foretold the subpoena. Behind the closed door, he heard the shower.

It seemed like hours of waiting.

The door opened at last. Francesca stood in the opening, ghostly in her white nightgown, like a figure of mourning.

"Come," she said. "Come to me." He turned off the light.

Chapter 8
The Circle Closes

Francesca's hand trembled as she read the letter.

"Dear Mrs. Becher, I heard from Mrs. Dalton about some of the distressing problems at the UW along with a hint that you may be affected. I'm very sorry to hear it, since you've been through so much already, but if there is anything at all I can do to help, please feel free to get in touch with me. I want you to know there are others who admire and support you."

She dropped the letter on her desk and stared at the signature: 'Harold Goddard'—simple, direct, without a flourish. She could still see the slight figure on the podium. This caring note was as moving as it was disquieting. If word about her situation was out and had reached the ears of a scholar as far away as Wisconsin, she must be in deep trouble.

It had not seemed so at first.

Gerald Dougherty, that sinister angel with the convivial smile, had not called again, which gave her faint hope that the whole thing might have blown over. But their last meeting had left her with a nagging worry. Why Gregor Matthäus? She'd asked a knowledgeable professor at the university's art department what he knew about the painter. He had never heard of Matthäus, and first learned about him by searching the departmental library following Francesca's inquiry. If the artist was so little known in America, how did news of his political role in Italy and her own article reach a legislative committee in far-away Seattle? She raised the question with her recent adversary, Mike Simonetti.

They ran into each other on campus in front of the library. He spotted her immediately and fell in step beside her, turning toward her with a friendly grin. "You look preoccupied, worried, or both."

Francesca, amused at his 'Li'l Abner' style of dressing—a colorful shirt and old-fashioned overalls—relaxed a bit. His cap was still turned around. She waited, unsure whether she should trust him.

"Do I?" she asked, marking time.

"Let me guess."

Only now she realized how tall he was, squinting down at her through wire-rimmed glasses. "You look to me like a person in need of some powerful advice."

She felt none of the anger of their first meeting, none of the sharp sarcasm. She decided to talk. "Do you have time for a cup of coffee?"

"For you, any-time."

The moment they sat in one of the coffee shops on the avenue, Mike launched into one of his political declarations. He began without the slightest preamble.

"They've got no right to hound people like you, but you have no right, either, to make us buy the story that you were never involved with the Communists. I repeat, all of you were involved, whether you liked it or not."

Francesca was very quiet. After a time, she locked eyes with him. "Do you want to listen to me?"

When he nodded, reluctantly, shifting his eyes away, she presented her problem. It had nothing to do with the partisans; it was Gregor Matthäus.

"Never heard of him."

"Jacob did know him, personally, I mean. I introduced them during those euphoric early days of liberation. But he has no idea where Gregor stood politically. And though I knew him lots better, neither do I." She paused briefly before posing the haunting question. "How on earth did they get his name over here? We can't explain it."

Mike's face lengthened. "Sounds to me like some ambitious politicians over here got wind of him and were told he was being persecuted by Communists—by folks like you, I suppose—so they put him on display as a victim of the Commies. I know where you stand—" He raised a hand to stave off her objections— "but once the machine gets hold of your name, you're trapped. It hurts me to see that happen to people."

"You might as well know. I wrote an article in an Italian newspaper in '46 attacking him as a covert Fascist. Under my real name, yet! But Mike, I repeat, how did they know about him in the first place, when even our art department doesn't seem to know he exists?"

"Politics," Mike Simonetti repeated. "International politics. You need a lawyer."

ଔ୦ଔ

Francesca called Harold Goddard in Madison, whose letter had given her the courage to think of him as a friend. Fortunately, he picked up after two rings. He was pleased to hear from her but not surprised that her situation was becoming more serious. Considering the late date and their level of sophistication, however, he sounded amazed to hear the Bechers had not yet consulted a lawyer. His words were cautious, polite. "I don't know how these hearings work, but I think you need legal help... just in case."

"Another friend has also just advised us to get a lawyer."

Goddard was relieved. "I don't know how these hearings work, but your case is different. You must know that."

"Because I'm an alien?'"

"Yes, and though being an ex-officer's wife gives you some protection, you can't count on that alone. We don't know enough about their plans. I wouldn't be a bit surprised to see them go after some graduate students as well, and—"

She interrupted. "You're right, of course, Professor Goddard. And then there are all those rumors about a German painter I used to know, Gregor Matthäus. I attacked him once as a Fascist in a newspaper article, though I'd been his friend. Very complicated. You're right," she repeated. "I do need a lawyer. How do I go about finding one?"

Goddard did not know any attorneys in Seattle, but he remembered their one-time hostess, Mrs. Dalton. A well-known activist, she would be an invaluable resource. "In case you might feel awkward approaching her on such slight acquaintance, I'll give her a ring myself. Better she calls you."

ଔ୦ଔ

The incessant ringing of the phone jarred Francesca out of a gloomy reverie.

"My dear, Gretta Dalton here. Professor Goddard called. I'm sure things can't be easy for you these days. I'll do what I can."

Francesca let out her breath in a long sigh of relief. She would drop by the Dalton house the following afternoon. Alone.

The meeting was reassuring. The rooms where the party had been looked oddly changed on this ordinary gray day, cluttered with knick-knacks, with comfortable, overstuffed furniture. Mrs. Dalton, too, looked different in a blue tunic and tweed slacks, her hair loose, flowing over her shoulders. Only the clever eyes behind those thick lenses were the same. Francesca sat on a nearby rocking chair and looked up expectantly.

Mrs. Dalton plunged directly into the subject. "My friend Harold Goddard gave me an idea of your problem. If only part of it is true, you may be in greater trouble than I thought."

Francesca nodded. "I'd be grateful for your advice, Mrs. Dalton."

Her hostess's magnified eyes studied her face. She smiled. "Call me Gretta, please. May I call you Francesca?"

"Of course." Francesca's mouth curved in an answering smile. The offer made her feel safe. "The whole thing worried me—and Jacob—terribly. And the subpoena makes it even worse,"

"Maybe I can help, dear, though it's awfully late. We do need an attorney who knows something about the politics of your situation along with your legal rights. Unfortunately, we can't impose on John Laughlin, whom they honor by calling him the 'commie lawyer.' He's already working for Professor Pembroke among others and has his hands full."

The late-afternoon sun cast patchwork patterns on the book-lined walls. Gretta Dalton rose from the sofa and, remembering her role as a hostess, offered drinks.

Francesca sipped her sherry. "You see, there were—are—many problems with placing our, I mean my future in the hands of a lawyer, no matter how big he is or how much he's admired. Partly, it's money, of course."

"Don't worry about that…"

"You're enormously kind, but for me, personally, money's not the whole thing."

Gretta looked puzzled. She waited, hands clasped around her glass of bourbon.

Francesca shifted in her chair. "You see, I'm going to be a lawyer, and perhaps that's why I don't want to depend on lawyers. I hope I'll be different. I pray I'll be different."

"Different in what way?"

"I don't know about America, but in my country lawyers pry into your whole life once you call on them. They want to—they think they have to—take over, especially if you're a woman."

"I understand. It's not so different here. Maybe some-time, on a better day, we can talk about this, because I think lawyers can be kept at arm's length. You'll see when you practice law yourself. But, Francesca, my dear, this is not the time for an abstract discussion. We've got to make the system work for you right now." She handed her a sheet of notepaper with a name and phone number.

"Why don't you talk to him, then decide. He's an ambitious young politician, pretty much on the Left. Or used to be. Most of them are changing, of course."

"It's good to find someone who sees how political pressure can cause those allegiances to shift."

"Try him! I've a hunch he may work out. Your history with that mysterious Matthäus is too scary. Another drink?"

Her first impulse was to decline politely, but with a lift of her chin, she held out her glass with a flourish. "Wish me luck!"

Their eyes met. "Your luck is our luck," Gretta Dalton said gravely. "Let's drink to that."

ဆဝဃ

His name was James Ahern. Smiling with apparent enthusiasm, he was a brisk thirty-two in his tan summer suit and regimental striped tie. Francesca and Jacob sat in his airy office, gleaming with metal and glass that reflected the morning sun streaming through the wide window.

"Gretta Dalton told me your story, Mrs. Becher. It's an important and affecting story, but I'm not sure I can represent you—at least not at this late date."

They sat in silence, expecting to hear more. Ahern said quickly, "Of course, money's not the issue. I told Gretta her help in this wouldn't be necessary. It's an important matter, and if I take it on, I'll do it *pro bono*. But I have serious doubts." Until that moment, his eyes had moved from one to the other. Now he focused on Francesca. "Tell me your situation—the way you see it. Your own angle."

Her concern had been justified. She was being asked to reveal herself. Nevertheless, she began to speak, telling Ahern about Matthäus and about her life in Florence and the suspicions aroused among her friends by his questionable connections with ex-Fascists and similar characters. She spoke in a measured tone, keeping her own person out of her narrative as much as possible.

In the end, Jacob burst out, irrepressible. "The whole thing's preposterous! Word got around she'd been in the Resistance and that means 'Communist' to them! And her article in that Italian newspaper seemed to support that. But how they got hold of that material all the way over here remains a mystery."

"I can swear I was not a Communist neither in my war service nor since." Francesca volunteered, her eyes fastened on the lawyer.

"That cuts no ice." He had been writing busily on a yellow legal pad while Francesca was talking. Now he looked up. "It's a problem. Regardless of where you actually stand, that article puts you in a bad light. But I don't think you need to fear an accusation of perjury, because no matter what they say, you never were in fact a Communist... or were you?" His mobile eyebrows rose toward his hairline, then drew together in a frown.

"No," she repeated. Her voice was firm, even as she lied.

"Good. Then there's no need to worry." Since she had not in fact been a Communist, he declared, neither the charge of perjury nor the threat of deportation under the McCarran-Walters Act would apply to her. Now he turned to Jacob as well. "But make no mistake, they'll push you hard—both of you."

Jacob sat quietly, sunk into himself. He brushed his blue-and-white seersucker jacket, as if there were crumbs on it. "Yes." He looked up. "I know." He began to drift.

ಬಂಗ

He'd been having those nightmares again, evocations of what he most feared. The latest one had been powerful. He was a teenager, walking in a foggy park, its trees mere ghostly silhouettes. Crunching footsteps followed him along the gravel path, coming nearer. Then a hand on his shoulder, spinning him around. Two jack-booted men in uniform with high-visored caps stood in stark, clear contrast to the swirling gray background. The tallest man spoke.

"You're one of them. Unmistakable. Look at that hair, those eyes, that nose. Don't tell me we missed some of you. Where's your family? "

"Y-you l-l-leave my family alone!"

Two shouts of laughter. "Come along with us. We have ways of finding your family ..."

He pulled away, staggered back, caught his balance and ran. The crunching footsteps followed, coming nearer.

ಏುೞ

Ahern's cheerful tone brought him back to the present. "Let's do it this way." The lawyer glanced at his watch. "I stay out of this for now and see how it develops. But I'll organize my thoughts in case it's necessary for me to jump in."

His apparent optimism led him to suggest that their youth and innocence unburdened by legal complexities would probably help with the Committee. "You'll be all right on July 19th." But despite his assurance, worry lines reappeared around his mouth and eyes. "At least that's how it looks now. We'll play it by ear." He admonished them to be sure to get in touch if something threatening happened.

When they walked into the street, Jacob, still under the spell of that remembered nightmare, took Francesca's arm and held it tight against his side. The brilliant summer day glowed mockingly all around them.

ಏುೞ

Francesca's last conversation with Gerald Dougherty clung to her like burrs on a sheepdog. His pointed questions troubled her, about her history, her politics, her associations. And the sudden insistence on the role of Gregor Matthäus in her former life back in Italy was unsettling. She had long since dismissed him as ancient history and now found him again directly on her doorstep. Their visit to James Ahern had done nothing to quiet her fears.

Intense nights spent rehearsing their fears drove a wedge between them. They were still close enough to sleep intimately, curled up together like a pair of spoons, usually nude. They had done so through most of their nearly two years of marriage, but the threat that combined and divided them was too great.

One night the warm body next to Jacob abruptly detached itself with a sharp pull that jolted him out of his drowsy half-sleep and left him exposed and shivering.

He opened his eyes and saw her standing tall beside the bed with her rich dark hair disheveled. She had put on her dressing gown that had been thrown carelessly over a chair and was pulling it tight around her.

"This is *my* body!" she shouted in Italian.

"Wha—What happened?"

Still on the border of sleep, he scrambled out of bed.

He saw two frightened eyes.

"Nothing I can say clearly." Her voice was toneless. "Just ... I'm not sure I can be with you like this anymore. Yes," she contradicted herself. "Yes, something *is* happening. Ever since that character Dougherty came after me again the other day ... Please leave me tonight." And in German, "*Bitte!*"

He said nothing, collected his abandoned underclothes and slipped into the living room next door.

It became a very long night. Groping in the dark to find the floor lamp, he let himself down slowly into his favorite armchair. He searched for an ashtray, matches, and a package of cigarettes. Jacob smoked rarely, but nearly always at a moment of crisis.

Now he took long-playing records from several shelves and put them on his phonograph. Keeping the volume as low as possible, he smoked, only half-listening.

The music lulled him, and he sank into himself, drifting down into an inner chaos, a realm peopled with nightmares from the past jumbled together with fears for the future, subconscious realms that had begun to divide him and Francesca from each other, encasing each in a separate ice-walled emotional cell. He relived their past, the seemingly long trek from the explosion that opened the gate to their life together to his quick rescue, snatching her from the ex-Fascist police, to the long wait he suffered with her while she was scrutinized on board her ship, to the present. Each moment was marked by the fear that had brought about their union and was beginning to divide them. Francesca's fear for her liberty caused her withdrawal this night, just as his own inner struggle shut her out: his memories of being a Jew and a dissident living in Nazi Germany had led him long ago to a nightmarish vision of life under a delayed sentence of death, forgetting in his anxiety that much had changed in Germany since he left. And yet, he barely understood her even now.

How would they survive?

Several hours later, when the last record—a Beethoven quintet—had sounded its final chord, Jacob stretched out on the worn sofa and looked at the gray dawn creeping through the curtains.

Then suddenly it was full daylight—he had dozed off—and Francesca stood in the middle of the room, an apparition with a drawn face.

"Dougherty," went through his mind, the name that connected them. Fear knotted his stomach.

"I'm sorry," he heard Francesca say in English. "I was scared."

He shook off his own fear and asked indifferently, almost ludicrously, "Scared of what?" He glanced at the clock on the book shelf. It was a teaching day.

She swept his flippant tone aside, preventing his attempt to escape. "You were lying so close. Again, once more, we were … together on—"

"On the threshold of death." Sobered, he repeated the words she hadn't spoken for a long time.

"Something like that. I panicked. I thought I had lost myself. All my desire to be close to you got turned around." She repeated, "I was … I am … scared."

The image of his wife, standing alone and distraught before him, remained with him as he rushed to the car and sped to the university, late for class. The nightmarish vision of life under threat, his own vision, had touched her as well. He finally understood that something irrevocable, something utterly destructive was happening to them, and he didn't know how to prevent it.

༄༅

Francesca, left alone with her fear, tried to find a footing in the whirl of events that were largely beyond her control. It wasn't easy to stay calm in the face of the danger of deportation, prison maybe, which threatened her entire being—body and mind. She knew that Dougherty had not believed her declarations. Her recent denials about past Communist connections weighed on her almost unbearably. And though she had decided to take Ahern's advice and keep further worries to herself during these last two weeks, she was only partially successful and counted on the partner who had undergone similar persecution to understand her need to withdraw.

Jacob, however, did not seem to understand. Outside threats should bring endangered couples together, not separate them, she told herself. From that first dreadful night on, she knew he only acquiesced to her need to isolate herself, to be alone with her apprehensions, to please her. She shut herself off, now rebuffing even his most casual embraces. Though she accepted him in their bed, they seldom touched. Yet, when she looked at him with great affection, the meaning of her gesture appeared to elude him; he seemed sure they were one step short of becoming lovers again.

I know what you think," Francesca said at one point, speaking in German again. "But I can't come back, not with this threat hanging over me. I'm again where I was in Florence back in 1945, when we started on this road. I need a friend, a brother."

Jacob responded as if he understood. But he could not. Increasingly, his own fears took over like weeds in a wet spring.

He consulted Katya. "What can I do? She hardly speaks to me. We're both in the same boat. I was subpoenaed, too."

But Francesca's friend offered no help. Katya had also received a subpoena, but because of her work in the AYD, which, after all, was a successor to the Young Communist League, she was far more endangered than Jacob. She had little sympathy. "It's hard on all of us. If I had a lover or husband, I don't know what I'd do. Fortunately I don't have either, but I would probably feel just like Francesca. Besides, you two aren't in the same boat. She can be deported."

The mornings were worst of all. Getting up in silence, walking past each other in full or partial undress but quietly separate, became for Jacob a subtle form of torture. And yet, in other ways, Francesca came closer than she had ever been. They sat and talked deep into the long summer evenings. He finally became the brother she needed. She told him anecdotes about her intense involvement with a Communist youth group at the University of Turin, how suddenly fulfilled she had felt to rise above the self-satisfied, vainglorious patriotism of her family, to identify with a cause all her own in a new kind of freedom. And she also told him of her break with the communist youth.

"They were self-satisfied, too!"

And she described how she found a way out by serving in the Resistance but joining a non-Communist wing. "Quite a feat of independence," she said proudly. "I was barely twenty." She paused. "So, you see, Jacopo, why I told Dougherty and Ahern that I wasn't with the Communists. I lied, but it happened that way." For the first time, she confided in Jacob completely about her political past. For the first time, Jacob heard the whole truth. She placed herself in his hands.

They were sitting in the garden behind their house, and Francesca turned a shadowy face toward him. "I'm telling you this to purge those memories. I'd rather not think about that time."

"And afterward?"

"You know the rest. How could they dare bring those idiotic charges against me? Embezzlement at that German headquarters, where I risked my life every agonizing day?" She paused. "Who imported Gregor's name and politics into America to taunt and possibly entrap me? How could his influence be so important *here* when he is merely a minor figure *there*?" Jacob did not interrupt. At last he spoke. "I understand now what drove you to despair that bad night. I see how we suffer the same fears, and yet we're alone, each of us. That's what brings us … holds us … together—both together and apart."

He gave her a mournful glance. "I'm sorry all this is coming at you again. My love! How can I help?"

"You can't."

She pulled her shawl around her against the cool summer night.

He rose and caressed her hair. She bent her head back and let it happen.

୨୦୯ଓ

Sunday, July 18. They sat together and talked—Katya and Elmo, Jacob and Francesca—on the porch of Elmo's ramshackle house, lounging on a motley collection of rough wooden chairs, worn easy chairs, and a sagging sofa. They had just lunched on ham-and-cheese sandwiches brought by Katya. Elmo provided the beer.

There was no need for Francesca to bring up her problem, though Katya did. Francesca responded with studied nonchalance. "I can easily deny those Communist connections they're fishing for. They really don't exist—at least not in the way they think. What do they… what can they know about my distant past?"

Elmo, the prudent pessimist, answered. "I wouldn't be so sure of that, Francesca. Their naïveté's deceptive, and they have their own idea of Communism. It takes in everything left of center. So, don't fool yourself. They have an effective research staff—spies, that is—and they're well connected with the FBI in Washington. They'll dig things up."

"Yes." Jacob reached out to squeeze her shoulder, affirming his solidarity by repeating what they all knew only too well. "We're all endangered, but none of us as much as you. We'll fight."

"That's all we can do," Elmo added quietly.

Francesca turned toward Jacob, transfigured by an affectionate glow, and they both knew what they saw: not the light of courtship and marriage, but their embrace on the threshold of death on the side of a far-away mountain.

Assault and Betrayal
(July 1948)

Chapter 9
Monday-Wednesday, July 19-21, 1948:
"The Committee Will Come to Order"

Francesca scanned the hearing room. They had chosen the last row
of the section reserved for witnesses. The scene was drab, bland, even
humdrum. But the air around her vibrated—almost tingled—with tension, fear and anger.

9:30 A.M. The hearing room on the second floor of the thick-walled
armory became stuffier by the minute in the growing summer heat. In
anticipation of protests and pickets, the windows were closed, curtains
drawn tight. Several busy assistants were rushing to the dais at the front
of the room and out again on last-minute errands.

Benjamin H. Pratt, the chief investigator, stood at a small table below
the dais, shuffling papers, preparing for the witnesses who waited in
rows of uncomfortable metal chairs to be called once the session began.
The longer witness table, with its empty chairs facing the dais, awaited
the first person to be called. One hundred and fifty spectators, including
newsmen for radio and print, had crowded into the chamber, while a
much larger crowd would listen to the proceedings in a room below by
closed-circuit radio transmission.

Francesca and Jacob maintained their outward calm, dressed as if for
a day's teaching—she in her navy blue suit, Jacob in sober gray with a
wine-red tie, a newspaper in his hand. Its headline read: CANWELL
COMMITTEE OPENS HEARINGS TODAY. She sensed his glance at
her profile but did not meet his eyes. Instead, she looked for Katya but
could not find her.

At a few minutes past ten, Albert F. Canwell appeared on the
dais. He looked young, lanky, and surprisingly unmilitary. Two state
representatives and three state senators made up his entourage. They
found seats behind the table, their faces severe. Below the dais, Pratt,
the chief investigator, looked over his potential witnesses and the

audience. His back was turned to the assembled committee. He, too, looked severe. Representative Canwell raised his gavel and brought it down on the table with a hollow thud:

"**The committee will come to order. The Second Public Hearing of the Washington State Legislative Committee is now in session.**"*

The words pounded inside her brain, like the gavel on the table's surface. The knot inside her tightened, and so did her fists. She opened them and stared at her fingernails, then looked up, her eyes roving over the room jammed with spectators and reporters. She wiped her forehead, already perspiring in the oppressive morning heat.

Around them, the band of unfriendly witnesses seemed like thirty damned souls lost in the antechamber to Hades. In the same section, a vast space—in spirit, not in fact—separated them from a different group: the so-called friendly witnesses—self-confident men and women, who were chatting amiably with each other, shouting up to several officials on the dais. Some of them looked painfully familiar. Francesca turned her eyes away, staring at the ceiling, at the clock.

A man in a brown suit tiptoed among 'the damned,' whispering intensely, turning right and left. He must be one of the attorneys for the defense.

When her mind refocused, she heard: "**We will proceed with proper dignity here; no demonstrations will be tolerated, no speeches from the audience … any violations of that, these instructions … summarily dealt with … orderly procedures at all cost.**" Should they have alerted Ahern after all?

The man in the brown suit looked up, listening to instructions and the warning that concerned him and his colleagues.

"**We will proceed in a moment to call the list of subpoenaed witnesses. I wish to state that these witnesses may have, and many of them do have, counsel.**"

Francesca became increasingly restless, wondering again why they had not insisted on Ahern's presence.

The voice went on. "**I want it understood that position of counsel is strictly in an advisory capacity. They may freely advise their clients whether or not to answer, they may not argue before the hearing.**"

Now the chairman had her total attention. Jacob reached over and took her hand.

"We are not going to debate any of the issues regarding the constitutionality of this committee, or its method of procedure."

A pause.

"Will you proceed, Mr. Pratt?"

Someone interrupted from the witness area. "Mr. Pratt and Mr. Chairman..."

A gasp of disbelief came from dais and audience alike. In a calm voice, the brown-suited lawyer asked that his client be excused at certain hours of the afternoon to teach his classes. The air filled with a flurry of whispers like moth wings around a lamp at night. She could not be sure whether the request was granted. Pratt's voice droned on. Her fist tightened as the next name was called. "Katherine Claiborne Rombeck." Katya's hand went up. Then followed more names, more responding hands.

Professor Pembroke of the Philosophy Department was in New York, teaching summer school at Columbia University. He had refused to come home to face the Committee, but had been compelled to change his mind under university pressure. His return was now expected, but he had not yet arrived. What to do? It presented a grave bureaucratic puzzle. At last, the voice ended with the names of four people who had refused to respond to their subpoenas.

The two 'friendly' witnesses, asked to testify first, seemed frightening, each in a different way. One, a Mr. Patterson, was a former Army Intelligence and Security officer, now running a detective agency. He sounded like the person who had infiltrated the communist faculty club to which a few of them still belonged, though others had left long ago. The other, Dr. Walton, a professor of American literature and the current chairman of the department, was expected to speak also. He knew all of them well, had socialized with them invited them to his home, eaten dinner at theirs. And yet he would now betray them.

Francesca stared at Patterson, the former intelligence officer, with the horrified insight that he had once been her husband's comrade-in-arms. She turned abruptly, freeing her hand from Jacob's clasp, her glance now fixed on his tense profile.

This time it was he who did not meet her eyes.

She questioned herself inwardly, *Army-Intelligence—counter-intelligence probably—where would he have been? In Italy? In Germany or*

Japan since the war? Did he expose Nazis, Fascists, high officers in former enemy countries, or… Communists over there and now Communists here?

When Pembroke's name came up, Patterson spoke with undisguised contempt for academics, a sentiment clearly shared by the questioner. Four rows ahead, Francesca could see Katya squirm. Pratt's line of questioning seemed like a noose, slowly tightening, threatening her as well as the friend she admired.

Katya, dear friend, be strong!

But how strong will WE be? This is just like the old days. Where will it end?

As if she'd spoken to Jacob aloud, his eyes met hers. He nodded, and she knew he understood.

Patterson explained that he had been to several meetings in the 'subject's' home. Francesca almost leaped up in anger. This odious person was obviously untroubled by testifying against Professor Pembroke, a man in whose home he had often been welcomed. Still, Katya was foremost in her mind as she listened to Patterson describing those cell meetings with relish.

Katya, dear friend, be strong for us all!

Pratt was still questioning the detective. **"Did you ever hear Professor Pembroke reprimand a member of the Communist Party, because he was afraid to belong to the communist faculty club?"**

Patterson began to waffle. "Well," he said finally. **"I don't have to confine it to a single incident.** " He went on to describe more generally the anxiety of some of the people he had met—**"those who were active and those who were not … One member in particular … He was quite nervous, I observed."** Patterson became almost incoherent. **"And he so stated that … and, of course, he was upbraided …."** The witness was asked not to name that man **"right at this time."**

If Patterson frightened her in one way, Arthur Walton did so in another. When he was sworn in, she turned to Jacob, grasping his upper arm and squeezing it hard to communicate her shared sense of his pain. Both Waltons, husband and wife it seemed, were prepared to name names. She sat transfixed, her stomach clenched at the betrayal by a colleague. And yet, she was not surprised. She had seen it too often in Fascist Italy. The testimony droned on as colleague after colleague was exposed.

The noon hour struck. "Adjourned for lunch. To be resumed at 2 P.M."

"Dear Lord." Jacob said aloud as he rose from his chair, and she gave him an understanding look. Outside, they turned into the leafy street as if it were the rose garden, but fear and depression followed them.

ଓଔ

Jacob walked silently beside Francesca, his gait almost jerky as he recalled the scene he had just witnessed. He could still see Walton, a stooped, scholarly man, explaining laboriously how he got into the party, and how he got out some time later. So much of that story felt familiar, including the attraction of a communist commitment and the underlying fear of its danger, its seductiveness, and its regrets. Walton had no doubt begun by teaching Upton Sinclair and Theodore Dreiser, and Jacob could understand how easily, in the course of pursuing social justice, this man could have been drawn into an intellectual quagmire, which he was about to vilify in public.

They ambled mindlessly along a footpath outside the armory. He stopped in his tracks and spoke his thoughts aloud. "That string of betrayals! All those names slipping almost by rote off Walton's tongue, the names of his friends, his colleagues and ... even their wives? Where will all this end? So many caught up in this mess!"

"It's so damned familiar, Jacopo. Under interrogation, people will do unimaginable things to each other. I've seen it before, but I thought I'd put all that behind me."

He began to recite the names, ticking each one off on his fingers. "There's Melville Jason, in anthropology—the students really love him—then there's Harold Enders and George Anthony, both of them Walton's colleagues in English literature, and, damn it all, he even dragged Hubert and Florence Chadwick into this. That's the couple that runs the Repertory Playhouse. Dear God! We all stand at the brink."

"I know." Francesca's head was bent, her voice barely audible as they drifted back into the building. "Think of Mabel Walton. There she was, called to the witness table, such a harmless figure—matronly really, with that perfect perm—and with that unquestioning allegiance to her man as if by marriage he'd become part of herself."

She mumbled that she needed to use the restroom, threw an arm around Jacob, gave him a squeeze, and walked away.

Upstairs, outside the hearing room, she saw a man looking very much like Gerald Dougherty talking to another man whom she hadn't seen before.

"Ah, Mrs. Becher. Good to see you." Dougherty turned quickly to his companion, as if remembering his manners, and held out his hand in a perfunctory introduction. "My colleague, Mr. Bentley, Mrs. Becher."

The other man, a lean, well-dressed fellow in his thirties, stood holding a cigarette. He nodded briefly, but his eyes betrayed his professional interest.

She thanked Dougherty politely and acknowledged Bentley with a nod. Dougherty's presence surprised and disturbed her, though there was no reason why he shouldn't have been there.

Dougherty went on. "Mr. Bentley is director of the Committee staff." He turned to his colleague. "Mrs. Becher recently joined the teaching staff at the University."

As if he already didn't know, she thought. Aloud, she said, "And I do have a class to teach later this afternoon. I hope this will be over by then."

Mr. Bentley removed his cigarette, addressing Francesca directly, "You're under subpoena, aren't you, Mrs. Becher?" He looked stern though he had an unexpectedly pleasant voice. "And you might be called and should be on hand. I think it would be wise to dismiss your class."

"But ..."

"You've got two hours to do it, Mrs. Becher." With that, he turned back to Dougherty to resume their conversation. She fled.

Outside the armory, pickets protesting against the committee marched up and down, chanting angry slogans. A brisk wind had risen, blowing away remnants of the suffocating indoor heat. Like a tonic, it cleansed her face, scouring away the dirt of that slimy proceeding. Yet the residue of her past still clung to her: the paranoid probing, the hypocritical pretense at virtue, encouraging the witness while soliciting betrayals—it stuck to the skin of her consciousness.

She felt alien and isolated. As she walked ever faster along the tree-lined street, she felt overwhelmed by the need for decisive action—the need to fight back. They must escape this legal trap. It would help Jacopo, too. For that, however, she had to be herself, with freedom to act.

She found a public telephone and called Ahern. The phone rang six times before someone answered. Lunch hour, of course.

"Hello."

To her surprise, it was a male voice and she thought she recognized her lawyer. "Hello, Mr. Ahern? This is Francesca Becher … Mancini-Becher …."

"Oh, yes?" He had clearly expected another call.

"Mr. Ahern." She spoke quickly. "Please help us. You said you would."

"What's happening?"

Considering his past assurance, he seemed surprisingly hesitant, aloof, and almost absent-minded. "What can I possibly do at this point?"

Now the adrenaline poured into her system. "I don't know, sir. I'm not yet a lawyer, and I come from abroad. But something must be done to help us, advise us. Some people are accompanied by counsel. I really think we need one too."

"Well …"

"Can you come this afternoon? I'm not sure, but one of us may be called."

"Impossible. But I can look in tomorrow." He sounded indefinite, even in his assent.

"Thank you." She hung up coolly, politely. More help was needed.

She fished out another coin and called Mike Simonetti. They had met once or twice and phoned since their last talk, and the more they saw of each other, the more they found they had in common. They shared similar recollections of the Italian war, though from different angles. Now she was eager for his advice.

He answered at last, after five rings.

"Mike, this is Francesca. Francesca Mancini. Mancini–Becher," she corrected herself.

"You're in trouble."

"How do you know?"

"Word gets around."

"What word?"

To her distress, he mentioned their subpoenas, his concern amplifying her own worry about her ambiguous past. But why did he imagine there would be a problem? She didn't need to ask.

"Jacob," he said with a note approaching sadness in his voice. "He's worried; he told me so."

She hadn't known he'd talked to Mike or to anyone else. Mike's voice broke into her thoughts.

"Do you at least have legal advice now?"

"Someone we could afford and trust? We have a lawyer—more or less. He's amazingly reluctant—seems he doesn't want to enter the combat zone unless absolutely necessary. I'm not sure he'll ever find it necessary. I just talked to him. He says he might come tomorrow. Who knows? I'm afraid I don't trust him."

"I wish I could help, but being new in town, I can't scare up a lawyer—certainly not now at the last minute."

"I know, Mike. I just wanted to hear a friendly voice."

"I wish we'd put our heads together before this. When are you on?"

"I haven't yet testified. Nobody knows the exact schedule. But Jacopo or I, either one of us, might be on later today."

"Hmmm. Let me think about this. Meanwhile ... good luck." Mike hung up and she slowly replaced the receiver. She suddenly remembered to dismiss her class. A quick call to her office.

Half an hour later, when she slipped back into her seat in the stuffy hearing room, Mike was already sitting in the row behind her, his baseball cap perched on his knee. Amazed and pleased at his instant response to her distress call, she flashed a tiny smile and waved. He nodded in return.

The words from the podium assailed and further oppressed her. For the fourth or fifth time, she heard the admonition to answer audibly and to spell unusual names, because the testimony was being recorded. The 'friendly' witness currently in the box was well received and well prepared. Pratt and Canwell were deferential. He was the Research Director of the famous Martin Dies Committee, and a distinguished crusader against Communism. "Would you detail for us," she heard Pratt's grating voice again, "some of the objectives of the Communist Party in the field of education?"

The eager witness launched into a lengthy explanation, starting with *The Communist Manifesto* and culminating in questioning the loyalty of the country's scientific elite from Harold Urey to Albert Einstein, even raising doubts about General Eisenhower. Amazingly, these allegations were all based solely on the assumption that even the slightest deviation from orthodox thinking was subversive. Francesca looked down at her lap, her eyes burning with an internal fever. Was this possible? Into what strange regions of time and space had she been banished in her flight from her own troubled world?

Despite the closed windows, she heard loud shouts in the street, whistles, and the quick, sharp explosions of backfiring motorcycles. Catcalls and shouting took over the hearing room as well.

"I am going to ask for the State Patrol to take drastic measures," the chairman shouted, infuriated by the disorder. "I am going to ask for the arrest of the participants."

Jacob again reached for her hand, but she withdrew it and covered her face instead.

"We are not going to tolerate a communist interference with the legislative process ..."

The sharp sound of a whistle came through the closed window.

And now almost a plea: "I suggest that the State Patrol make some arrests out there if this continues."

Francesca imagined Canwell's eyes meeting hers, penetrating them like ice picks.

"These people out there are the ones who are supposed to be interested in free speech, and academic freedom, and all the civil rights, and they're giving a typical Communist demonstration of what they really believe."

As the afternoon dragged on, it became less and less likely that either the Bechers or Katya would be called. But by then Francesca felt that it would have been a relief to meet the people on the dais instead of having to listen to the same tortured arguments alleging 'guilt by association' and the interminable recitations of suspect organizations that included everything from the National Council of the Arts, Sciences, and Professions to the Consumers' Union. She looked at Mike behind her. He was leaning back, looking bored. He raised his eyebrows at her. She recovered.

By five in the afternoon, the current 'friendly witness' had not yet finished his testimony, but the session was adjourned.

The day was done.

૪૦ Q

The next day began much as the previous day had ended: with further elaborations by the Research Director sent from Washington D.C., followed by further lectures from ex-Communists, all under the guise of testimony. But as Jacob and Francesca began to settle into a wearisome routine of sitting and waiting to be examined, apprehension caught them again. The ex-Communists may have been entertaining and depressing, but the real drama was enacted by the 'unfriendly witnesses.' One stressful scene followed another in a parade of predictable confessions and refusals, punctuated by the chairman's haughty reprimands of any professors who refused to state whether or not they had been members of the Communist Party, or whether they had favored the wrong side—the one opposed to Franco—in the Spanish Civil War, or had shown scruples about the use of the atomic bomb.

Ahern appeared briefly. He had indeed been busy, and the armory was not easy to reach, but was reluctant for other reasons. He knew by now that working under the conditions imposed by the committee would be extremely difficult for an attorney, since any defense, any attempt at cross-examination, instantly provoked angry denunciations and expulsions from the chamber. It seemed to Francesca that Ahern had put in a perfunctory appearance to keep his word with the least effort. She did not expect to see him again.

Everyone testifying fell short of total defiance, aware of the power emanating from the dais. Everyone shared an acute sense of danger. But though no one was downright heroic, some were more principled than others. While Arthur Walton cooperated fully, many, like the Renaissance scholar Gerald Anthony, drew the line at any attack on his personal principles.

To Jacob and Francesca, Anthony's behavior as a witness seemed at first disturbing—wheeling and dealing, squirming and equivocating—until they realized he would stop short of betraying colleagues. When the interrogation reached the point of "naming names, he stopped, making clear he was willing to talk "unreservedly" about himself but refused to implicate his friends and colleagues."I told you," he announced, referring to earlier unofficial conferences, "that I was unwilling to name other persons as Communists or possible Communists for two reasons. One is that I didn't have knowledge about the membership. And the other is that my own particular code of honor forbids that kind of naming persons to their possible injury." And with perfect poise, Anthony cited Polonius' famous advice from *Hamlet*: '*This above all: to thine own self be true…*' That is my position, sir."

The audience was silent for a moment. The statement moved nearly everyone except the Committee. Francesca could have foretold the result. Pratt launched into his interrogation, as though those words had never been spoken.

"Dr. Anthony, have you ever attended any Communist Party meetings with Harold Enders?"

And when, as expected, Anthony declined to reply, Pratt went on to the next name, and the next name, and the next, with studied disregard of the person at the table. Francesca whispered in Jacob's ear, "Just like Fascism. Debasing. Dehumanizing." She stared at the littered floor.

"We will not permit this to go on!" Canwell shouted. "Either you will answer the questions, the proper questions of this committee, or the questions we believe to be proper, or you will step aside until we wish to call you to the stand again!"

At that moment, the hall exploded in a burst of applause. People leaped up in spontaneous anger, their loud shouts of protest penetrating the thick walls, pouring down the stairwell and spilling onto the sidewalk outside, where the pickets were marching.

The gavel banged: "If there are any further demonstrations by the audience," Canwell announced in a sharp voice, though still under control, "we will ask the State Patrol to remove those participating in said demonstrations, and upon removal said demonstrators will remain out of the hearing room during the course of these hearings."

He called a hasty ten-minute recess. Francesca pointed outside and turned to Mike behind her and to Jacob at her side, "This, at least, is *not* fascism. Thank God for that!"

Mike avoided a response. "Let's go and get some air."

As they reached the entrance, Jacob raised a dejected face to the intense blue sky. "What a beautiful day. What a waste!"

༉ C�

Not everyone passed muster. On Wednesday, Sarah Maher joined James and Mabel Walton in naming the names of those with whom she had worked and socialized for years. In the past, she had used mainstream, middle-of-the-road organizations as cover for her communist activities, such as branches of the Democratic Party, where she had acted as head of the Women's Division. Now, she repudiated her past covert activities and cooperated fully with the Committee, confirming and commenting on every name of every suspected university professor in Canwell's and Pratt's book.

Maher attempted to destroy several reputations. By mixing innuendo with fragments of truth, she succeeded in destroying Bob Gerson, the famous professor of psychology, and in the same way nearly ruined the courageous philosopher John Richards, an active progressive who was not a Communist, but whom the committee was eager to 'unmask.'

Her attack on Hubert and Florence Chadwick of the Repertory Playhouse, accusing them of harboring communist ideology under the guise of dramatic productions could prove lethal. Jacob and Francesca, who loved the work of the theater, looked at each other in dismay and foreboding.

The attack on Gerson hit Jacob with devastating power. Jacob knew him as his much esteemed friend and colleague, and had always admired his civic courage. Seeing these strong persons and powerful thinkers humiliated, derided, chided, and treated like naughty children, offended them both deeply, as though their own fates were already written, inscribed by a pitiless recorder.

Footnote
* In Chapters 9-11, involving the hearings, quoted passages in **bold** are taken verbatim from *Second Report: Un-American Activities in Washington State, 1948*. Participants even within the quotations, however, have been given fictional names except for the chairman—Albert F. Canwell—and the chief defense attorney—John Laughlin—whose names have been retained for historical reasons.

Chapter 10
Thursday July 22, 1948
Tightrope Walking

Day four of inquisition. Jacob, Francesca, and Katya sat together enjoying the sunshine on the armory steps, munching tuna salad sandwiches in willful oblivion of the continuous threat that now dominated their lives. They were late getting back.

The trio entered the hearing room, trying but failing to be quiet and unobtrusive. They were greeted by Pratt's monotonous voice reading from a document:

"James Ipswich, **of lawful age, being duly sworn in under oath, deposes and says …**"

The speaker interrupted himself to explain that this deposition was by a former drama student at the University of Washington, now living in San Francisco, who had discovered, as part of his research for a paper on communist propaganda, that a woman named Katya was in charge of Marxist discussion sessions at a 'communal house' on East Forty-second Street near the campus.

Francesca heard Jacob's almost inaudible gasp before she could react. She glanced at the faces she could see, looking for reactions. Had she heard right? Yes, the address was correct. An inner storm raged. She clasped her hands, startled by their icy coldness, and locked them together. Her eyes searched for her friend several rows ahead, sitting stiffly erect, her knot of brown hair tight against her neck. Francesca imagined reaching out, cold hand to cold hand, across the rows of seats.

The content of the document struck her as farcical, conveying the startling intelligence that men and women lived together in that co-operative and that when he visited the place at nine on a Sunday morning **"they were all dressed in their pajamas and appeared quite relaxed with each other."** The hearing room was quiet, though she was gratified to hear some suppressed giggles. She could not bring herself to laugh at this lesson in 'communist immorality,' however.

The official voice droned on, but drowsy listeners became alert when Katya was summoned to the witness table.

"Are you a member of the Communist Party?" Pratt demanded.

"Yes, that's right. I've never hidden the fact."

"We understand that you have developed a youth group, the so-called American Youth for Democracy." The question came with a sneer.

"Yes, the AYD."

"Tell the committee the names of that organization's officers."

"Sir, I cannot do that."

"Michael Forrester, president. Is that correct?"

"I respectfully refuse to answer. I will neither name names nor confirm any."

After a litany of names and answering refusals, the focus shifted to her Marxist Discussion Group at the 'Commune,' as Pratt derisively named the co-operative. After a few further questions, Katya was dismissed for now. The air filled with rustlings and whispers of surprise that she was not interrogated more intensely. Evidently, Pratt and Canwell were in a hurry to get on to their star witness, Professor of Philosophy Pembroke, the man they had brought back from New York to lay the groundwork for a comprehensive charge of communist activity at the university. He had just returned, but had at once gone into seclusion before his appearance, now due in a few minutes. They could always return to Katya if needed.

Pratt peremptorily summoned Pembroke to the witness table, using the tone commonly employed for calling a dog. Francesca winced at the sordid treatment. A spindly man with receding gray hair, a ruddy face and sharp nose, the professor fixed his opponents with narrowed blue eyes while he held his ground. His refusal to answer the standard questions about his communist politics was met with scolding and ridicule.

One of the questions carefully postponed since Patterson testified at the opening session became the first salvo fired at the militant professor.

"Why did you scold a colleague for being reluctant to stay in your subversive club? I won't mention his name, but you must know him."

If Pembroke was surprised, he didn't show it. He looked at his adversary with a steady eye. "I refuse to answer, sir."

After half an hour of wrangling, it was all over. Finally, the expected word: "You may stand down."

During the ten-minute break, Katya looked frightened, not for herself but for her teacher and friend.

"Did you hear that exchange?"

Francesca merely nodded and touched Katya's arm, then drew her down the stairs and out the front entrance where they could not be overheard.

"I wish I'd sat with you." She put her arm around Katya's shoulder while they moved along the busy street, reliving the interrogation they had just witnessed. She was fuming.

"Outrageous! It was worst of all when Pembroke was trying to explain why he wouldn't answer either 'yes' or 'no' to the Big Question. And Pratt was whining like a child, '**Mr. Chairman, he's attempting to make a speech!**' Such unbelievable arrogance, treating the professor and his attorney as if they were children!"

Katya looked at her friend with dry eyes. "It's intended to be destructive. Sure, Pembroke is a committed Communist, just as I am. But he never made any bones about it. Where's the First Amendment? They asked him to implicate his friends—knowing full well he wouldn't—just to see him squirm."

As they turned to make their way back to the armory, three students barred their way. Francesca remembered that they had attended her talk in the New Life Cooperative.

Katya's face brightened. "Friends, thank you!"

Beth took off her wire-rimmed glasses and began polishing them. "We had to see you, you and Professor Pembroke, and ..." She glanced briefly at Francesca but turned back to Katya. "These are bad days."

Hal's arm described a generous arc that even included Francesca. "We just wanted you to know we're with you. All of you."

Jean looked at her feet, at first saying nothing. When she spoke, her subdued voice betrayed her emotion. "Where's Professor Pembroke?"

Beth nodded. "Yes, where is he? We need to see him, too. He 'shook us out of our bourgeois slumber,'" she said, misquoting a pompous line that had impressed her somewhere from a different source. "You know. You both did." She smiled at Katya. "But he has the deep knowledge."

Katya stretched out both her hands to them. "He'll see you, I'm sure; he should be in his office."

Hal's face reflected his disappointment. "Yes, probably. It's just that we were hoping to see all of you together, to let you know that we're here with you, what you're going through." He lifted his hand in a wave, and the three turned and walked away. Francesca and Katya stood alone for a moment.

Katya turned back to her friend. "They take my breath away. We are all in such danger." She clasped her own hands. "Francesca, it could be even worse for you. You could be deported at once if you cross them. Don't refuse to answer outright. Don't antagonize them!"

They walked on, Francesca's arm around the shoulders of her shorter friend. "I'll do my best. But one thing's for sure: I won't rat on my friends. Those kids are enough to keep me from making the slightest concession, no matter what those inquisitors do."

ಬಂಡ

When they topped the armory stairs, Francesca noticed a familiar slim figure with very short hair. As she came closer, to her astonishment, she saw James Ahern waiting for her in the hall, prepared, it seemed, to help at last.

How did it happen? Where did he find the time and courage? Had Gretta Dalton intervened? Francesca had not seen her at the hearings, but perhaps she had sat in the crowded chamber without making herself known or had listened downstairs.

She introduced Katya and at once asked her to call Jacob before turning her attention to her lawyer. "I don't know how much time we have. I'm supposed to testify this afternoon. At least that's what Gerald Dougherty, that independent investigator, told me when he stopped by just before noon. He didn't seem to know exactly when. And so … when did you get here?"

He responded apologetically. "I've been here a while."

She nodded as Jacob came bounding down the stairs and rushed up to Ahern. "Thank you for coming. I was going to call you later. Things are much tighter than we expected."

The lawyer drew them into a corner and came at once to the point. "The way I see it, the main issue will be the allegation that Matthäus was vilified by Communists and that Francesca was alleged to be one of them."

"How hard will that be to beat?"

"We'll do our best," Ahern's voice was soothing.

Gerald Dougherty appeared out of nowhere, his worried face again becoming jovial with relief. "Mrs. Becher, here you are! You're wanted at the witness table." He turned to Ahern. "You're their counsel? I didn't know they had one. You won't be needed, sir, I assure you, but you're entitled to come in."

Dougherty led the way upstairs with a determined air. Why did he shepherd them as if they were his personal charges? Wondering, Francesca followed closely behind him.

ℰℭ

She walked to the table, her body stiff, frozen outside and in. She raised her hand for the oath. Ahern had sat down next to her, notebook open, pencil poised.

Her eyes dropped from Canwell to Pratt, who stood one step below him, facing her directly. His eyes seemed enlarged tenfold behind rimless glasses. She could feel the packed audience in the hearing room.

The question came at once: "Are you or have you ever been a member of the Communist Party?"

She'd had made up her mind not to be a martyr, thrusting behind her any lingering doubts or ambiguities. Her voice rang out firm and clear in the dead silence.

"No."

To her relief, she was not asked the usual next question designed to compel the witness to inform about colleagues and friends. Evidently, the committee already knew from her bouts with Dougherty that she could supply little information about matters more easily investigated elsewhere. For the moment at least, they refrained from harassing her.

Instead, Pratt chose a different tack.

"During the recent war, as an Italian citizen, you were a so-called partisan, were you not?"

Ahern stirred next to her. Pratt went on without waiting for her answer. "As a partisan, you were involved in communist organizations or units, were you not?"

"I knew of such units," she answered. "But I was not involved. I served only with a non-communist faction of the Resistance."

"How so?"

"All I was interested in was fighting the Fascists—Italian and German—though sometimes I ran across Communists. In a fluid war situation, you can't always pick your fellow soldiers. But I never worked with them."

"Did you know the German painter Gregor Matthäus?"

"Slightly."

"Just a moment." Ahern addressed the chairman directly. "May I consult with my client, please?"

"You may," Canwell conceded stiffly. "But you do not have the right to call and cross-examine other witnesses."

"One moment." Disgusted, Ahern turned and spoke in her ear. "Be careful now, Mrs. Becher. Be sure you say nothing you can't back up later."

Francesca nodded gravely, but a knot had formed in her stomach.

"How slightly?" Pratt asked when she turned back to face him. "Personally? Professionally?"

"Both. I saw a great deal of him at parties when I lived in Florence."

A snicker passed through the audience.

Pratt forged on. "But you wrote an article about him, attacking him. Doesn't sound very social to me. Did you know he was a bulwark against Communism in your country? Were you not conspiring against him because he wouldn't follow the party line?"

Ahern got to his feet. His reticence had dropped away and his eyes were alive with anger.

"In the name of my client, I object to this insinuation. It is… "

"Sir! Mr. Adams, or whatever your name is! Let me repeat. You have no standing before this committee, except strictly as counsel for your client. You may advise your client as to her responses to our questions. Nothing, but *nothing* else!—Sit down!"

"But you insinuate …"

"I'll ask you one more time, Mr. Adams, to be seated. One further word of protest and I'll have you removed from this room."

The silence cloaked Francesca, a palpable, smothering presence. She broke it, speaking slowly, weighing her words. "My attack on Gregor Matthäus, a former friend, had nothing to do with Communism. I wrote in defense of my Italian homeland."

It was true. Communism had not been the issue in her article. As she saw it, cronyism had led that well-known painter to hobnob with Florentine Fascists. With her attorney's warning in mind, she said nothing further.

Pratt was not satisfied. "But you were a Communist, weren't you? Perhaps you are one even now."

"You heard my testimony, sir. My answer is 'no.'" The clock on the wall showed 4:00 P.M.

No one except Jacob knew the untruth of that denial.

Looking skeptical, Pratt changed the subject. "Why are you here?"

She deliberately misunderstood. "Because I was subpoenaed."

"In Seattle, madam. In the United States."

"I came here to marry my husband, former Lieutenant Jacob Becher, whom I met during the war."

"Were you aware of our fight against the communist conspiracy when you came here two years ago? Or were you more interested in supporting your dubious friends in Seattle?"

His vicious blow caught her in a vise. Either she denied her friends or made herself vulnerable to attacks from her enemies. She felt naked, exposed.

This attack was too much for Ahern. Used to the give and take of the courtroom, he momentarily forgot the rules of the hearings and leaped out of his seat. "You have no right! My client's personal life … irrelevant here! Privacy … just fishing for nothing!"

"Officer!" Canwell shouted for the State Patrol. "**Please escort this man from the hearing room. He will not be permitted to return!**" And, turning to Francesca, "You will have to consult your counsel out-side. He will not be allowed to interfere with the legislative process." And, to Ahern as the state policeman was about to escort him outside, "Sir, take note. Your own practice is on the line."

She watched the door close behind her attorney.

"Now then," Pratt resumed. "You certainly made the rounds among subversives and their meetings."

"The people I spend time with are not subversives."

Pratt's grating voice assaulted her one more time. Almost as if closing a dramatic circle, her interrogator, freed from interference by a meddling lawyer, reverted to the initial question—but with a difference.

"Mrs. Becher," he insisted, his voice almost comically fraught with menace. "Will you tell the committee one more time what you have already told our investigator—that you are not and have never been a member of the Communist Party or an active sympathizer?"

"That is correct. I say 'no' to all of these questions."

"I remind you that you have so stated under oath repeatedly—once when you spoke to our immigration officer on arrival, and again here this afternoon. Also, you so assured our associate, who inquired in our interest. I take it, then, that you affirm this fact with two solemn oaths and your personal testimony."

"Yes, sir." She still sat erect. She felt secure—only Jacopo knew her full past.

"Very well. You may stand down for the present. But keep yourself available to the committee. Your case is not closed."

She sighed and stood down.

Jacopo met her and took her hand. They left the hearing room and walked slowly down the stairs and out of the armory, leaving its thick walls behind them. Outside on the sidewalk men and women of all ages marched up and down, chanting.

"*Don't muzzle the teachers!*" A heavyset woman directed a group of boys and girls of all ages with hand-made signs. "*Abolish the Canwell Committee.*" An older student carried a sign: "*Your university is under attack!*" State troopers looked on in discomfort. The contrast with the hearing room could not have been greater.

"Let's go somewhere," said Jacob with relief in his voice. The tension was ebbing. "You need a drink."

"Not really, dear, but I bet you do. You go."

"No, no, I'll stay with you."

"All right. Let me call Goddard first." She turned into a nearby phone booth and rummaged through a purse full of quarters. She reached his secretary and left word that she hoped to hear from him. She needed his reassuring words.

When she emerged, she looked for Katya.

Chapter 11
Friday, July 23, 1948:
Betrayal

Jacob climbed the steps behind Francesca and watched her sweep into their living room without stopping to look at the mail. Her gusty sigh floated down to him. He stooped and gathered the envelopes that had been thrust through the slot in the door. His breath caught in his throat. A letter from the Canwell Committee! His fingers stiffened as he tore at the flap. The letter was short and formal:

> Dear Professor Jacob Becher,
> Your presence is requested on Friday, July 23, 1948, at 11:00 A.M. in Room 103 of the Armory. You will be interviewed, prior to your scheduled appearance before the committee at 2:00 P.M., by the official investigator of the Albert Canwell Committee, Mr. Gerald Dougherty. You are expected to attend both meetings.
> Yours very truly,
> Benjamin H. Pratt

He looked at his watch. Past ten at night, but he'd risk calling James Ahern. Maybe he would understand even if he'd gone to bed already. But an alert voice answered.

"Yes? Jacob? No, I was still up. An interview with Dougherty, you say? No, no, I wouldn't worry. You have nothing to fret about as long as the facts are clear in your mind."

"But this summons makes no sense, Mr. Ahern. I've never been a member of any political organization. It must be—has to be—because of Francesca."

James Ahern's brief silence meant he agreed. "You know about guilt by association, don't you, Dr. Becher? It's practically proverbial these days. If she's caught in their sticky web, you're caught. She's your *wife*." He paused. "But I'll be there, Dr. Becher. You'll find me in the hall downstairs."

"I'm in line to testify at two."

It was Jacob's turn to sigh. He replaced the receiver, relieved at the change in Ahern's tone and responses. The tension in his body seemed to drain away as his confidence increased. Maybe he would sleep tonight, at last.

₧₨

A clock in an office somewhere chimed eleven, each stroke reverberating inside Jacob's skull. Sleep-deprived after all, despite last night's conversation with Ahern, he knocked on the door of Room 103. The man who opened for him surely couldn't be Dougherty, the menacing figure Francesca had described. The round, friendly face, further broadened by a comfortable smile, made a reassuring contrast with Canwell's and Pratt's grim demeanor. Unlike the committee personnel, this man seemed worldlier, more humanly accessible. He extended a hand, shaking Jacob's with a firm and warm grip, then took his place behind a large steel desk.

"Welcome, welcome! I'm Gerald Dougherty. Have a seat, please!"

Despite his joviality, the interrogator got right to the point. He had positioned his desk so that sunlight seeping through the blind on the high window glared in Jacob's eyes, dazzling him.

"Lieutenant Becher, I know you're no longer using this title and have chosen not to stay in the Reserves. Even so, I can't help thinking of your important military service, where you were often in harm's way. You also used your wits on your country's behalf as an officer in Army Intelligence." He paused to let that sink in. Jacob felt flattered in spite of himself.

"Of course," Dougherty continued, "the war did something for you, too." The smile shifted, bordering on a smirk. "You brought a beautiful wife home with you." The offensive smile remained. "I met with the lady twice, as you know. She's formidable." The smirk became more definite. "I assume you love her, yes?" The man asked it casually, making it sound irrelevant.

"Very much," Jacob responded. He looked about furtively, feeling trapped. He rubbed his sweaty palms on his trousers, hoping his questioner wouldn't notice. "Would you mind adjusting the blind, Mr. Dougherty? The sun's bothering me."

"I'm so sorry, Lieutenant Becher."

He rose to adjust the blind, then sat and leaned forward with an expression that became almost lewd. His voice took on an insinuating purr. "Tell me. How did the two of you meet? In a bar? An officers club? Or did she ...?"

Jacob interrupted on a harsh, warning note. "Please don't continue."

Dougherty leaned back, his face bland. "But then tell me. This is personal, I know, but surely not privileged information." He repeated his question. "How *did* the two of you meet?" He looked surprisingly benign; his eyes crinkled at the corners.

One part of Jacob's mind knew better than to trust appearances. But despite himself, he couldn't dislike the man.

"We met under shell-fire. In the field. We almost died."

Dougherty looked serious. "I can see how that *would* bring you to-gether."

Jacob was unexpectedly moved, his disgust at the betrayals he had witnessed all week momentarily obscured by the empathy he heard in the man's tone.

"Do you remember her clothes?"

"Not sure ... some kind of fatigues, I expect."

"A red armband?"

"I ... really don't recall. I don't believe so." He could see by Dougherty's slow nod, his head on one side, that he was believed. The next question came from another direction.

"You and your wife have a pretty restricted social life, don't you?"

"What do you mean?"

Dougherty repeated the committee's formula. "I mean most of the bunch you go around with are Reds. You spend a lot of time in that commune."

"Reds? Nonsense! That's not a 'commune,' it's a student co-operative dorm. I don't even know most people's politics there."

"I guess I stand corrected—so far." Again that odd transformation, a sympathetic crease between the brows, the head inclined. His hands with their stubby fingers lay flat and relaxed on the table as if he had nothing to hide, and his tone was mellow. "Lieutenant Becher, don't think that I don't share a desire to create a better world, but unlike you and your wife and friends—"

Jacob interrupted. "We're certainly not out to destroy the Republic."

Dougherty raised his hand, palm out. "I know, I know.... Perhaps not you, but you've heard these subversives all week, their machinations, their pleas, their poisoned messages undermining the young. And you... perhaps you don't want to undermine the state, but you're certainly following the crowd."

Jacob pressed his lips together, the wall clock loud in the silence.

Dougherty's regretful eyes locked on Jacob's. "I'm sorry we don't see eye to eye, but you must understand that we investigators are under pressure."

Is he trying to read my mind? At least, he speaks with conviction. Jacob remained silent, and his interrogator continued.

"Yes, I see that you have an honorable record in Military Intelligence. Did you ever uncover hidden facts that weren't noticed at first glance? Things different from what they appear?"

Jacob laughed briefly. "Along with dodging incoming shells and mortar fire, we did have some donnybrooks."

"And sometimes you had to use deceit, to wear a mask, when trying to get some information out of civilians or enemy soldiers?"

Jacob shrugged.

Dougherty continued to purr, his smile almost conspiratorial. "Lieutenant, I do understand. Really I do. I spent some time in college. I did my stint in the service like everybody else. I met lots of folks like you in my life. All of you think that if everyone got the same share of everything, the world would be a dandy place."

Jacob exhaled and let it pass. The peace offering was, of course, ludicrously simplistic, but despite its trivializing, it was a relief to face an adversary who seemed at least to try to meet him part way. Nor did he object to the assumption that he shared his friends' socialist credo. He straightened as the investigator continued.

"But you, an intelligent man, must see our side, too. Our country is in great danger, my friend—all those A-bombs out there and the Soviets will soon have that hydrogen thing, too. Look at the tension in Berlin, the airlift all summer long!"

Jacob began to lose his moorings. Unable any longer to distinguish the man's apparent openness on one level from his devious purpose on another, he attempted to reach out.

"You may know some things about us, but do try to understand us better."

Dougherty would have none of it. "You people *do* work against us from the inside. Did you listen to them upstairs undermining our system all week long? It's a frightening time, Lieutenant. Aren't you scared?"

"Not at all."

"I know." Dougherty's round face broadened again with his indulgent smile. His eyes were still gentle, even mournful. "As far as internal subversion is concerned, you aren't scared, of course, or you wouldn't be in the spot you're in right now. But outside danger—from the East—*that* must scare you."

"No, it doesn't."

His adversary still took no offense. He held out his open palm, "My friend. You and your wife may be perfectly sincere, but you're caught in a huge conspiracy. I recognize this danger, and you must, too, as a good citizen concerned about this country." Dougherty's eyes were still warm, friendly. His voice was mesmerizing. "How can I convince you it's real?"

Now he turned to a different subject. A touch of severity crept in. "When you were on leave in Florence, Lieutenant Becher, dating your present wife, did you ever meet a German painter by the name of Gregor Matthäus? Forgive me for prying into your personal affairs, but it has become an important matter."

Jacob started at the name. Dougherty had found his mark. "Yes. What about him?"

"We already asked these questions of your wife, as you must know. Her vicious article published before she emigrated gives us much food for thought. Ever since then, Matthäus has complained of a bad press, for the most part inspired by Reds. Could it be that your wife was one of them at the time she wrote that scurrilous piece—before she came here?"

"Certainly not at that time. You heard her deny Communist Party membership before the committee yesterday."

A moment of silence.

"You just said 'not at that time,' Lieutenant. I'm assuming she must have had prior connections with Communism, in her young years, perhaps. It would be only natural."

Sleepless, his mind foggy, in a numbing breakdown in volition, Jacob felt himself drawn to this man who exuded understanding, acceptance. He was smiling at him even now.

Jacob answered almost automatically, unthinkingly. "Of course, it would have been impossible to grow up in Italy during those fascist years in good conscience without taking a political stand. Communism offered her a means to resist. It was just part of growing up, a young student's struggle to survive as a responsible person."

The glint of triumph in his opponent's eyes told him it was too late. His mind cleared. *Any* admission of a communist past was enough to leave Francesca open to the charge of perjury. He tried to retract some of what he said, to alter it, belittle it, put it in a different context. But he'd said it.

His interrogator mixed his triumph with a touch of sadness. "Lieutenant Becher, your wife stated otherwise." Silence fell. "I warn you not to forget these statements when you testify at the public hearing at two."

He should have known all along who was wearing the mask.

ဆင်္ကြ

Jacob closed the door and stood still, his mind reeling. What *should* he do now? What *could* he do? He turned and flinched at seeing the group of well-wishers gathered in the hall by the stairs. Most conspicuous was the imposing figure of Gretta Dalton, her hair draped loosely over the collar of a dramatic black cloak. She peered through her thick lenses with cheerful encouragement. Next to her stood Jim Ahern, trim in an elegant seersucker jacket. He, too, offered an encouraging smile. Mike Simonetti had brought Francesca, wearing a light blue summer dress against the July heat. Scanning Jacob's tense face for a clue, they all began to look worried.

"One down, one to go!" Gretta exclaimed. "How did it go?"

"All right." His voice was dull, flat. How could he say otherwise?

"Let's go eat lunch," Ahern proposed. "Talk some strategy. There's a place down the street by the water. My treat." Mike excused himself and ambled away.

As the others filed out of the armory, waving at the pickets, Jacob took Francesca's arm. She responded, seizing his hand. "You look worried. Scared."

"I am." They trudged down the hill behind the others.

Gretta turned toward them at the next corner. "Dear Jacob," she said warmly. "Was it that tough?"

He compressed his lips. Francesca glanced at him, then filled the silence, relieving him.

"It looks like it," she said. "Mine seems to have been a piece of cake by comparison."

"I wasn't there," Gretta apologized. "But I'm glad Jim could be with you."

Francesca forced a laugh. "Not for long, though. And I gather they won't allow him back for Jacob either."

Jacob groaned, "Oh, no!" His last hope for a barrier against Pratt flickered out.

"That's what I heard. Why don't you check with him, Jacob?"

Ahern had overheard their exchange. "It's true. That's why I suggested the strategy lunch. I want you ready to cope with the tactics they'll be using on you this afternoon."

They had barely sat down in the small restaurant when Jacob pushed back his chair and stood. He paused behind Francesca's chair, his hands pressed on her shoulders as if they were his only support.

"Forgive me. No strategy can help me. I need to be alone."

Francesca half rose. "Do you want me to come?"

"No, darling, enjoy your lunch. I'll see you there." Over his shoulder, he caught sight of her apprehensive face.

He didn't *want* to be alone; he *was* alone, except for fear and self-loathing. He walked up the hill past the chanting pickets and found a bench across from the armory. Leaning back, he closed his eyes and let the warm sun pour over his face. His eyelids trembled as he absorbed the light that bore down on him with unexpected force and shimmered red on his retinas. They would take a while finishing their lunch at the water's edge, and he still had almost an hour before the time of his ... execution, his moment of reckoning, of being discovered, revealed as the coward he was.

Could it be 1948? Yes, a hot July day in the Pacific Northwest, not in Germany ten years earlier, but his temples beat with the same fear. He was transported to a cold day in 1938. He and his students sat in utter silence, trying to pretend it was an ordinary class. But they knew. Barking commands startled them at intervals, breaking the school building's all-pervasive, tense stillness. Now they heard boots marching in regimented cadence through the halls, harsh voices issuing orders. He knew they were arresting all teachers to take them to the concentration camp on the edge of the city.

It was their turn. The door banged against the wall. A man in boots had come to take him, too. Jacob remembered the faces: the contemptuous, arrogant stare of the arresting officer, his cheeks ruddy with manufactured fury, and the ashen face of his talented fellow teacher, Artur, already arrested. Tall and gentle, his warm voice had led hundreds of students to love poetry. The officer marched the two of them down the hall toward a waiting police van. The eyes. Those eyes remained in Jacob's memory across the years: a sharp pair, greenish blue and triumphant, and Artur's light brown pair, glazed with dread.

Jacob opened his own eyes and stared at the armory before him, the irrational conviction welling up that he would soon disappear.

Footsteps came near. Someone sat down next to him. It was Ahern. "They delegated me to look after you. We all feel you need help."

"Kind of you, Mr. Ahern."

"Call me Jim."

"Thank you, Jim. But I'm beyond help, believe me. You're all too kind." Jacob sat up, alert. He repressed the scenes that had flashed through his mind. Surely they were memories only, not a vision.

"But there must be something I can do. I'm your attorney, you know."

"No, I don't know. For one thing, legal counsel doesn't help with this crew. You must realize that by now better than I do. They make up their rules as they go along. But for another, I'm in too deep, too far away for anyone to help me. But thanks just the same."

Ahern's silence spurred him to try an explanation. "When I say far away, I mean in time. Maybe it won't make sense to you, but ..."

Ahern waited.

"It goes back a long way." Jacob spoke slowly, haltingly. "Francesca, I love her. We're both pursued by the same ghosts—*my* ghosts, Jim." He stopped again. "It goes back to Germany when I was teaching history in a Jewish big-city school. Somehow, now, facing that armory, waiting to be called to testify, those memories keep coming back and I can't get away from them. *My* ghosts, Jim! It was ten years ago—Crystal Night, you know."

Ahern nodded, still waiting.

"That image … clear … unforgettable. We teachers were expected to go on with our classes while the SS was taking over the place. The arresting officer came up to me, marching my friend and fellow teacher ahead of him. He shouted at me, 'DU, RAUS—he used the familiar form of address to show contempt—YOU, OUT!'

"'But my students?' I asked, my voice taut and strange.

"'WE take care of that! GET MOVING!'

"Artur and I were loaded into a police van with other teachers. We watched another van pull up, watched the school emptied of Jewish adults. We were hauled to the edge of the city. Makeshift barracks of rough lumber had been set up to house all adult Jewish men in the city. We endured blows, verbal abuse, lack of food and sanitation. We were told this *"Aktion"* was meant to avenge the death of a German diplomat in Paris at the hand of a young Polish Jew.

"Most of us were released in three weeks—some sooner because of lack of space—but I found out that Artur had disappeared. We had belonged to the same dissident youth movement, but he had ranked a step higher than me. The SS had even arrested me a few weeks earlier, took me to headquarters, interrogated me. Why I got away from the camp and Artur didn't, I'll never know. Maybe their bookkeeping is not as perfect as their reputation would have it.

"My family had been preparing to emigrate and go to America for some time already. As soon as I was released, we packed our belongings. Four months later, fearful but undisturbed after the *Aktion* was over, we embarked like ordinary citizens, with all our luggage and good clothing.

"I was safe, Jim. Artur was not. I wonder how he reacted to them, Jim, a sensitive man, but brave. When you're a prisoner, it's the strange intimacy of the thing, Jim, the abject intimacy. Silently we asked for mercy, not even for all of us, but each for himself. We wanted to appease … to *appease*, Jim. Say what you like, but the same impulse still lives in me. I understood my cowardice then, and I know I'm just as frightened today. That's what I'm afraid of, and that's why you can't help me when those same self-righteous men come for me to finish the job."

Ahern's voice betrayed his fear for his client's state of mind. "Nonsense, Jacob! That's a lot of nonsense! The two situations aren't comparable; you've got to realize that. But tell me, what happened with Dougherty."

His reply was no answer, his words now stumbling, obscure. "Just that ... Just that if you're just afraid, not angry, *afraid* and can't hate, all you want to do is please the other, even make him *understand* you—if that can make an end of it."

Ahern stared at Jacob, his face a mask of worry. He exhaled a gust of air, leaned forward, planting his elbows on his knees, his head in his hands. They sat together silently, each sunk in his own thoughts. Jacob rallied and looked at his watch. Ten minutes before two. He rose and saw the rest of the group walking up the hill. He had eyes only for Francesca, her tall figure, her gestures, her sad but encouraging smile as she waved to him.

"See you later, people," he forced himself to say. "I have to get ready."

He escaped but not for long. He would be on trial, his inquisitors merging with the men of 1938. Francesca could no longer lessen his anguish. July 23, 1948. They would all be waiting. Dougherty would be waiting. Pratt would be waiting. Canwell would be waiting, too.

ഹോ

He had never felt more exposed. Sitting slantwise before the dais, he swept the crowded chamber with a glance, while the chairman's gavel continued to pound the table. He half listened to the droning exhortations about the importance of giving clear answers, loud enough so they could be heard by the recording system. He scanned the still faces—eyes he knew and eyes he did not, eyes he loved and eyes he feared and hated. He fervently hoped his father hadn't come, yet his friends were out there in force. Katya sat with Elmo. There was his Francesca, unmoving, flanked by Gretta and by Mike, stiff and erect. And, yes, there, sitting apart from them all, he saw the impassive face of Dr. Otto Becher the man he had begged to stay away.

Adversaries were also in evidence. Glen Arnold, the angry student at Goddard's lecture banded together with several companions in a conspicuous enclave, glaring and hostile. Newsmen bustled about everywhere with their notebooks and cameras, shooting pictures with blinding flashbulbs, seemingly at random. When the gavel ceased its imperious hammering, Jacob straightened to face his interrogators.

The routine began. Canwell administered the oath. Sitting with his back to the audience, Jacob felt hemmed in. A drop of sweat trickled into his left eyebrow but he didn't reach for his handkerchief, feeling the eyes he loved and those he feared focused on him, burning the nape of his neck.

Pratt peered down at him, his slicked-down hair glistening in the electric light. "Lieutenant Becher ... are you now or have you ever been a member of the Communist Party?"

Jacob had his answer ready, the same answer he had heard several times a day, all week long.

"I am prepared to respond to your question for myself only. The answer is 'no' on both counts."

Pratt's thin lips widened in an ironic smile, then he went on as if Jacob had not spoken.

"You were an intelligence officer with the United States Army in Italy during the war, were you not?"

"Yes, sir." His voice was expressionless.

"I understand you came originally from Germany, a refugee." Pratt paused, peering over his glasses, giving himself an air of gravity. "Yes, of course, you fought well for this country." He paused again, no doubt for dramatic effect. "So perhaps you can tell us how Nazi oppression differs from communist oppression?"

"They are both oppressive."

"But you do consort with known Communists."

Jacob remained silent.

"Or at least with people who lie about their communist past?"

The words came over him like a flood, suffocating, drowning. Behind him existed only the eyes he loved, unseen, burning.

"I—"

The Chief Investigator did not allow him to say more. His bland face was now contorted. Jacob feared the man's anger, which to his horror, made him cringe. He became desperate to escape.

Pratt spoke with stinging sarcasm: "You live with a woman who hid her communist past. You so testified to our associate. You live with a woman, *your very own wife*, who covered up her communist connections. She is known as a person who defamed, with a poison pen, a celebrated German painter, a man who had been a vigorous fighter against the communist conspiracy. Your wife, a woman who has perjured herself on two occasions ... your wife, your very own wife, and you admitted it! *You said so yourself!* Didn't you, sir? Didn't you, Lieutenant? Didn't you so state to our associate, Mr. Gerald Dougherty this very afternoon? Didn't you?"

Jacob Becher was silent. He heard a gasp, a muffled outcry.

Canwell intervened. "I remind you that you're under oath and required by law to answer our questions—all of them"

In a regular court of law, Jacob knew he could not be pressured to implicate his wife, but this was a hearing, not a court of law, and such rules were more laxly applied. He saw no exit, no escape from the chairman's towering anger, his knuckles tightening around his gavel, his lips compressed, his face flushed. With an angry edge to his voice, he repeated the charge, "Your testimony to Mr. Dougherty shows incontrovertibly that your wife, the former Francesca Mancini, lied on two occasions under oath about her communist affiliation: first at the port of entry in New York; second, in sworn statements to this committee. Simply repeat for this committee what you have already stated."

Jacob trembled, his sweat congealing in the in the hushed, suddenly icy room. Refusal meant jail. The Fifth Amendment? For a brief moment, he felt strength inside him: his jail term rather than hers! But ghosts were rising from the past, terrible ghosts he had always felt compelled to appease.

Pratt was ready for him.

"The words of your testimony are quite sufficient. You will be charged with criminal contempt for lying to a legally constituted state authority if you deny them. Now then, once more, and quite explicitly, was your wife, the former Francesca Mancini, also known as 'Olga,' knowingly involved in the communist movement in Italy, the United States, or any other country, in the present or in the past?"

At this moment, Jacob Becher's vision replaced two bland American officials in civilian clothes with two men in black uniforms, death's heads on visored caps and swastikas on their sleeves. For a fateful, hallucinatory second he faced himself alone: his abject surrender to destruction

that was the intolerable burden of his history, his life. In his confusion,
for that brief, decisive instant, the fears he had harbored throughout the
war years irrupted into reality. He was back in their power, and it had to
be so, as he sacrificed the person he loved most to appease his enemy.

"Say it!" Pratt spat out. "was she or wasn't she?"

"Yes," he whispered.

It was too late. Irrevocable now.

Chapter 12
Francesca's Farewell

A moist hand gripped Francesca's shoulder. She turned to meet Mike Simonetti's grave eyes in a drawn face. Momentarily paralyzed, stunned and dizzy, she gasped for air.

"Let's go. Now!" Mike edged gingerly along the row of chairs, squeezing past spectators' knees.

She rose but paused when she saw Gretta's face. The older woman's expression was momentarily blank before her hazel eyes locked with hers, conveying a world of regret and worry before Gretta let her go.

Where's Ahern? Then she remembered her lawyer was not allowed in the room. They pushed along sideways and people let them pass without resistance.

"This can't be true," she whispered.

The scene around her seemed to recede in psychic distance. Beyond her shock, beyond the ache—deep as a physical wound—she reached for her wartime discipline, hardening inwardly as she followed Mike in his inch-by-inch progress. They reached the side aisle, where they could move more freely but where they were plainly visible and in danger of being stopped.

She knew the danger, but brushed it aside. *He's been closer to me than I was to my own self.* Grim-faced, with teeth locked, she had become Olga again. She felt Mike's hand placed lightly on her back. He leaned toward her left ear, whispering even as they moved, "I was afraid of this. Now we've heard it, seen it."

They continued to head for the doors that would hide them from view. She scanned the audience. *Odd. They seem mesmerized by that whispered 'yes.' They're only glancing at us, not taking in what they see.* Shock overcame her self-control for a moment, and she staggered as a violent tremor shook her body. But force of will mastered her body's weakness. Her instinct for self-preservation urged her toward the door ahead. She would be less conspicuous if she passed through it like someone headed for the women's room. The door closed slowly behind her on its spring, and she walked sedately down the stairway to the still empty lobby.

She had just reached ground floor when pandemonium broke loose in the hearing room upstairs. The frozen silence had been shattered at last. Cat calls, whistles, shouting. She heard the gavel bang, Canwell's excited voice: "Order! Order! Officer. The State Police will arrest... "

The noise inside ignited noise outside. The hearing-room audience, at odds with each other, some furious at Jacob's treatment by Canwell and Pratt, others outraged at the betrayal, turned into an indignant mob that spilled down the stairs and rushed past her into the street, joining the protesters outdoors. It was the last moment to escape arrest.

Jim Ahern hung up the downstairs public phone where he'd received an emergency call. He saw Francesca and moved toward her, visibly puzzled by the noise and the commotion. His mouth opened to speak to her, but she shook her head with a wave as she passed. Jacob would have to deal with him.

At the entrance, Katya waited. She must have left the hearing even before Mike had alerted her. Her friend's eyes glistened with tears.

Francesca took her hand and pulled her outside. "No time for weeping. We've got to get out of here."

Mike, following on their heels, put an arm around them both, and the three strolled casually down the street.

"Hands off our free education!" Pickets chanting slogans stood in clusters on the sidewalk. Uniformed and plainclothes state policemen were everywhere, but were too preoccupied with the chanting protesters to notice three people walking with unconcerned faces through the milling crowd.

Running footsteps behind them made them freeze in alarm. Beth!

"I was downstairs, listening on the public address system. I heard it all, Francesca. I'm so sorry, I misjudged you—your commitment, I mean." The girl faltered, embarrassed, then seized Francesca's hand and shook it with a firm grip. "Good luck, wherever you go, whatever you do." She darted away.

They reached Mike's car, which was parked not far down the street, as if he'd expected this turn of events.

Another surprise. They found Elmo leaning against the car, waiting. Who had told him? Why was he there? He spoke to Francesca a little shyly. "I had to see you. Mike hinted that it might come to this and I found his car here."

Though pleased, she did not respond to him directly, questioning instead. "What went wrong with Jacob? I mean deep down?"

But why ask him? Because he's a clergyman? What could he know?

Elmo answered simply. "We're not surprised." He shook her hand without answering her question, his brow creased in sadness. "I guess this is good-bye, at least for now. God be with you and protect you always, Francesca."

Katya jumped into the front seat next to Mike while Francesca stretched out in the back. She spoke harshly, the pain a hard knot under her heart. "If I hadn't seen with my own eyes and heard with my ears, I wouldn't have thought it possible."

Mike snorted. "He's an anxious man. That made him an easy mark. Now he has to live with himself." He maneuvered deftly through a busy intersection.

Her Olga-self spoke: "Yes, he'll have to do that, but not with me."

They were leaving the suburbs, and she looked around her, disoriented but feeling safe with her friends. "Where are we going?"

"Any place but home," Katya answered. "There's no place to go but north."

♟♣

Francesca never went home.

Her friends drove miles north on US 99 through late rush-hour traffic in the sunlit afternoon. The road seemed endless, clogged with long lines of cars and heavy trucks creeping in both directions on the two-lane highway. She closed her eyes. The sun glowed red through her eyelids; her head pounded. Looking out again, her glance slid over black, impenetrable walls of pine and Douglas fir on both sides of the road. A vision of that long-ago ride with Jacob replaced reality. Winter, with icicles hanging on the trees and patches of ice glittering on the rutty road. But Mike, not Jacob, sat behind the wheel. No one spoke. Sunk in grief, they pondered the ghastly turn of the day.

"We've got to get you across the border," Mike said finally. "And we can't hide you."

Francesca managed a wan smile. "Of course you can't. I'm too big."

Katya looked at both of them, her forehead creased with worry. "What do we do? Mike, you told me you have a plan."

"Don't worry," Francesca cut in. "I have my passport, and it's still in order."

Nothing more was said for several miles. But when they were within sight of the Canadian border at Blaine, Washington, she exclaimed with a momentary explosion of pain: "Please, is there no other way?" She longed to stay with the loved ones she had left—her friends. A futile outcry.

The customs house came in sight, and she saw the raised arm of the Canadian guard. The officer, trim in his well-fitting uniform, glanced at all three, his friendly blue eyes peering from under his visor. He wasted little time on Mike and Katya. Now he turned to the dark figure in the back-seat to ask the usual questions about birthplace—Turin—and citizenship—Italian. Francesca didn't wait to be asked for her papers. "Here's my passport." She pulled it from her handbag, hoping the officer would not notice her trembling hand.

"Italy, eh?"

He turned and ducked inside the building, reappearing after a few moments. She stared at the fresh entry stamp as he handed the passport back to her and waved Mike on, anxious to get to the next car in the line that had formed behind them.

"We'll be in Vancouver soon," Mike announced, his voice light with relief, "I know a place where you can stop over for the night. I stay there when I'm in the city. It's a rooming house, you know, nothing special." After a pause, he added, "Shouldn't you be in touch with someone in your family?"

"Yes, my parents. I suppose I should cable them, but it's too risky. I'll wait a while."

Mike's question and her answer brought a sharp picture to mind, the last glimpse of her mother in the bus in Florence, her face hidden behind the cascade of her brown hair as she bent to pay the driver.

Mike's voice broke her reverie. "Money?"

"I have enough. I'm an old operative, you know. You don't forget, Mike. We were under subpoena after all. I half expected something to happen that might make us run, though God knows, not like this—not alone."

Twilight was fading into night when she remembered Goddard. It seemed ages since she'd left the message for him to call. Only yesterday? By now, he'd have tried to reach her and would have gotten Jacob instead. She shuddered.

She leaned forward. "Katya, could you call Goddard for me, please, and tell him whatever you think is wise. I had left a message for him to call me, before …" She choked. "Don't say I'll be in touch. Say anything. I can't phone him now. Or ever." Her voice broke. She scribbled his number awkwardly in the moving car. "Thanks a lot."

Their headlights illuminated the gray stucco rooming house as they rounded a corner. Her friends helped her reassure the landlady by mentioning that her suitcase had been delayed. She reserved the room for two nights. Next day, she would buy what she needed and on the third day, she would board the eastbound train to start her long journey home.

Now the three stood together on the porch. Francesca hugged Mike in gratitude. She kissed Katya. "My friends," she said quietly, filled with a new kind of love, a hard love, drained of all sentiment.

She gripped their hands. They were gone.

ഇൻൽ

The first dream came in her early sleep. Jacopo sat in the familiar, worn easy chair in the living room reading a book. Her dream self watched him, knowing she would never see him again. The reading lamp shed a benign glow over his brown hair. An earsplitting crash! The lamp became a missile that fell and struck his head with great force, igniting the room, the man, and all the familiar things with a blinding flash and an explosive roar. He vanished as if cremated.

She started up, eyes wide. A door rattled somewhere and heavy footsteps moved down the hall. Her windows were open to the sticky, heavy summer night, filling the room with stifling humidity. Thunder rolled in the distance, and a toilet flushed downstairs.

She lay down again, and her last glance at the radiant dial of her watch told her she'd been awake for an hour. Then she was in Italy. Her mother sat across from her on the bus in her severe Army raincoat. "My dear, do what you must." The words, long buried and now suddenly exhumed, rang in her mother's clear voice. The bus rattled and swayed, taking on more passengers until riders filled the space between them, and it became hard to keep her mother in sight. "My dear, do what you must," she repeated, and a moment later, more words from that last unhappy visit in Florence, "For us, dear girl, it's beyond understanding." Only Jacopo, she thought, could save her, but Jacopo was now dead.

This time she lay awake in the darkness, dissecting her dreams. The lamp—the bomb—had killed Jacopo in her first dream, and his death became accepted fact in the second. Henceforth he was dead, dead for her. She sat up and propped herself against the headboard. She would never see him again. In his collapse, which she might one day understand but could never forgive, he had crossed a no-man's-land into the impermissible. He had loved her, she knew, and they'd been betrothed by that blinding shell, but in the end he had sent her into exile.

Fully awake, Francesca stared with dull eyes at the shimmering July dawn. Exiled, perhaps, but not adrift. She would build.

Groping in the half-light for paper and pen, propping herself up in the bed, she looked in her purse at the roll of bills in high denominations, drawn from several places with Jacopo's approval, that would pay the train and boat passage back home. She began to write:

"Dear Mama and Papa: I will be coming home to Florence—not to your house in Turin where I grew up, but to my own world ...." She lowered the pen and gazed vacantly out the window. How much would she explain? Yes, that her marriage had failed, but no details of the betrayal. Now that she was forced to leave the States, she would tell them she intended to continue her law studies in Italy and would once again request their financial help. She'd tell them, too, that she hoped for reconciliation, but expected them to meet her half-way. And she would send her love. Her father might greet her overture with cynical rejection, but she accepted that risk.

She finished the letter and continued sitting in the bed, hugging her knees, reviewing images from her first dream: Jacopo, cremated in the flash and explosion after the lamp shattered over his head, the husband who had betrayed her in his weakness, who had broken his vow to be faithful unto death. Now, as Olga, she had the strength to go on. She'd say good-bye to him somehow, but she feared a telegram could be traced. Instead, she wrote a postcard to her former address. She would mail it when she was far away.

She wrote in German, their first mutual language. *"Jakob: Die Granate hat uns doch erreicht. Wir existieren nicht mehr.* The shell has hit its mark after all. We exist no longer. Olga"

The war was not over, but she had survived the blast.

Part Two

Purgatory

"I have lost the sight of the sun above…which was known by me too late." –Dante, *Purgatorio*, Canto VII

Chapter 13
Jacob's Grief
(1948-1962)

"Francesca!"

Silence.

"Francesca! Where are you?"

His voice echoed in the empty apartment. "Don't leave me! I'll reverse it. I didn't mean to hurt you ... I might have refused ... risked jail. Francesca, please, where *are* you?"

For a few heartbeats he felt reassured. Her hat and winter coat hung on the rack, her dresses in the closet, her things untouched. He found her extra handbag, even her keys. He opened the drawers in her dresser and rifled through them in search of some clue to her whereabouts, spilling stockings and underwear on the floor. Her desk! Student papers, uncorrected, were piled on one side, unanswered letters on the other. Surely, she would be back. She was a conscientious teacher.

With an effort, he cleared his mind. She must be with Katya at the cooperative. Someone there might know something by now, more than two hours after the session was over, nearly seven o'clock. He dialed, heard the phone ringing in empty space. Where was everybody? Finally, someone picked up: a male voice. He knew nothing about the events of the afternoon. "No, Katya isn't in the house. Francesca? No, I haven't seen her in days. Hearings, you know. Try again later, maybe."

Finally, he called Elmo. To his relief, the pastor's voice was warm and compassionate.

"I'll be right over."

As good as his word, Elmo now sat across from him on the worn easy chair, listening gravely as he poured out remorse and self-accusation.

"Where is she, Elmo?"

"I don't know. Safe, I guess. Let's hope she's safe."

Jacob rambled, desperate to talk, to explain it all to himself. "She got away at least for now, thank God. But Elmo, I had no chance to

... I couldn't explain why ... why ... how it happened. I couldn't beg her ... to understand, no, not to forgive, just understand."

Covering his face with his hands, he mumbled, "No time, no time, Elmo, no time."

A sharp ring of the doorbell jolted them both. Two policemen, a younger man in uniform and an older one in civilian clothes stood silhouetted in the doorframe.

"Where is Francesca Mancini Becher?"

Her absence had finally been noticed, and now the committee's arm reached out for her. Francesca's often-told scene in the shabby office in Florence was replayed before him: the same two officers of the law on the same errand, seeking her arrest. Had he rescued her then to have condemned her now?

"Dr. Becher? We have a warrant for your wife's arrest."

Jacob shook his head. "Not here."

"Where is she then? You don't know?"

Jacob's face drained of color. He didn't know or, under such pressure, he might have betrayed her a second time. The old fears hovered, ever-present.

"I really don't know. Believe me!" His words tumbled over one another. "I couldn't find Francesca when the committee adjourned at four-thirty and she wasn't here when I got home."

Hearing himself rehearse the last few hours, his fresh loss stabbed him with increased pain. His self-control nearly failed him in front of these policemen, men who had become his enemies, but he held on to himself, preserving his dignity—and hers. He repeated, "She wasn't here when I got home."

"You'll hear from the committee. Meanwhile, make sure your wife contacts us." The detective sergeant's stance became menacing. "We'll be back with a search warrant if necessary. Being a fugitive is an art, not to be practiced by amateurs."

Francesca's voice echoed in Jacob's ear, telling her Italian story: the final threat by a departing cop. He felt close to the woman he loved for a few precious seconds before reality set in.

"Yes, sir."

The sergeant in civvies glowered, and Jacob noticed sharp brown eyes and a small mustache. "I have no warrant for your arrest at this time, Professor Becher, but you're under suspicion of shielding a fugitive from justice. You're not to leave the city until further notice."

He was hardly aware that they had left. Though they'd told him he would not be arrested, a fresh wave of terror shook him. What were they waiting for? Why torture him—making him wait like this?

At last, he expelled an explosive breath, his muscles functional again. He heard the men's steps fading away down the stairs. Elmo was still with him, and the stalwart presence filled him with a surge of gratitude. He made coffee, and for a while, they sat together in silence.

At last, Jacob choked out in a barely audible voice, "When I saw those men walk through the door, I was terrified again. Overwhelmed by dread. Shadows from my past way back in Germany possessed me again, just like this afternoon, facing the committee. But now I'm no longer afraid." His sigh almost became a sob. "Why not this afternoon when it mattered?"

Elmo stood, crossed to Jacob, and put a hand on his shoulder.

"God understands."

This was the first time Jacob had ever heard his friend, the Unitarian minister, invoke God in a private conversation. To his surprise, the answer made sense.

The high note of the ringing phone cut short their reflection. Jacob leaped up. "Francesca!"

His face fell. It was Professor Goddard calling from Madison.

With Elmo in the room, Jacob felt self-conscious, and he almost stuttered, because he couldn't bring himself to tell Goddard the truth. Not yet. He was sorry, but Francesca wasn't in just now. He hadn't known she expected his call. Yes, this had been a very hard day. He'd tell Francesca he phoned. Elmo winced. "Thank you so much for calling, Professor Goddard."

When he hung up, Elmo looked at him, shaking his head. "Lying won't help you, Jacob. He cares about Francesca, too."

Stricken, Jacob all but shouted, "I just couldn't admit she's gone, Elmo, that it's over, that our 'marriage' under shell fire was for nothing. My marriage. My everything. All those hopes and plans. I need just a little more time, just a little longer before I can take it in, let alone accept it."

Again, the hand on his shoulder. Elmo moved to the door.

"You're in pain, Jacob, but lying even to yourself won't help. Nothing you'll say or do will bring her back, at least not now. You have no choice."

They walked downstairs together. "Let me drive you home, Elmo."

"No thanks, I need to think."

They stood awkwardly in the driveway. "Thanks, friend."

Elmo nodded and walked away. Tree-filtered gleams from the setting sun accompanied him down the street.

Jacob glanced toward the stairs to the apartment and winced. The emptiness that awaited him there so appalled him that he took refuge in his car. He drove aimlessly, finding himself near Volunteer Park after an hour's meandering. The sound of the doorbell inside his parents' house woke him from a near trance. His mother answered but he remained on the doorstep, not knowing why he had come, ready to escape. She was embarrassingly cloying, her worried face studying his to see if he had suffered any harm.

His father appeared in the hall behind her, the porch light reflecting on his bald head, reticent in his welcome. "I like her," he said, coming straight to the point. "We disagreed a lot, but I like her. Where is she now?"

Jacob shrugged. "I have no way of knowing, Papa."

"I hope she's safe. She's a refugee like us."

"How safe are you?" His mother clasped and unclasped her hands.

"Only they know, Mother. Only they." He turned and fled.

The days immediately following were loud with a roaring absence, a painful, palpable void that continued without letup. He remained under suspicion of concealing Francesca's whereabouts and endured repeated interviews with Gerald Dougherty, still retained by the committee. The investigator never believed that the Bechers' separation was more than a gesture. He refused to consider the possibility that Jacob's capitulation had destroyed his marriage so completely that he could not be expected to know where his wife had gone.

Jacob hoped Francesca had fled to Italy, but the thought remained mere speculation without evidence, which he would never share with the authorities. When Dougherty pressed him again and again, he decided to consult Jim Ahern, the nearly forgotten lawyer who had tried to be helpful before his downfall and Francesca's flight.

He hadn't visited Ahern's office since that bright June day when he and Francesca had sought advice about the hearings, nor had they met since his shameful breakdown and his wife's disappearance. He called the lawyer and brought him up to date. So much had changed since their first meeting, so many assumptions about the committee, its deadlines and range, had proved fatally wrong. When Jacob entered the sunlit office, the sense of *déjà vu* became so strong that he turned his head, expecting to see Francesca behind him.

Ahern rose and walked around his desk to greet him with a warm handshake, seeking Jacob's eyes. "It's been just a few weeks, hasn't it, but—"

Jacob interrupted. "Don't we wish we could play it all over again, starting with our talk on the bench? Where was my mind then—back in Germany in '38... Crystal Night?"

Ahern shrugged, not without sympathy, and pointed to a chair. "I might have done more." He turned back to his desk. "I should have been paying more attention to the radio all along." He reminded Jacob that the widely publicized hearings of the House Un-American Activities Committee were broadcast not too long ago. His cheerful manner faded visibly. "Really, we should have known them better. It's been obvious for years that their side is very strong. Why did we ignore it?"

Jacob interrupted Ahern's train of thought. "I hope you'll advise me one more time, despite my screwing it all up and sending Francesca into exile. It could have been avoided, you know."

Ahern gave a barely perceptible nod.

"I've been interviewed by Gerald Dougherty several times since," Jacob went on, "and I should have gotten in touch with you three weeks ago when it started. Jim, it's always the same stuff. He always wants to know the same thing. I guess he figures to wear me down. 'You *know* where your wife is hiding, so you'd better come clean, Becher. *Where is she?*' That's all he ever asks. Believe me, Jim, I'd be happy to know the answer so I could fly to her. Anyway, I didn't want to trouble you again after our—my failure."

Ahern's voice was resolute. "Let's get over this now. Nothing is gained by blaming yourself. We have work to do."

Jacob looked up, admiring the lawyer's firm response.

The attorney's chair creaked as he leaned back. "You have the right not to speak, you know. Be warned, though, Jacob, if it comes out that you might have known where Francesca went, you'd be obliged to tell them."

"I think I know why, but you're the lawyer. Tell me."

"It's what the arresting officer said, that you'd then be shielding a fugitive from justice, which would make you an accomplice."

"I swear I don't know where Francesca is! Believe me!"

Ahern's eyebrows rose, and he cocked his head. "Of course it's hard to prove whether you know or don't know. Still, this frequent badgering amounts to harassment."

Jacob wasn't sure whether Ahern was baiting him or questioning his veracity. He waited.

The lawyer's lips widened in a smile. "Just tell Dougherty to leave you alone, politely, of course. And call me if you need help. Your own case worries me more. Are you still under subpoena?"

"I think so. I wasn't told anything about it, one way or the other. As for Francesca, I'd give anything in the world to know where she is and I'd never betray *that* secret."

There was nothing more to say. They shook hands once more, and Jacob went on his way. He still felt ill at ease, knowing he'd be unable to keep Gerald Dougherty out of his life. Ahern's legal advice had fallen short of expectations on that score, but even so, Jacob felt less alone. Knowing that his lawyer had grasped the gravity of the situation and sensing he had Ahern's backing, he was able to turn away the agent's constant questions about Francesca's whereabouts unapologetically and with confidence.

ಬುಡ

The months passed in mourning. Jacob hoped to be consoled by shared misery, for he knew that many of his friends and colleagues were worse off than he, under pressure and plagued by uncertainty. Yet his anguish, born of isolation and personal failure, did not abate. Francesca left a void where there had been support, barren loneliness where there had been warmth. As the university followed the

Canwell Committee in cleansing itself of any suspicion of being "soft on Communism," Jacob felt himself a stranger in the place of work he loved. Lost, he resumed driving through empty streets at night and striding through dark paths on the university campus.

He seldom tried to imagine just what Francesca was doing now, convinced that she had escaped to safety. His relief that she was able to take out enough of their money to help her flee did little to lessen the overwhelming sense of loss that shut out all else.

Memories flooded him after a night of wandering, when exhaustion stopped him beside the impressive fountain where the rose garden began. In the deceptive light of early morning, swaying blossoms stretched down the gentle slope for what seemed like miles. That last time, the garden had been an expanse of mud in the driving rain. Now it was in full bloom as the sun opened the day, shedding dazzling beams over a sea of red, pink, white, and yellow. Jacob, head bowed, leaned against the tree where they had kissed. The memory of that moment glowed with the colors around him, blending with the lush green of the lawn.

He spoke aloud, feeling sure he would not be heard. "Francesca!"

But he was heard after all.

"Mister!" shouted a man in blue jeans and a checkered red shirt, "What do you think you're doing?"

Jacob waved across the flowers, recognizing a campus guard. "I'm Dr. Becher in History. Just taking a walk!" To his relief, the man turned away. But his mood was broken. Without Francesca, the rose garden was no longer theirs.

ಐಂಚ

At last came a verdict. Professor Jacob Becher, on his way to class in the driving rain, clutched a copy of the morning paper and rehearsed the sad news he knew he'd find. The early broadcast had already announced the disaster for him, for his colleagues, and for academic freedom, but details had been sketchy. It was hard to accept what had happened to him and his entire community. Perhaps, he thought, it was all to the good in the long run, for it would galvanize the entire profession. Or would it? Six tenured men had been singled out for punishment: three for direct dismissal, three for a severe reprimand that would shackle them for life, and all of it done for the 'preservation of academic freedom' by the university's own Committee on Promotion and Tenure.

As Jacob hurried up the footpath to the building where his class was waiting, he repeated to himself the words of the judgment that burned themselves into his brain. Anthony, the English professor who had annoyed the Canwell crowd by the famous quotation from *Hamlet*, was one of the victims. So was the philosopher Pembroke and Bob Gerson, Jacob's favorite experimental psychologist. Jacob shook with indignation.

Suddenly, two tasks loomed before him. He must perform them, or he'd never again be free. He must break his ties with an institution of higher learning that would soon spew him out like the others, and he had to reach Katya once more and hope to be forgiven.

Resigning his teaching post turned out to be the easier of the two heartbreaking tasks. Immediately after his class, on an impulse fuelled by anger, he burst into his chairman's office. John Henderson pretended not to be surprised. Tall, gray-haired, a historian of American diplomacy, he looked as distinguished as the diplomats he taught and wrote about.

"Good to see you, Jacob." He paused, troubled to see the congenial young professor so distraught. "What is it, Jacob? I'm sorry things are tough for you these days. How are you making out?"

"Not great!" But before he could express his anger, his chairman began to speak of Francesca.

"My regards to Mrs. Becher when you get in touch with her. She impressed me a lot."

Jacob's throat grew tight as anger escalated. He barked a reply, "I haven't heard from her and wouldn't know where to write. But I—"

Henderson continued without a pause. "To be quite honest with you, Jacob, nobody believes that."

"They'd damned well better, John. I have no idea where she is. None."

In the tense silence that followed, Jacob clenched his fists and locked eyes with his chairman. "The administration of this place has no balls. You can call *me* a coward if you like, but look at the lot of *them*, betraying the people, the faculty members, whose work justifies their very existence. They're living like parasites off our teaching. *We earn their bread and butter!*"

"Jacob ..."

"And damn the craven faculty on the Committee on Promotion and Tenure! They've sold out their brothers and sisters to please a filthy bunch of autocrats—the Canwell Committee."

Henderson leaned against his bookcase, arms folded and legs crossed. He stretched out his hands, making patting-down, calming motions. "Professor Becher," he said, formal all of a sudden, "get hold of yourself. Now that you're here, let's talk about your situation in the department after the decision we heard this morning. The worst seems to be over."

Jacob's eyes narrowed. His chairman seemed to believe he was capable only of self-interest, that his anger was a symptom of worry about his status. He gnawed his upper lip.

Henderson continued. "Our weak-kneed administration seems to have done its worst and the committee's about to shut down. All things being equal, Becher, you're OK for a while and I'd fight to keep you, except ... except for the situation with Francesca. The two of you know too many people Canwell and his crew have investigated. She's shrouded in all sorts of mysteries, and you're a long way from tenure. I like her a lot. She's very impressive. *But you must stop shielding her.* Everyone, from the FBI to the president's office, believes you must know where to find your own wife. If you don't do anything about it, we might not be able to keep you much longer."

"Of course, *sir*, I knew that."

Henderson raised his eyebrows with an intake of breath. The sarcastic tone seemed to unsettle him. Jacob continued, "My colleagues and I, *sir*, we all certainly know that."

It was foolhardy, but in this one decisive moment he was joining Francesca in becoming footloose, wandering.

"I resign, Professor Henderson." His voice rang out, sharp and defiant.

"But, Jacob! Get hold of yourself! I was just warning you. There's plenty of time. Things are changing, and Francesca will be with us again!"

Jacob didn't believe a word of it. His eyes were clear. "My mind is made up. There's no place for me after these hearings. And this morning's news sealed it for me, for me and Francesca, wherever she is. I—we—go before we're forced to go."

John Henderson looked at the man blazing with defiance before him. He dropped his eyes and Jacob detected a measure of respect. "Well, if you want it this way…"

Jacob didn't let him finish the sentence. "Thank you, sir. I enjoyed working with you."

The door banged behind him.

ഇരു

The second task was a heartache. He knew Robert Pembroke was among those dismissed, and Katya would be doubly in mourning. She had lost a beloved professor, and both had lost their Francesca.

It was early evening when he rang Katya's number, and she came to the phone at once. "Hello, Jacob."

"I'm calling about Pembroke."

"Thanks for thinking of me. What can I say? He never hid the fact that he's a Marxist, a Communist."

Jacob answered quickly. "I know. There was no subversion, no concealment; we all knew where he stands, and so did his students."

Katya's voice was sad: "Maybe he'll win out somehow after all, but I doubt it."

She hung up with an abrupt click. For all the sadness they shared, Jacob knew he had been dismissed. He had never asked about Francesca. An inexplicable inhibition held him back. Part of him now wanted to cry out: "How is Francesca? Where is she? Please!" But it was too late. He wouldn't call back.

Chapter 14
Without Francesca

Jacob had taken his fate into his own hands. Meanwhile, the authorities remained interested in Francesca and therefore also in him. Her article in *Il Tempo* exposing Matthäus had led them to think of her as far more important than she actually was. But having impulsively burned his bridges at the university, Jacob felt freer to challenge Dougherty, his benign tormentor. He still had to endure a few more uncomfortable sessions in the investigator's downtown office, but the agent's power over him had diminished.

Dougherty addressed him with a thin smile. "Professor Becher or Lieutenant Becher... which should it be this time?"

Jacob didn't answer. His adversary, however, sounded determined. "You were in intelligence, so you know what I'm doing." The same catch words designed to unsettle him, the same faintly threatening posture.

Jacob mustered the courage to speak with quiet dignity and determination. "Mr. Dougherty, I'm no longer employed by the university, as you know. I'm what we used to call strictly a civilian. And I've done nothing to offend you or the State. Why do you keep after me?"

"You can fix it easily, sir. Just tell me how we can get to your good wife Francesca Mancini."

"I don't know. I have no idea. We've split up for good." And with a cry of anguish, "Leave me alone, *please*. You've done enough."

Jacob was saved by the Italian police, who located Francesca back in Florence.

Dougherty's unruffled demeanor finally slipped the day he telephoned Jacob with the news: "No need to pretend any more, Becher. They found her back in Italy, where she belongs. Congratulations!" He hung up with a decisive click.

The discovery of Francesca in Florence relieved everyone. The fugitive made it clear that nothing could induce her to return from Italy to rescue the man who had betrayed her, and those in America who hunted her were finally convinced she wasn't important enough to bother fighting for her extradition. She would have been deported anyway in the end, and her escape, though illegal, avoided trouble and expense. Her case was quietly dropped, and therefore Jacob's as well.

When his job ended formally at the end of the term, Jacob had little reason to stay in Seattle. He had seen less and less of his parents and was pleased they agreed that his looking for work elsewhere would be a good move. In the lonely quiet of his changed existence, he decided to leave Seattle, the place of his marriage and his betrayal. Overtly, most of his friends did not break with him, but he couldn't ignore the barriers that recent events had raised.

One person remained uncompromising in his hostility: Mike Simonetti. Guilt and the search for absolution made Jacob call his name one day when he saw him leaving the university bookstore. They nearly collided. Mike turned away to walk down the street, pretending not to see him. But when Jacob caught up and touched him on the shoulder, escape was impossible. Seeing his cold eyes, Jacob regretted his compulsion but was unable to leave.

They stood face-to-face. Beside them, cars honked, a lumbering bus came to a stop and unloaded a crowd of students carrying notebooks and briefcases. For a moment, they seemed hemmed in by hurrying people.

"I'm sorry," Jacob croaked.

No answer. The silence continued for nearly a minute. The traffic light at the corner turned twice. Passers-by stared.

Mike ignored the apology. "In case you're concerned, Dr. Becher, she's OK. Safe, I think, I hope. But no thanks to you." He paused. "It's best we don't speak again." He turned, dodged the heavy traffic, and vanished from sight.

Jacob remained on the sidewalk, transfixed. Slowly, he turned away to walk down the avenue. The humiliation had brought with it a kind of cleansing.

A greater shock arrived with the indirect news from Francesca. On her anonymous initiative, a speedy divorce had been arranged between a Florentine attorney and James Ahern, who brought papers for Jacob to sign. After sitting for a few minutes with his head in his hands while Ahern waited, he signed them. All formal ties were severed. Might there still be informal ones? But Seattle, even this apartment, no longer felt like home.

Once he could face leaving the place he and Francesca had shared, he gave notice. But the decision had been agonizing, and he procrastinated until the end of the semester. He gave away all the familiar furniture, left some important mementos with his parents, emptied what remained of his bank account, and for no reason except a whim, headed for New York.

It was painful to cross North Dakota by train, this time in bright daylight alone. He imagined her in Florence, at the Arno, on the patio near the Duomo. Sunlight flashed on the glass of brown vermouth as she raised it. "The war is over. I can be myself again."

ഇൗരു

Francesca had gone from his life. Not even Olga remained. Yet, from now on, through all the years to come, Jacob Becher would cling to her at the core of his memory. Enfolded in his mind, a perpetual image of that intense face, those penetrating eyes, that body filled with reluctant desire, that reserved figure suddenly bursting into a festival of love, would bob up and down within the current of his life.

"Francesca!" he cried within himself, "Forgive me, my love. It was only the lapse of a moment, that 'Yes.'" He replayed the scene differently each time. "No, sir. I won't answer. Mr. Dougherty was mistaken about what I was supposed to have said." At other times, "I take the Fifth Amendment. I'm her husband. I can refuse to answer. You say I can't? I refuse anyway. Put me in jail." In bed that night they would turn to each other, relieved. He would enfold her in his embrace.

Jacob's pleas, mostly spoken in silence, could sometimes burst forth in audible speech, covered at once with a shy smile, a furtive glance. "Francesca!" he would call out as he boarded a crowded bus. Faces turned to him, then away, discreet, embarrassed, disapproving.

"Francesca! It's raining outside. Remember our kiss in the rose garden?"

"Don't you hear the shell? See it? The bright light and the roar? Huddled like insects on the mossy ground? We, *Geschwister*, brother and sister on the threshold of death, *auf der Schwelle des Todes*? Your words, not mine. My sister! Come back!"

He refused to relent or to adjust. And he treasured these moments.

He continued to lead a double existence. His growing desire for a normal life struggled with his obsession with the ghost of Francesca. It possessed him even as he concealed it from the professional and social world. So far, he had not heard from her directly, even when all dangers had passed, and they could have exchanged letters with ease. The divorce had been handled in the utmost impersonal way.

Her heart, once opened so generously to him, had turned to stone. She kept her private address from him. Only once a distant echo came to Jacob's ears. A casual acquaintance, without realizing that Jacob even knew her, heaped praise on a "helpful attorney" in Florence who spoke excellent English. That was how Jacob discovered that she worked out of the Florence Office of the Prosecuting Attorney as one of the prosecutors investigating war crimes. He was tempted to write her there, but knowing her efforts to shield herself from him, he left her to her isolation.

ᎦᎧᏏ

Much happened during the next ten years. In New York, he first found a congenial psychoanalyst who helped him as best he could. After a lengthy psychoanalysis and many conversations, he recognized Jacob's grasp of psychological problems in others and his ability to help them. He then suggested that Jacob might train as a therapist himself. He suggested a "Postgraduate Center for Psychotherapy" on Manhattan's East Side, an institution for training therapists that had grown up in the 1950s, partly in response to the needs of veterans still bearing psychic scars from World War II. Also, it extended help to professionals in a number of disciplines who, like Jacob, had been shut out of their original fields by the growing wave of McCarthyism. It served the need to replace strict medical training, traditionally required, with an equally strict regimen in psychiatric theory and practical work in outpatient clinics and settlement houses.

Jacob substituted this new endeavor for his past commitment to European intellectual history and slogged through the required eight years to qualify for this very different profession, choosing psychoanalysis as his main theoretical orientation. He didn't regret having left history behind, for he enjoyed being directly engaged with people rather than only with books and ideas. In fact, he was so zealous in his work that he was offered a staff position after graduating, which he accepted with pleasure.

He was very effective, for like many wounded people, he sought to heal himself through continual contact with the wounds of others, continual contemplation of the human condition and his relation to it. He repressed his sorrow and anger at himself, finding it easier to read and "cure" those feelings in others rather than deal with his own. He enjoyed the collegial atmosphere in the Center's austere brick building. It was there that he met Lisa Wertheim, a brilliant young woman, a student-apprentice, and in a mixture of guilt and boldness, he proposed a short time after they met. He had allowed himself to become quickly enamored, moving from attraction to a growing desire, fanned by twelve years of celibacy, even though the shadow of Francesca hovered continually behind him. But Lisa was young, a promising professional, good to look at and full of lively talk, and at that moment the shadow was absorbed by the sunny day.

Still, it was an awkward scene. They were walking west on Fifty-ninth Street heading for Central Park when Jacob suddenly stood still in the middle of Park Avenue as the light turned red.

"Francesca!" he called out inwardly.

Aloud he said: "Forgive me, Lisa. This sometimes happens to me. I don't know why."

Determined, cheerful, Lisa did not probe. Instead, she gave him a sidelong glance with her piercing blue eyes and touched his arm.

"Wake up!" she laughed. "Come on. Let's get across."

When they finally maneuvered through the traffic and reached the other side safely, he stood still again. He turned towards her. Her eyes still rested on him, her lips curved in a slight smile. He held both her shoulders.

"I'd like to marry you," he said simply. "If you care."

The year was 1960, in the spring.

ജ‍ഗ

An announcement appeared in the society pages:

NUPTIALS: Mr. Edmund Wertheim, President of the ExecuCheck Banking Conglomerate and Mrs. Felicia Wertheim, née Schwartz, announce with pleasure the forthcoming wedding of their daughter, Lisa Ellen, to Dr. Jacob Becher, Psychoanalyst and Historian.

The wedding was a sumptuous affair. Guests flocked to the platters laden with smoked salmon and turkey breast, pâtés and pots of caviar, bowls filled with rainbow-hued fruit. An elegant bar served wines, liquors, and mixed drinks with the swaying sound of old dance tunes in the background.

The father of the groom waylaid his son just as he poured himself a glass of burgundy. "Great food, great wine!" Scrappy and elegantly bald, he recalled the simple first wedding twelve years ago and added with some force, "Beats our old Meany Hotel in all respects but one."

His father had found his vulnerable spot. Jacob surveyed this splendid second wedding, which dwarfed the modest gathering of the first.

Seattle. Francesca as a bride in a blue silk dress adorned with the delicate orchid Otto had pinned on her shoulder, contrasting with the strong, beautiful face of the former partisan.

"What do you mean, Papa?" The question with its trace of belligerence betrayed his discomfort.

Otto allowed him no escape. "Just for a second, Jacob, let's remember our Francesca." He paused. "I know you had to do what you had to do. Still ..."

The music swelled in the background. Jacob, transfixed, stared at his father, wineglass in hand. He knew Otto had not intended such a sweeping exoneration.

Waves of anger passed over him. "This is my *wedding*, Papa."

"True," Otto went on unperturbed, adjusting his glasses, straightening his tie. "But we mustn't forget her. Francesca Mancini was a refugee like us. She was a great daughter-in-law—the best. She knew Fascism, unlike anyone else here. We could talk to each other. It's been a dozen years. We let her down."

Voices and music surged around them. For a moment Jacob felt paralyzed, but he managed to choke out a few words. "She was hurt. So were we all." He studied the red wine, the light reflecting in the cut glass with a golden glint. Inwardly trembling, he now faced his father, seeing another anguished man. He put his arm around Otto's shoulders.

"We think the same, Papa, but we must learn to forget."

At that moment, Lisa, young and vibrant, came toward them, a fluted glass in her hand still half-filled with tired champagne, untouched since the toasts over an hour ago.

A shadow fell over Otto's face. "Please, Jacob. This is between you and me." He paused for a second as he watched his new daughter-in-law come near. "Only you and I," he murmured hastily, "only the two of us must keep on remembering. Leave Lisa out of it! This isn't her struggle. Keep her future clean, for her and your children."

The shadow dissolved before Lisa reached them. The old man smiled.

"My dear!" He looked at her tenderly, at the young face flushed with excitement. "My dear," he repeated and, wiping his eyes, he slowly walked away.

"A lovely man," said Lisa, watching him disappear in the crowd.

"That he is." Jacob stood still, mesmerized. He looked somber. His father had touched him with his contradictory plea.

৪০Ⳅ

Otto died a few months after the wedding. Jacob hadn't realized how ill he was. Would he have thought or acted differently had he known? Perhaps not, but as he stood in the cemetery in Seattle, he knew he had lost an irreplaceable treasure. The day was blue and bright. They gathered among sunlit tombstones and trees, every leaf delineated in unusual clarity.

He'd not known the dimension of his loss until he stood at the open grave. Supporting his mother with one arm, his other arm around Lisa's shoulders, he knew that, with Otto's death, the most crucial connection that tied him to his betrayal was gone. He was free now, asserted one part of himself, but, asked another, how could he continue? He felt once again those eyes burning behind him as he faced his inquisitors at the hearings in Seattle, eyes that knew about investigations and threats, knew about the enemy and about the victim's fateful bonding—those eyes would no longer see him. No one to put a hand on his arm, understanding without forgiving.

Would it be possible to live?

Chapter 15
Francesca's Second Farewell
(1962)

In the fourteenth year since the Hearings in Seattle, a shadow of change seemed to stir.

Now, in the spring of 1962, a break occurred. That cool and rainy day, as he sat in his modest office in the Postgraduate Center for Psychotherapy, Jacob Becher, PhD received an odd phone call. A man with a distinct German accent was on the line. "My name is Egon Scheffel," he announced in a loud voice that reverberated in the receiver. "You don't know me, but your name was given to me by friends in Italy as someone knowledgeable about art. Could you fit me into your schedule for perhaps half an hour?"

Jacob was puzzled. Who over there could possibly think he was an expert in art? But then, with a start, he knew: It had to be that malevolent ghost, Gregor Matthäus, to whom, indirectly, he owed the loss of Francesca. Clearly, he had to meet this caller.

He glanced at his diary. "I have a cancellation the day after tomorrow at three o'clock."

"Thank you, sir. I'll be there."

Jacob hung up slowly and scratched his chin. Their meeting would surely be about Matthäus, but what could be the reason? Although McCarthy was long gone, his spirit, like those of Canwell and others like him, still lingered. He felt a nagging anxiety.

The man entered with a self-confident stride. He was tall but not as overpowering as his telephone voice suggested. A receding hairline indicated he was at least in his forties. Jacob shifted slightly in his chair, pierced by the other man's sharp brown eyes as they scrutinized each other briefly in silence. Jacob had felt secure behind the rampart of the desk, but for Scheffel it was no barrier. He reached across it to shake Jacob's hand, a ritual Dr. Becher had neglected.

"What can I do for you?"

"I've come to ask you about a matter, which is a great worry to an important painter and his admirers. He's living in Italy now. Gregor Matthäus. You know him?" He turned the statement into a question, speaking fluent, idiomatic English as he fixed Jacob with a steady gaze.

"You speak German, of course." It was a peremptory assertion and Jacob nodded, feeling reluctant.

Scheffel continued in that language. "Herr Matthäus knows about you and asked me to look you up. We're colleagues and friends. I'm a bit of a painter myself, though I'm mostly an art dealer."

"But how can I help you?"

Scheffel pulled his chair within a few inches of the desk. He sat without dropping his eyes, deep pools in threatening weather. He went on in German, "Just after the war, an article appeared in the Italian press that showed my friend in a very bad light."

Jacob looked away to hide his emotion. Francesca hadn't come back as he often imagined in his daydreams, but she was intensely present in the room, dragging an unfortunate piece of history behind her.

"Such a scurrilous piece of garbage!" he heard Scheffel's booming voice. "It attacked him as a Nazi, a Fascist—and it has done my friend a great deal of harm." Again his sharp brown eyes pierced Jacob's. "It damages him even now, Dr. Becher, believe me, in 1962, sixteen years later."

Jacob merely nodded.

Egon Scheffel continued with great warmth. "I'm sure you agree that Herr Matthäus is a brilliant artist. Deep down, he's a German artist, but he has a great following in Italy. His oils and watercolors are shown all over—in important galleries in Rome, Florence, Milan."

Jacob's mouth felt dry. *Why tell me this?*

Oddly, the man across the desk became subdued. He looked self-absorbed as he lowered his voice.

"We know the author of that article. A woman who was once close to Herr Matthäus, one might even say a very close friend, especially after the German Army cleared out of Florence and he could come out of hiding."

Jacob was gripped by a sharp pain of anticipation. Had she become more militant again? For a moment, his present life, his marriage to

Lisa, faded into the background. He envisioned his lost love coming back to him: the woman in white, standing in the bedroom door. Her voice echoed in his mind: *Come to me!*

Scheffel's next words brought him back to reality.

"I'm afraid she never believed in his innocence. He could never escape having been a German officer, although his own people were after him with all their cruelty when it came out he loved men. After the war, the support of his fellow artists in Florence crumbled once he became successful. Gregor wondered what was the source of their suspicion. Was it the art lovers who flocked to him? His admirers? Of course, some of them *had* to be former Fascists!"

Scheffel's voice shook again. With mourning? Regrets? Indignation?

"But did that mean he'd betrayed his friends? You see, that's why it hurt so much when he received his worst blow from one of his dearest friends in that bitter article in *Il Tempo* in 1946, attacking Gregor as an instrument of the Fascists left behind after the German retreat."

Scheffel forgot himself and all but shouted.

"Dammit, she knew better! She knew Gregor well. But we hear she hasn't changed her mind even now, at least not officially. And she has good connections. She used to serve in the prosecutor's office for the Florence area, but we understand she's a defense attorney now, in private practice, representing revolutionaries and such. *Francesca Mancini!* Gregor used to call her *Olga.*"

The names, rolling off the man's tongue, struck Jacob hard, like successive blows. And he even added her partisan alias! But how did he know of their connection? He wondered, as he followed the drift of Scheffel's speech, whether he knew that Francesca had been his wife. Then he remembered climbing that stairwell in Florence, and the painter opening the door. He heard Gregor's delighted shout, "Olga!" Perhaps Scheffel was there that night.

The man went on. "She's a genuine crusader—*eine echte Kreuzfahrerin*—out to nail him." Scheffel's voice now vibrated with urgency. "We know you were her husband. Please help us stop her!"

Matthäus and Scheffel knew the connection between Jacob and Francesca, but not the whole story, nor that he was remarried. He was beginning to feel less uncomfortable with the man. He appreciated genuine passion, which he sensed in every word and gesture. Perhaps, Jacob realized, he might actually help, and gradually his sense of his visitor shifted from discomfort to that of a possible opening, a way back, somehow, into Francesca's good graces. Her hurt about the artist she had once loved might have changed since 1946. Sixteen years had passed since then, and she might look at him and Matthäus in a different light.

He heard Scheffel's voice as if from a great distance. "Are you still talking to each other?"

Jacob shook his head, confirming the break without owning up to its cause. Perhaps he could find out Francesca's private address. Could there possibly be renewed contact? Would she accept Lisa? Even become a godmother to any future child? His mind leaped far ahead. He didn't mention his new marriage.

Scheffel's voice intruded again, insistently. "All we ask is that you convince her that this fine artist must not be destroyed by such false accusations."

Jacob phrased his response carefully. "Here's the crux of the matter, Herr Scheffel. How could I possibly know more than Signora Mancini herself about things she already knows well? Why not ask her directly?"

"Because we think that, in your position, you might carry more weight with your former wife. Besides, she would probably rebuff us."

Jacob was tempted to accept. Still, he hesitated. Did Francesca know he was married again? Wouldn't that make him less effective? Wasn't this an impossible daydream anyway? Yet it might open the door for him as well. If only they could all meet freely!

"Let me think it over." A scab might have formed over her wound. Jacob saw himself flying to Italy, waiting at her door until she finally opened it, like a priest to a penitent.

In the ensuing silence, they were suddenly aware of voices in the hallway. Egon Scheffel stood up to shake hands and spoke with a touch of timidity.

"Would it be awkward if I invited you to visit my place? It's on Central Park South, a friend's apartment I'm keeping warm for him.

And, let me tell you, he's a great fan of Gregor Matthäus. He has some wonderful examples of his work—I'd love to show them to you."

Jacob hesitated for a moment, but when Scheffel urged him once more, he accepted.

≫∞≪

Jacob arrived at the flat that Scheffel was "keeping warm" after sloshing on foot through blocks of Manhattan rain. His host opened the door at the first ring. "Dr. Becher. How good of you to come!"

Casually dressed in khaki trousers and a navy blue turtleneck sweater, Scheffel welcomed him at once into a spacious living room illuminated by myriads of small recessed spotlights. Looking around discreetly, Jacob noted a few sparse items of modern blond furniture—a coffee table, two easy chairs, a comfortable sofa. But when he lifted his eyes to the wall, he saw a huge canvas, an abstract painting filled with dancing colors—intense blues floating upward from ebony black, startling yellows shading into orange, with accents of blood-red.

He stood in awe. Now at last he grasped the power of the man Francesca admired, the man she had put on a pedestal—a place now occupied by his canvas—the man she tried to destroy in her anger and disappointment. He was unable to take his eyes off the canvas. And he felt a sudden kinship with the absent painter. *She loved us both, and we both betrayed her.*

"It's Matthäus at his best," Egon Scheffel exclaimed. "Look at this!"

He offered scotch while the two men stood together in the middle of the room, sharing their admiration. Jacob at last gave voice to his first impression. "What a festival of colors!"

Francesca! Please take us back!

Egon Scheffel pointed at the sofa, and they both sat. "Have you thought it over?" he asked.

"Of course I'll try, or I wouldn't be here. A lot has happened to all of us since those early days." This was as far as he felt he could go in signaling a change in his life.

They were both thoughtful after that, each hoping for Francesca's change of mind, each for different reasons, yet both looking toward an absent woman to redeem them. They stayed together for nearly an hour in quiet conversation, drinks in hand, Gregor Matthäus's achievement glowing before their eyes.

ৡৄৎৠ

The next day, during a quiet hour in his office, Jacob began his letter. Writing in German, their old lingua franca, he tried to compress sixteen years of longing into his fervent plea.

My dear Francesca.

A hundred times I was tempted to reach out to you, the last time just before my new marriage to Lisa after twelve years of waiting for your forgiveness. I hoped to make some contact, some connection that doesn't deny the past. Each time, I stifled my impulse, but now an occasion has presented itself that gives me courage to approach you. It's about Gregor Matthäus. I don't need to tell you how deeply I shared your pain when you told me about the change in him, how we shared his role in our lives and how together we detested the Dougherties of this world who seemed to have been his helpers, even as they used him. I know you admired him greatly as an artist, but despised his political machinations. Your article in Il Tempo must have been painful reading for Gregor, for suspicions and accusations began just then and seem to have lasted until today.

Last night I visited one of Gregor's German friends—Egon Scheffel, an art dealer. I stood with him in a private salon in New York, and we admired a painting that glowed like a comet among pale satellites, a magnificent abstract by Matthäus. Herr Scheffel asked me to put in a good word for Gregor, to persuade you to try to undo the damage to his reputation your 1946 article caused. Gregor's friends know that we were once married, but I'm certain they wouldn't have chosen me as a possible intercessor had they known the cause of our estrangement. This tells me that you have never betrayed my betrayal.

I hesitated to write this letter, knowing how you felt at the time, but I don't know how you feel now—about him and about me. Gregor Matthäus is an important artist. I'm a mere head doctor. But we have one thing in common: We both loved and betrayed you.

Are we again worthy of you? Will we ever be? I'm taking this chance to plead my cause alongside his.

Jacopo

Though I've been married again for the past two years, your place in my inner life has remained unchanged. Ever since the shell nearly struck us, now and forever, you are a part of me.

ജരൂ

For four weeks, Jacob walked on air, thinking that with each passing day a welcoming reply, or at least a friendly note, would surely be on its way. When, during the fifth week, an airmail letter with the familiar handwriting arrived at the office, he dared not open it at once. Instead, he called Lisa, telling her he would be late, put the unopened letter in the inside pocket of his jacket and, after seeing his last patient of the day, hurried out of the building and began to walk the streets.

Uptown to Grand Central Station, east toward the river, dodging traffic. When, finally, he saw a small café that suited his purpose, he selected a booth with some care as though preparing to wait for a friend, and ordered coffee. Only when the sullen waitress had placed his cup before him, did he take out the envelope. And only at that moment did he realize how thin it was. His hand trembled as he tore it open. He read:

Friend Becher. I do not exist for you nor you for me—with or without your new connection. Please accept my non-existence in your life. Matthäus will take care of himself.

Olga-Francesca Mancini

No open door, no word of absolution, not for Gregor Matthäus, not for Jacob Becher.

Francesca had written her second farewell.

ജരൂ

Eight years later, in 1970, when he was fifty-three years old, Jacob Becher and his small family (then including a little girl named Teresa) pulled up stakes. Jacob had been offered a distinguished job in a private clinic in Seattle—the unlikeliest of places. Still, after some thought, he decided to take it—to deliver himself from his past, to confront the ghosts and lay them to rest. It was a daring and precarious move. Lisa, ignorant of what had happened there, was happy to support the change as a refreshing new start for them all.

Francesca's silence continued.

Part Three

Teresa's Search

Terri sensed that her father lived somewhere between two women. His moodiness had spread a pall over her childhood, like a haze that dimmed the sunshine.

Starting Over: Another Generation
(1996)

Chapter 16
A Caribbean Birthday

The penalty of death is qualitatively different from a sentence of imprisonment however long.

The phrase pierced Jacob Becher's mind as he looked over the restless expanse of the Caribbean bay. He leaned back on his deck chair and took off his horn-rimmed glasses, fingering them impatiently, lodging their earpieces on either side of his knee, to stroke his gray goatee. A light rain sprayed his face. He and his wife Lisa had chosen to spend the first month of his official retirement here in the resort hotel, and their only child, daughter Terri, had joined them to celebrate her thirtieth birthday.

The penalty of death … These stark words had leaped at him from the news summary of the *New York Times*, produced by courtesy of a caring management. The phrase, without context, sliced through the subtropical unreality around him, as slender palm trees began to bend in the growing wind. On the patio facing him, where a coffee urn and croissants invited early risers, the light wind lifted the starched white tablecloth, curling the edges. Jacob got up quickly to draw a cup, then settled back under the awning to survey the near-deserted beach below—the few swimmers stroking toward shore in the cool dawn, the kayak bobbing on the increasingly choppy water. A premonition invaded his mind that the impending change in nature would soon be mirrored in his life: orderly paradise upset by a brief, violent storm.

A tall waiter looked out from a wide glass door under the vaulting roof spanning the dining hall, its teak structure shimmering in the hesitating sunlight. Jacob turned toward the man and away from the sea, but was startled when, quite suddenly, he saw a bolt of lightning reflected in the dark island face. The waiter moved away briskly as sheets of rain came down like a deluge. A moment's darkness, then, as boat and swimmers scrambled for the beach, Jacob's eye caught an abrupt opening in the sky. Trembling on a sudden beam of light shot by a penetrating sun, the brilliant colors of a rainbow arched over the green foliage below.

He was suffused by the light that followed the storm. The darkness ebbed away quickly as though the contemplative silence of this lush land- and seascape had never been disturbed. Banished for a blessed moment were violent thoughts, not just of capital punishment but of that long-ago war. Still, only for a second. That distant, yet ever-present inferno returned to plague him—a residual flash like lightning, a roar like thunder, two dark, frightened eyes under him.

Imprisonment however long?

Terri should be up by now. She had come in last night while he and Lisa were already in bed, worn out with waiting for her arrival. He had tried to read, then had given up to keep from disturbing Lisa, who had finally dropped off, but sleep wouldn't come to dispel those memories that gushed over him like the sudden rain.

"Yes!" to the accuser, losing the light of Francesca's dark eyes forever.

Guests did not usually arrive in the night and Jacob had no longer expected his daughter, yet he was restless with worry as he'd been for most of the thirty years she'd been alive. He often imagined disasters that never occurred but which left him with debilitating anxiety. So, when those brisk knocks sounded on their cabin door, they stabbed him like heralds of misfortune. To his relief, he made out Terri's slender silhouette. She closed the door behind her and switched on the ceiling light. He focused on her incredibly bright blue eyes, their translucence set off by her short brown hair. They were all bathed in a white glare, disturbing Lisa, who sat up abruptly.

Terri tossed back her head and laughed, for a moment ignoring her mother. "I almost didn't make it, Dad,"

She turned to reopen the door a few inches, allowing a flow of cool dark air to freshen the room. She exchanged a few words with a deep male voice. Jacob heard the reciprocal good-byes and the steps receding down the path. Then silence.

"A fascinating man" had brought Terri across the bay from Tortola. That was as far as she'd been able to get from San Juan by air, having missed a late plane that would have taken her all the way to their resort on Virgin Gorda in the British Virgin Islands.

"I was extremely lucky that he offered to bring me here in his boat, or I don't know what I would have done this time of night." Her words tumbled out in excitement. "He's really great, a musician who also owns and leases boats. He's playing a gig here at the resort tomorrow evening. You could meet him there. You'll love him!"

"It's past midnight," Jacob heard himself say, slightly disgruntled, and Lisa, barely awake, "Darling, we're so glad you're finally here. Tell us in the morning."

In the ensuing silence, Jacob got up, padding to the door to embrace Terri before leading the way to the next-door cabin they had rented for her. Shouldering her canvas bag and picking up her valise, she followed him into the subtropical night.

"Let's get together in the morning," Jacob proposed before leaving. "I always write on the patio in front of the dining hall to escape from the mourning doves on our roof. Anytime before seven."

He wondered if she would come at that hour.

⁞⁞

To Jacob's surprise, Terri did come just after the storm had passed. He saw her ambling down the footpath toward him, spotting him immediately on the cobblestone patio, waving to him with unaccustomed abandon. She walked past the jungle-like bushes and low palm trees and emerged into the clearing with the reawakened sunlight on her face and hair. As she came closer she and the world around her were transformed: The Caribbean sun became the Italian sun, decades slipped through his mind like sand on a beach and Terri's face, framed by the lush green around her, became the face of the past—a young Francesca's unchanging presence.

The picture faded as Jacob got up to greet his daughter.

"Thanks for the invitation, Dad. In my wildest dreams, I couldn't have imagined a lovelier place to celebrate my thirtieth birthday. How did you find out about it?"

Jacob smiled. "A secret …. I still get around." An undisclosed pain cut through his pleasure. He managed to say, "I'm glad you like it here, but you've barely arrived. There's much more beauty ahead."

As Terri turned away to pour a cup of coffee, he reflected on the pang that had invaded him. Whether it was the unexpected male voice in the middle of the night or some other more distant memory, Jacob could no longer maintain the bantering tone of their conversation. He half listened as Terri chattered about her trip and the excitement of her job in the art department of the *Times*. She had a *surprise* for them both! Her voice came to Jacob as if through a long, echoing tunnel.

She stopped as if sensing his distraction and picked up her bulging shoulder bag from the floor. She opened it and looked inside, then shook her head. Perhaps she had decided not to reveal her surprise just yet. Instead, she spoke about food.

"They're about to serve breakfast. Let's go in, *then* I'll show you my surprise. Will Mom find us there?"

He nodded and, gathering his papers, led the way inside to look for a table.

৪০৫১

Terri chose a place with a view, close to the window, and they sat silently while she studied the menu with total concentration. The pile of papers stacked on the chair next to him gave Jacob the sense that he might still realize his ambition. His decision to become a psychoanalyst had proved to be a fortuitous choice, for it had provided scope for his imagination and his search to help others while still allowing him to afford this comfortable holiday in an expensive resort with his wife and daughter—a radical shift in lifestyle and circumstances to a level he had never hoped to reach.

Terri's eyes followed her father's to the chair next to him heaped with papers, and she asked in a light tone and with a teasing smile, "I see you're on-to something else, Dad. May a daughter know what it is?"

He felt touched by her question.

"Still about memory, Terri. It's still about *Memory: the Fabric of Culture*. It's going to be a more popular sequel to my book since the original did so well."

"Hi! There you are!"

Lisa's happy voice rang out of nowhere, and he rose with instinctive courtesy. Unlike her husband and daughter, still frowsy with lost sleep, she looked rested and trim, her graying hair a neat cap above the same insistent blue eyes as her daughter's.

"I just want coffee," she announced. Then, turning to Terri, "Wonderful to see you, dear. Sorry I was out of it last night." She smiled at Terri and glanced back at her husband. "Dad and I had a long walk on the island, and I was bushed."

Terri, with a flamboyant gesture, delved into her bulky bag at last. "You didn't hear me, Dad, but I said I had a surprise."

"I heard you all right, but you caught me too early in the morning."

"A surprise?" Lisa's eyes opened wide in anticipation. "A surprise on your own thirtieth birthday?"

"It so happens," Terri answered, looking at her mother with a mischievous smile, "that your nice invitation here wasn't my only present."

The waiter interrupted, asking for their orders. When he left, Terri once more reached into her bag and, producing two folded copies of an arts section of the *New York Times*, handed one to each parent with a flourish. "See Page 4," she ordered.

And there it was!

"Art and the Exigencies of War." And below, "The Florentine Struggle of Gregor Matthäus" And below that, "Teresa L. Becher."

Silence.

Jacob broke it at last. "I didn't see it! Why didn't I?" *A hoax on her birthday? It made no sense.*

"It's not out yet," Terri informed him. "Look at the date."

Indeed, it was for tomorrow.

Lisa's eyes filled with tears as she took her daughter in her arms. "I'm so proud, darling! What a wonderful achievement!"

But Jacob felt doors closing, locking him away from his daughter and her success. He remained stone-silent, his eyes fixed on the paper in front of him with an unwavering stare.

"Dad!" Terri exclaimed, her voice anxious, uncomprehending. "What is it? What's the matter?"

Once again, the past surged around him like a tide. The name *Matthäus* had opened the floodgates.

Moving back to Seattle had begun a journey of rediscovery. He and Lisa went through old boxes filled with things he'd left behind with his parents when he fled to New York after the trial many years before. They pulled out old history textbooks, an old stapler and tape dispenser, and then Lisa had lifted out a package and unwrapped it. It was the picture *War and Peace* that Francesca had brought from Italy as a gift to celebrate their wedding, the beginning of a new life.

"How lovely!" Lisa had exclaimed, "What a beautiful display of gentle violets and fierce orange! A priceless watercolor!" And after a moment, "Who did it?"

He had not answered, and Lisa's face became grave, then suspicious. "Why did you hide it away? What's the story behind this? I'd like to hang it. I know Terri will grow up loving it!"

Rediscovering that painting with its heavy emotional freight, coupled with Lisa's insistence that it be brought out for all the world to see, had released a shock wave. Now Matthäus's ghost had found his daughter through this essay and would take her away, too. Back then, he had lashed out irrationally at his wife while his daughter had looked on, almost paralyzed. He barely suppressed an extreme reaction now.

Moments later, he looked up as if emerging from a trance. Besieged by his feelings, he still did not register his daughter's success. Where on earth did she find, among all the painters in the world, the one artist who might provide a clue to the part of his life that must never be reopened? Again, a flash of vivid detail: the vivacious young woman introducing him to a slender man with an ascot and graying hair *en brosse.*

"Gregor Matthäus gave us fresh hope." He heard her voice distinctly through the decades.

"I snuffed it out," his mind responded. *"I failed you."*

He barely noticed Lisa and Terri embracing before he heard his own voice, tight and troubled. His words were utterly inappropriate for the occasion.

"How did you get onto *this* subject?" he asked, still without a word of congratulation. "A minor artist like him shouldn't be worth your trouble."

Terri's surprise and hurt at his reaction were palpable. He regained enough control to try to smooth over his apparent boorishness. "But forgive me. It's great you got this assignment. I was just too moved to be articulate." He reached out to hug his daughter, but was rebuffed. Terri could not bring herself to gloss over her father's inexplicable hostility to her triumph.

"What's going on with you, Dad? As for 'getting onto this subject,' a colleague at the office told me about this artist, who, he thought, needs an introduction here ages after he's been well-known in Europe. It was a fun assignment. But here's the funny part: When I looked at his paintings, I remembered that little picture hanging in our dining room all my life, and realized I'd known Gregor Matthäus all along. So, you see, I couldn't *not* write about him." She paused, then continued, her tone sharp. "Does that answer your question?"

Lisa wiped her eyes. "Jacob, please! This is such a great moment."

Caught between the shame of his past and the compassion aroused by Terri's stricken face, his reaction was still inadequate. "I'm so sorry, Terri. I had no right to speak that way. Please forgive me."

But Terri held her ground. "What's going on, Dad?" she repeated, "What's Gregor Matthäus to you?" The angry tone gave way to suspicion. Her eyes narrowed. "What *about* that picture? Did you know the painter?"

He failed to frame an answer, and finally murmured, "You know how I sometimes fly off the handle before I have time to think." He glanced down at the paper before him. "But I'm very happy for you. I'll read the piece later today. My daughter's first! I'm very proud." He reached out and this time succeeded in taking her into his arms.

The tense lines in Terri's face dissolved, and her question came in a cordial voice. "Let's go to the concert tonight? It'll be fun."

The waiter arrived with their breakfast. Of course, they'd go.

ଞଠଖ

The music began early. They could already hear it from their cabin. Arm in arm, Jacob and Lisa made their way down the footpath back to the patio in front of the dining hall where the band was set up. They were struck by the profusion of light, the pounding rhythm, and looked forward to meeting the man who had delivered their daughter safely to them, remembering a mere voice, a few muffled sounds.

"Bye for now." "Thanks loads. You were a lifesaver." Footsteps receding.

The music stopped, and he suddenly emerged on stage with a beaming Terri at his side, mingling with his musicians, a tall, broadshouldered black man with a trumpet under his arm. The musicians tuned their instruments: brief barks of horns, trumpets clearing their throats before the next number. The players looked relaxed, smoking and talking in low voices while knots of their listeners stood about or sat on garden chairs, waiters scurrying to serve them drinks.

They were a colorful group, most of them black islanders, all male, wearing the bright blue, green, and red patterned shirts and wide-bottomed trousers that their patrons had come to expect. In the brilliant light of the sun, slanting to dip towards a Caribbean evening, Jacob observed Terri's rescuer, his vision filtered through a sudden mistrust. Dark features under a crown of black hair that stood up straight above a generous high forehead, the wide, welcoming smile, the roguish lift of the chin and impressive large eyes.

He could see how his daughter might find this man attractive. The bandleader looked up and with a quick, vivacious stride approached him. A vibrant voice addressed him in a light British accent as he came. "Jacob Becher! I've wanted to meet you since I came across that interesting book of yours with a new angle on memory. It's great!" And when Jacob looked surprised that someone this far away from the 'centers of American culture' should have read his *Memory: the Fabric of Culture*, he added, "I especially liked what you say about time, the past always being with us in the present ... how that explains and shapes us. I'd really like to talk about it some time." When he still didn't get any response from Jacob, the man quickly introduced himself, "I'm Jeremy Taylor. I don't write books, but I buy and rent boats and play music and travel and that sort of thing ..." And after another pause, when the instruments sounded again, he added with pride, "I also lead this band."

Jacob's hesitation was obvious. He was stunned by his own reaction, and when he looked at his daughter, perceiving her radiance, the momentary silence became embarrassingly prolonged. His professional ease as a doctor of troubled souls had deserted him along with his social grace. Why? Was it a possessive father's instinct? The color of

Jeremy's skin? It was hard to determine, but the effect was the same.

"I'm *honored* you like my book."

With these cordial words he shook Jeremy's hand as Lisa introduced herself with enthusiasm. "I'm Lisa Becher, Terri's mother. Great to meet you, too. And thank you for rescuing our stranded daughter at that late hour."

"It was my pleasure, Mrs. Becher."

He met her eyes, then once more addressed Jacob. "A real treat to have met you, Dr. Becher, I hope we can talk more ..."

He stopped himself and looked at his watch. "Excuse me. I've got to get back to my band."

Terri, observing everything, said nothing at all.

ഇൗരു

Dusk settled, and the bright patio lights went on under the starry southern sky. Jeremy Taylor towered over his players as he raised his trumpet for the first tremulous sounds. He started the melody gracefully, then directed his band with easy gestures. His face was transformed as he reached out to his men before turning to the steel drummers, as if drawing them out to yield a pattern of ear-shattering sounds of his own design.

The pulsating rhythm washed over the audience sitting on wrought iron chairs, sipping the scotch and water and island drinks the solicitous waiters brought them. Terri stayed with her parents, grateful that they had come, but she soon felt drawn to the music—and to Jeremy. After the next number Lisa signaled that it would be all right for her to leave. From then on, during each intermission, Jacob and Lisa watched their daughter moving easily among the players with their bright, billowing shirts while Jeremy led her from one to the other. They watched her shaking hands, heard her ringing voice raised in laughter above the murmuring of the audience. A young Lisa, thought Jacob, but he knew better.

As he watched Terri moving back and forth among the accelerating notes of an ever-more-urgent music, he knew the dull pain in his chest was no longer connected with Taylor: it focused on Terri herself, *his* Terri, a vision that continued its disturbing alternation with the face of Francesca Mancini. Yet this picture was not called forth by Terri's presence among her new-found friends but by her evocation of

Gregor Matthäus, his enemy, in a brilliant essay that made him proud. He had read and reread it that afternoon, had rolled her fine phrases over his tongue and knew she would be recognized. Unknowingly, Terri had touched a painful nerve in her father, stirring up a past that overwhelmed him and pulled him back: Matthäus, the Arno, shadowy hope, and Francesca lost once more in the distant pools of remembrance.

ಬಂಙ

And then it was over. He took his wife's arm as they walked slowly up the footpath to their cabin. There was no sign of Terri. When they entered the commodious cabin, they could still hear distant voices, an occasional clanging of instruments. Lisa sat down on the bed, smiling, crossing her legs. "Our girl's really enjoying herself," she said quietly, tossing her head in the same unconscious gesture he loved in Terri. "A perfect contrast to her work. This joy tonight hasn't happened often in her life."

Her father was silent, ashamed of his hesitation.

They raised their heads. Footsteps were approaching the door, one set heavy, the other light, followed by a loud rap. Lisa opened the door to Terri and Jeremy.

"Don't go to bed yet!" Terri commanded, her face flushed, eyes ablaze. "There's going to be a party, and you're invited!"

Jeremy repeated her invitation in baritone. They were holding hands, Jacob saw, and it had been just a few hours! The man looked even more attractive in the mild light of the bedroom lamp. There was something easy about the way he wore his clothes, the red scarf flung lightly around his neck above a colorfully patterned royal blue shirt. Jacob hadn't noticed the small moustache, but he recalled the intense eyes.

"Come on, Mom and Dad," Terri called out, looking straight at her mother.

Lisa only glanced at her husband. "Let's go!" Her response was brisk and bright. She reached into the closet for a wrap against the uncertain night.

Jacob saw the group looking at him expectantly. Lisa beckoned, strands of her graying hair framing her happy face. Terri, in a flamboyant mood, smiled at him, pleasure dancing in her face. And there was the male predator, eager to possess his quarry, Jacob's only child. He knew better, of course, but he politely declined to join them nevertheless, claiming fatigue, the lateness of the night. He longed to be alone.

But suddenly he wheeled around to face Jeremy, knowing that his demeanor must reflect his hostility. He was shocked as he heard his own trembling voice. "Take care of my girl!"

Stunned silence. Wordless, Lisa turned to the door and, putting an arm around Jeremy's and Terri's shoulders, she steered them out of the room. As Jacob turned out the light, he caught sight of his despondent face reflected in the dark windowpane.

Chapter 17
Awakening

Where am I? Terri sat up, staring at the unfamiliar, wavering patterns of sunlight on the walls and furniture of her cabin. It was late. The sun, already high, sent its rays through the tropical foliage to sketch ghostly faces and fantastic animals on the space between two open windows. A flash from the mirror on her right momentarily blinded her. She closed her eyes. Outside, the ever-present doves continued their cooing—rhythmic, repetitive, insistent.

It had been almost dawn when she got back to her room. The night had not only been long, it had been extraordinary. It began with her father's attitude and the hostile tone of his remark to Jeremy to "take care of my girl." Knowing him as she thought she did, it made no sense. Her dad had never been a racist, but it briefly put a damper on their mood. They soon recovered. For the rest of the evening in the resort's noisy recreation room, Jeremy had been loving and tactfully tender, dancing mostly with her rather than indulging the other women guests in their beach-bright dresses, while his musical friends applauded from the sidelines. They touched constantly, holding hands whenever they could.

Her father … Just yesterday morning, he had reacted to her triumph at the *Times* with apparent hostility. She'd done her best to repress her anger, but it was hard to conceal. He must want to remain a controlling presence in her life—at age thirty, no less! How dare he judge her attraction to Jeremy; how dare he question her choice!

But unexpected things, good ones, had happened as well. Within minutes of their arrival at the party, Lisa dropped her reserve along with her shawl. With surprising gusto, she chatted with a trombonist here, a drummer there, and Terri was pleased to see how kindly her new friends responded to her mother.

As her eyes adjusted to the light of late morning, Terri's mind veered away from her recollections of the night. The sun warmed the tangy fresh air flowing through her windows and evoked visions of pure white sand under her bare feet, of transparent water shimmering above shells and cragged coral in the depths. It was a new day. She'd momentarily forgotten! How could she? Last night, after seeing Lisa to her cabin, she and Jeremy had embraced at her cottage door. He did not release her, but held her close as he murmured into her ear, "I'm running a cruise ship tomorrow. Would you like to go?"

"I'd love to."

They had kissed deeply, but then they parted. She had closed the cabin door and undressed in the dark. His embrace lingered in the night like black velvet.

❧☙

The gull skimmed across blue-green water rendered semi-transparent by a penetrating sun. Then Terri saw the heron, its huge lazy wings flapping as it passed overhead with shy determination. She heard a gull cry out, following the heron as they both searched for fish.

The boat's engine sputtered. Men in gaudy shirts and women in bright, flared skirts, bandannas, and fancy hats, wandered about, sipping scotch, gin, beer, Chardonnay, or Coke from plastic glasses. Dark sunglasses veiled their eyes; cameras hung from their necks.

A cry went up.

"Look to starboard—the right side of the boat." Jeremy's voice with its elegant accent came crisp and clear through the microphone. "Sharks passing through!"

Terri watched Jeremy instead. The sun glinting in his hair, his challenging eyes as bright as ever, he was a daytime version of last night's god. Today he was Neptune, statuesque god of the sea, standing behind the wheel, with the wind undoing his yellow neckerchief, whose ends flapped about wildly, glowing against a teal shirt. He gestured, holding his sunglasses with one hand while easily turning the wheel with the other. Caught by the extraordinary display of energy, she kept her eyes on him while the other passengers rushed to the starboard railing to peer down at the water.

She followed slowly. She was not disappointed.

As they looked down, they saw the long dark shadows passing under the ship from one side to the other, pointed snouts forging ahead as the slender aquatic figures sliced through the sea like small submarines.

"They're not dangerous," Jeremy laughed a deep rumble. "They're not the man-eating kind."

"How d'you know?" asked a lanky man with a full white beard.
Evidently, he was not to be deprived of his thrill.

But their helmsman was not provoked. Every inch the tour guide, he
began an informed explanation. Seeing that the man had lost interest,
he thought better of it and just grinned. He winked at Terri. The heron
came back, dipping its wing. He—or she—seemed to wink, too.

My parents would have loved this performance, Terri thought, especially Jacob with his penchant for irony, sharing in her mind his awareness of the contrast between the vast sea and the small, pompous crowd.
Why hadn't they been invited along? Despite the difficulties of the previous day, Terri wasn't sure. Would Jeremy have minded? He had after
all admired her father as the author of a book on memory he'd liked, and
he certainly liked Lisa. She pictured him lifting her mother off the dance
floor. For some reason, she dismissed the thought that the invitation had
been meant for her alone.

Jeremy's spiel, its professional gaiety borne on the wind, rekindled unaccustomed warmth. His baritone with its teasing inflexion explained to
his charges what they were seeing as they passed a cove overshadowed
by a tree-studded mountainside. Jeremy changed his position, most eyes
following him as if by command while he pointed out an elegant yacht
here, a flock of sea-birds there, as their boat skimmed the blue surface
of the bay. Terri felt a surge of pride in that tall sea god with the microphone as everyone followed his outstretched arm and stared at more
green coves and undulating waters.

As the sky had began to darken, Jeremy spoke into the mike once
more, taking in the sea with another grand gesture.

"Nature's closing for the night," boomed his voice. "So are we. Refill
your drinks before the bar closes, too. We're heading home."

The heron had vanished, but gulls still screamed.

Surrounded by garish colors and plump thighs, Terri watched the
straw-hatted women and men mill about, chattering and posing for
flashing cameras as the dusk deepened. She looked across the boat, her
glance straying to the sea before she again focused on the spot behind
the wheel where Jeremy stood, his eyes shadowed and indistinct as evening came on faster and faster. Her inner warmth receded for a moment,
then returned with tingling pleasure as she gave in to a sudden impulse.

She rose and scrambled across abandoned benches to reach him at the wheel.

"Did you have fun?" he asked gently.

She nodded silently, then laughed. "You're good at this," she said, pointing at the passengers still crowding around the makeshift bar. The boat deck, filled with gear and laughing people, shivered lightly with the hum of the engine.

"I know," he said, his hand reaching for hers, "but, you know, I don't envy people who have to do this day in and day out. I don't mind doing it now and then, but as a routine, it would really get to me."

"How?"

"You think they're amusing as you amuse them." He pulled a long face. "But, you know, they get the better of you in the end. You find yourself playing their clown. They always win."

"Still, you were great."

"Sure, it can be fun. But I'd rather play music."

The change came over them both as they were about to land. It was nearly dark. Lanterns were swaying on the dock as they approached. An old man with a frayed straw hat stood on the pier waiting to catch the rope and secure the boat to its moorings.

With pangs of regret, Terri watched as their guide closed down the tour, helping the passengers across the rickety gangplank, accepting their thanks, saying cheerful good-byes. She admired Jeremy's poise. More and more during the past twenty-four hours, her inhibitions had dissolved, and her built-in wall of caution had crumbled.

Now they stood on the dock, awkwardly, face-to-face.

Terri said casually, not really thinking, "I wish Dad had been with us. He would have understood what you meant, too. The irony of it all."

"Oh?" Silence fell between them. After a time, Jeremy spoke again. "We're playing on the other side of the island tonight and tomorrow." Terri felt the moment suddenly overcast by darkness and chill. "It'll be a bore. Let's get together when I get back."

Terri, seized by the cold, searched for a way back to warmth.

She missed the heron with its wide-spread wings.

ಬಃಂಜ

From that moment, Jeremy Taylor would be absent without further explanation. Terri's remark on arrival at the dock, evoking her father's uncomfortable presence, seemed light-years away from where he'd imagined her to be. He preferred to make his escape before becoming too attached. Terri captivated him with that open face she shared with her mother, guilelessness without loss of sophistication, brilliance untouched by arrogance. She seemed to reach out to him in her eager talk, to be open to something he dared not yet call love. He admired her loose-limbed, agile body, unself-consciously supple and direct, totally attuned to him as they danced.

Yet a warning held him back—her almost imperceptible awareness of his race, so he thought, as she held his hand all night and kissed him at dawn. Even so, he refused to believe that she might reject him because of his blackness; their closeness had been so evident, and yet ... He knew by instinct that her mother was not bigoted, but Jacob Becher was another matter. In him, a man she obviously adored, he felt a thinly veiled hostility.

All his life he had carried a heavy burden. His father, who had started as a tour guide and later in his life succeeded as an owner of boats, made crushing demands on his children, which Jeremy, his youngest son, had resisted with varying degrees of success. had been—and still was—under obligation at home and had to struggle every day for his freedom to be a musician, fighting against everyone who stood in his way until, at last, he'd begun to free himself.

He was used to fathers, used to anger, then he met Terri. It had begun as a relief. He saw no anger in her, none in Lisa, but he sensed it in Jacob Becher. Jeremy refused to take a chance.

ဆာ03

Sitting on the beach, Terri swallowed her longing. Finally, she rose, gave Lisa and Jacob a thin smile, draped her towel over the back of her beach chair, and went for a swim. The sun glittered on the water as she drifted on her back, watching the undisturbed blue of the sky, trying to sort out her hurt and what may have caused it. Fate, always hostile to her, decreed that Jeremy should walk by at that very moment. As she floated fifty yards offshore, Terri watched him stop to talk to Lisa. She waved at him, and he waved back, a mechanical gesture, it seemed. Then he walked on.

Terri's birthday week ebbed away in empty, disappointing days. Walking to her cabin in the dark, she listened to crickets chirping and, in her fantasy, saw the heron against the sapphire sky with its leisurely flapping wings. But Jeremy was not there, not *really* there, though she did see him from time to time. He often came to the resort on some business or other, and she'd detained him once as he crossed the beach. She had tried to make conversation, but somehow he managed to look past her. She could not fathom what had caused the sudden death of a budding friendship.

One morning she talked to Lisa. "I have no idea what got into Jeremy. Any suggestions?" She made herself sound casual, but there was a knot in her stomach.

Their eyes locked. Lisa looked away first, making a little grimace, and Terri was suddenly sure her mother knew the answer. "I asked him to your birthday dinner, but he couldn't make it. I'm sorry, darling." That night in her cabin, after her parents had feted her appropriately with a sumptuous dinner, Terri resolved to escape her increasing misery. She packed her things.

When Jacob looked for her in her cabin, he faced an empty room, rumpled bed-clothes, the door of the massive wardrobe ajar. Her backpack and valise were gone. So was Terri.

Her note began: "Dear Mom and Dad—You've been perfectly wonderful to send me off into my thirties with a flourish. I loved last night's dinner and I loved all your caring. But I feel overwhelmed and need to get away. After all, I'm thirty. I'm my own person now."

She added politely, "I'll phone when I get back to New York"

I'm my own person now.

Jacob felt himself peering down through decades stacked in his consciousness like transparent sheets of glass. Deep down, five long decades below, he found that phrase again, *I can be myself now*, etched in his memory.

It's all in my book. It never goes away.

Holding Terri's note in a hand that trembled, he left her cabin. Outside, the sun of the opening day burned again with fierce intensity and the doves cooed in their unmelodic way.

He looked up.

A heron flapped its lazy way across the sky.

Chapter 18
Communion

An August evening in New York. Terri's wrist fluttered in futile rhythm, fanning her dripping brow with a pad of lined paper. Her only air conditioner was on the blink, and temperature and humidity were both in the upper nineties. Of course, it would have to break down on a weekend, when no mechanic could be found. Her haven, her workshop, was stifling. Her thoughts drifted, evoking a gentler Caribbean warmth. She leaned on her fist. Those days in Virgin Gorda were ideal, and her parents had been so very generous to celebrate her birthday week amid beauty she could never have afforded. Guilt and regret weighed heavily in her stomach while she absently shoved papers—notes for articles and her book, bills—around her desk.

That first night, the night of her arrival, she'd had high hopes for the holiday: meeting Jeremy, who gallantly ferried her across to the resort, arriving with the big surprise in her book bag—but it had turned sour in the end. She bit her lip. Not just her dad and his cold reaction to her success, it was also Jeremy. He'd given her a glimpse of freedom, a window that promised escape from her loneliness. Then he shut the door. Why? Whose fault was it? What had she done? She regretted running away without confronting either her father or Jeremy. She'd left an inadequate note for her parents, but not a word for Jeremy. She rose, gave the papers a final shove, and paced the room, a jumble of anger, guilt, regret, and self-pity rising like a knot in her throat. Of course he hadn't tried to get in touch with her.

She glanced in passing at the draft for the book she'd started to write on Matthäus, the painter—piles of yellow pages in labored longhand. The heat darkened her mood of loss and futility: Jeremy lost, the love she never had, the futility of pursuing this biography, inspired by her recent assignment for the *New York Times*. She realized she would need more material and would have to go to Italy and Germany to get it. His paintings intrigued her as she moved from her earlier quick analysis to the core of the man's work. Why Matthäus? She thought once more of the little painting in the family dining room, but by now there was far more: a personal challenge, her father's stricken face when she displayed her essay, her mother's clear joy. Lisa probably told the truth: She knew very little. But why not share what little she knew?

It was too hot to write, too hot to indulge in futile speculation. The travel clock on her desk showed the time had come for the best escape from the heat: dinner out in an air-conditioned restaurant. Alone? With others? She would eat alone. In the corner of the Village where she'd lived for years, she had never allowed her contacts to become close. They remained more than acquaintances, less than friends. Perhaps she was afraid of being cut off, disappointed … Damn it all! Parents, potential lovers—they all demanded an intimacy she couldn't cope with. The modest success of her article exhilarated her and pointed to a career. Someone in her department apparently thought she had the right stuff, and a career would surely blot out her loneliness. Why should she suffer heartache each time her father escaped into the awful world of gloom neither she nor her mother could fathom? They all had their careers, Jacob still maintaining his office, Lisa seeing patients at home, soul doctors both, even in their retirement. She, Teresa Becher, had her own career, her own world. She could be independent of all of them—her own person.

The phone rang just as she was about to pick up her purse and keys. She answered after three rings. *Heavens above! Could it be?* A familiar baritone resounded like a bullhorn in her ear. Neptune with a slight British accent calling from the deep! The sharks were passing under the boat's keel like sharp-nosed submarines. It was unmistakable, but also mysterious.

"Jeremy? Jeremy! Where *are* you?"

"An ill wind blew me into New York. In case you're wondering, I got your unlisted number from Lisa in Seattle. She sends her love." And when that explanation seemed inadequate, he went on, "I hoped I'd be able to reach you. I wangled your parents' address from a desk clerk at the resort. He owed me."

For a few moments, the line seemed dead while Terri coped with the unaccustomed flood of joy that filled her. Then, recovering her poise, she spoke with a lilt in her voice. "I'm *so* glad you did, Jeremy! It's great to hear from you."

She looked down on her desk, at the calendar. She would mark this as a special day. "Listen, you just caught me as I was leaving to have some dinner. It's been a bitch of a day. I don't know where you are, but can you join me?"

"Sure thing. Just tell me where."

ဆသ

He spotted her at once, the slender young woman with light brown hair, bent over a magazine. A jolt of acute pleasure traveled through him when she looked up, her eyes sparkling with answering joy. She was the same person he had bumped into on a Caribbean boat dock not too many months ago, frantically searching everywhere, looking for anyone to help her get across. She welcomed him with a happy smile as he wound his way towards her past rows of tightly packed tables and chairs.

He held out his arms. She put down the glass of red wine and rose to meet him, taking both his hands. A brief silence hung in the air between them—an awkward silence as their feelings of intimacy outran what they could say. He watched her eyes travel over his city clothes, his elegant wine-red tie. He spoke the expected words:

"Good to see you."

She looked paler than he remembered. He noticed rings under her eyes.

They studied the menu. Not quite by coincidence, Terri told him, she had chosen her favorite Caribbean restaurant the moment he called. Now she grinned, looking up from many combinations of shrimp and crab. "This place should be like home to you. You know, I'll never forget those sharks coming up from under the keel like a flotilla of submarines. It was the first image that came into my mind when I heard your voice."

"I bet you can get a good dish of shark here."

She shook her head. "Not on your life. Not me! I couldn't eat one after seeing them so graceful." She changed the subject. "Now, tell me what brings you here."

The waiter arrived, and they ordered a bottle of pinot grigio to go with their soft-shelled crabs.

"Business," Jeremy told her. "This has to do with Dad and me. We're agents for sales of pleasure boats and so forth. There's a transaction pending in New York."

She sat back, giving him a long, appraising look. "Now, Jeremy, that's not a role I see you in, being a sales agent for millionaires. Granted, you look gorgeous in that business suit," she teased with a smile. "But the way I think of you is out captaining that boat. You looked like Neptune, god of the ocean, right out of the sea on that glorious day down there off Virgin Gorda. You were my *real* birthday present."

Flattered and a bit daunted by her poetic praise, he gave a mocking snort. "Humph! You didn't even mention my music!"

She laughed. "Oh, yes, that, too. I can see you right now, raising that trumpet to your lips. But this other business you speak of, renting and selling boats large and small; that will never fit the picture!"

They fell silent, and Jeremy asked himself, as he had done before, why he'd left Terri in March only to try to bring her back now, in August. He still saw her as she swayed sinuously toward him at the party, arms outstretched like a Mayan virgin prepared for a sacrifice. She'd alternately clung to him and held him at arm's length as they danced. Still, it was not until he heard her say how she missed her father on the boat tour that Jeremy felt the need for escape.

"Yes," he heard himself say as he emerged from his reverie, "I had a good talk with your mom. We've been talking now and then for a month or so. She's great."

"Yeah. But I'm hardly ever in touch with her, with them."

"I know."

She laughed. "What else do you know? I hadn't a clue you and she were in touch."

He ignored her remark as if he hadn't heard. "I'm really impressed by her. In a single twenty-minute phone call, we hit it off again."

It had been a moment of lightness, of freedom, interrupted by the waiter, arriving with two dishes of steaming crabs. But then Terri fell silent with a crease between her brows, drifting away from him in an apparent brown study.

As if to make amends for the change in mood, she began to chat about her life in New York and about her dreams of freelancing, still in the future. "I have an idea for a small book about a German painter. I did a piece on him for the *New York Times* just before we met. I'm not sure I mentioned it." She smiled at him. "You and I were too busy with more-pressing concerns ... The painter, Gregor Matthäus, lived mostly in Italy. I love his work, especially the water colors he did in Florence at the end of the war before he became really well-known. Even so, he's almost completely unknown in this country. I'll fix that."

She waited, sweeping him with that appraising look. She must be thinking he was bored, not following. But he proved her wrong. "He was German, you say? In Italy? Florence during the war? So, what was his political role at the war's end?"

Terri's eyes narrowed. Politics ... what were Jeremy's politics? Left? Right? She groped for an opening not only to Gregor Matthäus but to Jeremy himself. They had reached coffee, and Jeremy's contribution to their conversation had been only brief remarks, now this pointed question. She turned thoughtfully back to Matthäus.

"I really don't know where he stood. Nothing I can put my finger on. He was a German ex-officer, a gay man, apparently." She stirred her cup. "How did he get away with it in Florence; how did he manage to disappear as a civilian and actually paint? Someone was protecting him, that's for sure, but who?"

Jeremy supplied answers that showed he was no stranger to this way of thinking. "The Resistance? Perhaps even the Church?"

She went further. "Some Fascist bigwig? Or even someone high up in the German occupation? We really don't know. I just feel queasy about his politics, but you should see his work! Wow!"

Again that uneasy silence.

"I really don't know much about art ...That kind of art. Music, yes, any kind of music, but modern art ... ? It just leaves me stranded."

She could tell by his hesitations he expected her to disapprove, maybe to disdain him. But she reassured him with an understanding smile. Increasingly, the words they spoke and the subjects they touched—her work as an art critic, his as a musician—became less and less the point of their true conversation. Increasingly, their exchange became one of eyes and voices as they found themselves caught in their mutual attraction.

Once outside, the heat came at them like a moving flame after the chill inside. They looked at each other in awkward indecision as if they'd just met.

"Where do you live?" asked Jeremy as if it were the most natural question in the world.

"Quite a way over in the East Village." She replied, just as naturally. "On East Sixth Street."

She became apologetic, much to her annoyance. "It's been home for many years. It's *home* even if I could afford something better." And again as if warding off the inevitable, "My place is hot, though, sweltering hot. My air conditioner is on the blink."

"We'll manage."

Thus they completed the Caribbean journey they had scarcely begun. Their clothes formed two mounds on the floor.

ഇരു

Terri woke up in the gray city dawn and was appalled by the disorder in her room. The sun, barely out of hiding, cast geometric shadows on her two chairs piled high with books and stacks of papers. To her left stood her heavy oak table—a precious object bought in her early years in the city, with money she couldn't really afford to spend—and on it she saw a vase of late-summer flowers and an abandoned water glass next to her purse, which she had carelessly dropped there when they walked in. The window was wide open, a refreshing breeze blowing the curtains apart, and a bright ray of sunlight burst into the room.

They had been sleeping sprawled across the king-size bed in her sanctum, her bedroom study, where pillows and bedclothes were mixed with magazines, paperbacks, half-open letters on bed and floor. Terri's kimono hung limp over the back of her desk chair. She noticed that the floor lamp was still lit.

"Good morning." Jeremy, already awake, was sitting up, his elbows on his knees, his palms propping his chin, looking straight ahead.

"Good morning. Welcome!" She waved her arm at the cluttered room. "It looks pretty alarming by daylight, doesn't it?" She hurried on. "I always have coffee when I wake up. How about you?"

Without waiting for an answer, she got up and headed for the kitchen.

"Hurry back!" His eyes followed her as she padded naked down the hall.

They made love once more while the coffee was brewing.

Still, however close their embraces, puzzles plagued them that they could barely articulate, much less solve. Questions raised in the restaurant the night before still seemed to need answers. And neither of them was sure what the night they just passed would portend for their future.

They sat on the big bed, still without clothes, holding mugs of coffee to their lips. With her cup in her left hand, Terri put her right arm around his shoulders, feeling the moisture of another warm day spreading from his skin to hers, hers to his.

"You know," she reminisced, "when you stood in the middle of that room—remember?—and you sang out loud in that great baritone of yours, you were as naked as you are now." She paused, then added shyly, "And as magnificent."

He turned, pleased, leaning against her.

"Isn't that a bit much?"

But he completed her thought. "My singing made me feel close to you ... and, in a way, to Lisa, too."

"Why to Mother?"

"She's freer," he answered without explanation.

"You know," Terri said after a moment's reflection, "you're right. Lisa's freer than any of us. She's had her practice as therapist for worried mothers as long as I can remember. But there's something strange going on between her and Dad ..." The clue was clear. The moment Jacob Becher was mentioned, Jeremy withdrew with a glum face. She went on quickly, "I'm sure it's got nothing to do with you. Did Mom say anything about that? I doubt it."

He shook his head. "She talked mostly about your being so far away. That's all. Nothing mysterious." He ducked away from her arm. "Too hot," he explained.

Terri's mood echoed his glumness. "It's got nothing to do with you, Jeremy! It's Dad; it's part of his life. It's something *political.*"

"Don't pry then. It's his—no, *their* life. But you can't tell me that he isn't worried his sweet white girl is involved with a black island native. Remember him telling me 'to take care of my girl'?"

"Yes, I don't know what that was …. He'd probably worry about my virtue if you were a Nordic king. But I know him, Jeremy, and I'm sure it has to do with that painter. I can't say yet how, but I'm determined to find out."

"How can that be? What's that got to do with his rudeness?"

He couldn't follow her. She needed to explain to keep his trust. She decided to talk.

"There was something in Dad's life that still cripples him."

It was very quiet in the room as Terri closed her eyes. She moved farther away from him until nothing linked them except the bedclothes under them. Terri felt she had reached a solemn but also a heartbreaking moment. Was this her room, her refuge? She had invited him in, and so she must open herself—and her father—to an outsider. Yes, Jeremy was still an outsider even after their night, but she could come to love him. And if she allowed herself to love, if she opened herself to such a dangerous degree, there was only one path ahead.

According to the unspoken rules of behavior she'd absorbed since childhood, she would have to share family secrets that would amount to a betrayal of her father, of her family … of herself.

She shuddered. Her bare skin felt cold and prickly. But she had to hold on to Jeremy, who in one night had given himself and helped her glimpse happiness. She must make sure he knew that those who counted in her world would never think of him as a stranger because of his skin. She *must* tell those secrets, she must betray.

It wasn't a momentous betrayal as such things go. She wasn't condemning anyone to death or servitude. But to her, at age thirty, it was like tearing curtains apart that protected a secret known to no one but her father, her mother, and herself—and, ultimately, only to her father.

Their faces were turned to each other. Terri repeated: "*Something* happened in Dad's life that cripples him."

She sat up firmly on the bed.

"Once, when I was fifteen, when Mom was going to mention something bad in the past … I didn't even quite hear it … Dad turned all pale. I can't remember Dad looking so white before then and only once or twice since. His face was like chalk. And then something else happened: I'll never forget it. A word, a name, came up that has sent shivers down my back all my life but until then was never spoken to me out loud ... *Francesca!*"

She was quiet for a moment, then resumed:

"Naturally, I wanted to know what was happening. And that name 'Francesca'—it was all very scary, and you know what, Jeremy? It still is today. I tried to make myself believe it never happened at all. Dad changed the subject; Mom changed the subject. But I know it's serious, an unspoken secret that hangs over the three of us and never goes away. It has darkened my life, and I don't even know what it's all about. But it has nothing whatever to do with you."

She seemed exhausted after this long speech, spent, staring at the white expanse of the big bed still rumpled from their lovemaking. Her conscience gave her a sharp jab. She had betrayed.

Jeremy took her hand. "All that energy spent on something you can't help! Why let it get to you? My dad has skeletons in his closet, too, but I've stayed clear of them. Our family situation is bad enough without resurrecting those old cadavers. They're *his* problem, not mine." And after a pause, "It's *their* life, Terri, especially if, as you say, it really has nothing to do with me."

For a brief moment, Terri was not so sure she'd been understood, but just then Jeremy carried her hand to his lips. That gesture convinced her. But all at once, she realized that the dark blot in her family's past had spread over Jeremy as well, now that they were lovers. Something unexplained hung over them both before they had even taken the first steps. Abruptly, they became aware of the everyday world they'd left behind. The room was filled with sunlight, bathing them in its growing heat.

Jeremy stood and stretched. "Let's go someplace cool before it's too late." He remembered the painter. "Sunday, you know. Folks go to museums to be cool when they don't go to church."

"It's *political.*" Terri had the last word. "I don't know what else it could be."

They headed for the shower.

Tracking Father
(1996-1998)

Chapter 19
Discovery

A month later, Terri, sleepy and vaguely disappointed, looked up from reading microfilms of old newspapers in the basement archives of the Museum of Modern Art. A lonely fly buzzed near the recessed window. She had talked with Lisa on the phone that morning and felt a twinge of guilt that she had been in touch so seldom, especially now that she'd learned her mother often spoke with Jeremy. The fly and her thoughts distracted her from her work. At present, she had only this one afternoon to give to her hunt for Matthäus, for the solution to the mystery that surrounded her father. Her senses came awake, and she began to hear the coughs and rustling paper all around her, to see the cold light from neon tubes in the ceiling, the sharp, eye-piercing glare of the microfilm reader in front of her. A headache congealed behind her brow. Or was it boredom, the wish to do something else, yet the sense that, whatever her body might say, however it might try to distract her, her mind had to get on with this?

The material on Matthäus was useful, but far from exciting. As an artist, he'd been much more interesting to her last winter when she wrote the piece for the *Times*. But now she had a mission: to understand her father's startling response when she mentioned the painter's name. What was the cause? The connection? She must find the answer.

An attendant shuffled toward her, an old man with tousled gray hair, in a navy blue blazer. He eyed Terri suspiciously, pausing in the space between her desk and the window as she adjusted the microfilm reader. She glanced at the clock on the wall behind her to make sure there was time. She still had an hour. A whole hour to fill!

She sighed and ignored the man as she threaded a new film into the machine, returning her attention to the newspaper spools she had requested. Most of the papers were German and Italian, and she merely scanned any other foreign texts for the painter's name, finding only trivial notices. She found a few more substantial articles in the London *Times* and the *Guardian*; a long piece in the *Figaro*. Nothing from America. She took off her glasses and wiped them, but the improved vision didn't change what was in front of her, nor did it help her headache. They all praised Matthäus's oils, to Terri's dismay ignoring the early watercolors she loved. They made a few hesitant references to his role in the gay society of his time. None of it was new. Nor did the material contain any clues that might lead to her father. Terri reached up, about to switch off the reader and return the films, casting a last glance at a column of text. She sat bolt upright, her headache forgotten.

Francesca Mancini.

Memories flooded her of dark winter evenings during her childhood, sad and angry voices overheard when she was very small. Now, struggling with scanty Italian, she read on an editorial page of *Il Tempo*, dated September 13, 1946:

Fêting a Fascist. Gregor Matthäus—once a German officer, now an artist celebrated in our land— .... Two sharply worded columns followed. Terri read on:

During the Allied 'occupation' of Florence, vestiges of Fascist control remained and were even encouraged by our ostensibly benign occupiers. So were some dubious German characters who remained behind as the German tide receded: flotsam preserved and protected by holdovers of the old regime. Gregor Matthäus was such a man: a brilliant artist yet compromised by politics ...

And then The Name: *Francesca Mancini.*

Terri picked up a pencil to take notes, but the pencil remained suspended in air as recent memories overwhelmed her. She saw her father's stricken face when she displayed her article and heard his anxious questions before he had even acknowledged her work, much less praised her. She shook her head, wondering. What was his connection with Matthäus? What role did Francesca Mancini play in all this, if any? *Mancini ... Mancini ...* the last name seemed familiar but only vaguely. Was this the dreaded Francesca of her childhood?

Her father's history during the Italian campaign, as she knew it from his stories, coincided with the history of the controversial painter. And there was another coincidence: The small watercolor in their dining room was by Matthäus. Why in *their* house when hardly anyone else in America seemed to know him? Still another coincidence: The city of Florence figured in both her father's stories and the articles about Matthäus, but how? Terri was stymied.

The attendant reappeared, his eyes on the wall-clock behind her. It was five. She had used up the entire hour in her reveries.

Terri got up slowly, returned the microfilms, and made for the door. Outside, the shimmering heat of August enveloped her like a poisoned gown.

ೞೞ

When he answered the phone, Jeremy's voice sounded full of joyful expectation. He was in high spirits. He told her of the performances he'd booked for his band and how he looked forward to her visit in two weeks. It would be fun to have her in the audience at the major gig they were all anticipating.

She cut him off, afraid these happy plans might be endangered by her overriding need to know, frustrating as it already was with the regular demands of her job. Her next words bore little relation to his thoughts. "I'm finally trying to get behind my dad's secret, and I found something just a couple of days ago. It's about Matthäus, the painter."

Unhappily sobered, Jeremy waited.

"I came across an article by a woman named Francesca Mancini, attacking Matthäus for Fascist connections back in '46. That's around the time when Dad was in Florence. I found it yesterday in the Museum of Modern Art."

"So?"

The interjection threw Terri off the track.

"I … I heard that name when I was little. It's got to be the same person. Maybe Mother knows for sure. I can't stand this secrecy any longer. Come on, Jeremy, you must understand."

"I don't really. But let's talk about it when you come in two weeks. That's still on, isn't it?"

There was a moment of silence.

When Terri did not react, Jeremy spoke sharply. "It better be! Damn it, Terri! Here we just started on a life together, and you're making it into an obstacle course. That's not fair! Not to me, not to yourself either. Do you really want to do this now? Why not let your dad cope with this thing alone?"

"Jeremy!"

The room danced before her eyes in her indignation. "It darkens *my* life, too!"

He seemed a little calmer, but she wasn't sure she felt easier. On the contrary, what he went on to say ignited her even more. "I've come to appreciate him better as time has gone on. He isn't the hundred-percent bastard I thought him to be. He's lived with it for years. Let him be."

"Oh, don't be condescending!" Something in his response had wounded her. "Yes, he'll live, but how? Actually, if you want to know, dad has barely managed to live with it and, worst of all, he refuses to take mother and me into his confidence. There's always a secret hovering over us. Through the years, it's been like a cat-and-mouse game. *It has to end.*"

Terri's lover sighed. "Do what you have to. But please don't destroy what we just started." He took another audible breath. "Let's talk about it when you come."

Terri still hesitated. She felt his rising anger crackling over the long-distance line, matching her own. She almost smiled when he began a sentence only to interrupt himself. After heaving another sigh, he concluded the conversation on a hopeful note.

"Still, we love each other."

"There's that," she answered dryly. Happily, however.

Left to herself with a silent telephone, Terri was dubious again. She felt remorse about Jeremy, for she was by no means sure she could visit him in two weeks. She wanted to grow in their life together, but she felt she had to push him aside, temporarily, until she'd cleaned up this mess. She turned back to her papers.

ഞരഇ

Temptation got the better of her, and despite some reluctance, she flew to Tortola and Jeremy. She enjoyed three carefree days of island breezes and entrancing music, putting aside all thoughts of her father and his mysterious aversion to Gregor Matthäus. Velvet nights cemented their love, fortifying them for trials to come.

Once back in New York, however, time crept by slowly, and the New Year found Terri buried in research. Progress wasn't easy with all the interruptions that invaded even her home with questions, e-mail memos, and phone calls. Looking at the material about Matthäus, she found it rich and formidable, painstakingly culled from books about the region surrounding Florence and the Italian war—the result of weeks of work added to her bread-and-butter routine. When pooled with the information she'd gathered earlier for her *Times* article, Terri was able to reconstruct a possible chronology, linking the stories on Gregor Matthäus and Francesca Mancini with what she knew of her father's life during the final phase of the Second World War.

After concentrated work, Terri recognized that exploring her artist's miraculous survival as an escapee from the German army during the occupation of Florence would make good copy for her book, but it also compelled her to link it to her father's activities at the time. The events in Gregor Matthäus's life, as she was now able to reconstruct them, coincided with Jacob's stories about events in and around liberated Florence. She'd heard him tell often about the cold winter of 1944-45, when he was assigned to a headquarters north of the city between Florence and Bologna which was then still in German hands. Florence was no more than an hour's drive away, though often the roads were made almost impassable by packed snow in the mountain passes. Still, Jacob had told her how he'd enjoyed getting away now and then for a brief weekend of luxury: a concert, an art gallery, a night in an actual bed with white sheets, a hot bath, privacy.

It was during this time that Matthäus was holding court in Florence for intellectuals, artists, and art connoisseurs of all ranks in the American and British armies—men starved for anything that would lift them out of one hell or another: fighting or mindless routine. As a biographer, Terri still lacked any firm knowledge about Matthäus's career and his place among artists in the Florentine community. However, she was caught by the near certainty that the painter and her father were present in Florence at the same time, and therefore the fierce author of the article attacking Matthäus might be connected with either or both. She needed a plan of action, but before she could develop one, she had to know more, including the role played by the ominous Francesca, whose name had shadowed her early childhood.

Terri never asked herself why she was so determined to shoulder this burden, a commitment without reservations. At last, she would take decisive action. The obvious place to start was Seattle. She applied for a few days' leave and arranged the trip.

ഇൟൟ

Jeremy, engrossed in making music, his favorite activity, squinted in displeasure when a boy interrupted to announce the phone call. His musicians, seated in a semi-circle in front of him, placed their instruments on their knees and looked at him quizzically.

"Who's calling?"

The boy shrugged. "Some woman."

The afternoon sun slanted across the gravel and chased shadows up the stuccoed building that housed Jeremy's office. He set his trumpet on its stand with a decided click and strode off with a stiff stride to answer the phone. A flight of gulls punctuated the moment with raucous screeching.

Terri's voice abruptly reversed Jeremy's mood, but his pleasure became concern when he detected an unaccustomed tone of sadness.

"What's the matter, Lamb?"

Terri burst out laughing in spite of herself. "What did you call me? 'Lamb'? Don't you know how unlamblike I am?"

He laughed, too, but continued to worry. "It sounds like trouble. Tell me."

She told him at length, and he had to listen, standing in his cluttered office, furniture and computer covered with films of dust, his musicians waiting outside. She announced that there had been enough shilly-shallying, that she now really had to get to the bottom of Francesca's story—the shadowy woman who seemed to provide a key to her own and her family's past.

"I'm calling to tell you that I can't join you for that island tour as we planned. I'm going to Seattle for a few days. It's been a tough decision, but I've found a clue to my dad's behavior, and the trail leads me back there. I know you think all this is unnecessary, Jeremy, but please bear with me. I have no choice. I'm really sad, but this is the only time I can get away from work—I'm taking a week off without pay. Please understand."

Jeremy's silence was laden with disappointment. Discouraged, he suddenly felt weary, his enthusiasm gone.

"Don't worry," he heard her. "There'll be many more times—I'll see to it."

"And if you can't?" He hadn't meant to say this, but couldn't stop himself.

"I'm sorry," she answered. "I was looking forward to it, too."

Jeremy Taylor carefully replaced the receiver. He frowned. Her voice echoing in his ear filled him with alarm. As he walked across the courtyard, he tried to shake it off.

"Now then, let's go!" he called to his band. "Come on! Take it!" He raised his trumpet and a triumph of music spread over the yard.

Terri left New York the next day.

৪৩৪

At the airport in Seattle, Lisa and Terri missed each other at their prearranged places—the gate, the security check, the baggage claim—until they fell into each other's arms by accident in front of a newspaper stand. Terri's pleasure at their reunion was clouded, however. The close embrace revealed new lines marking the familiar face.

They drove to the city, exchanging trivial remarks about New York and the weather.

Terri knew from her mother's quizzical glance that she was not at all sure why she had come but was careful not to ask. She answered the unspoken question.

"I've come to help you, Mom—help *us*, I mean—get to the bottom of our family 'mystery.'" When her mother still said nothing, she added, "It's about Gregor Matthäus. And it came out of my article, soon to be my book, I hope."

"But what ..."

"Dad's weird response to my article—negative even—means more, surely, than meets the eye, but what *does* it mean? I must get to the bottom of it."

"Why now after all this time? Perhaps you're reading too much into it." She changed the subject. "You know I really enjoyed chatting with Jeremy on the phone. He's quite a guy ...."

"I know." Terri turned away to hide her distress at her mother's seeming indifference to her need. Whether or not Jeremy pleased

Lisa, her own life was on the line, her past, her future. Her distress subsided, shifting toward pleasure. "Jeremy really likes you, and I'm grateful." She fell silent. Would her mother help solve the riddle of the past?

They pulled into the driveway.

ໜ໐໕

"That Matthäus in there …" Terri began, asking her father again about the familiar picture she'd seen all her life. The three of them were sitting on the enclosed patio watching the sunset. It had been a lovely winter day, crystal clear rather than uncomfortably gray. Jacob had seemed both pleased about his daughter's unexpected homecoming and comforted by her warm embrace.

They enjoyed the waning light, the sun gilding the bramble hedge. Terri spoke hesitantly. "Please tell me something more about the artist. It was really this little water-color in our dining room and your explanation of it that made me so excited about that assignment."

Her father seemed to squirm, as if suddenly uncomfortable, as if he were asking, *How many times do I have to pass this quiz?* He shaded his eyes against the setting sun. His words, vague, distant, threw up the usual barrier. "Nothing much more to say."

Lisa was very quiet.

Jacob went on as if Terri had probed again. "I like his *work*. That's all."

His daughter exclaimed, her voice full of exasperation. "Oh Dad, please! Just tell me *anything* you know about him!"

"What more can I say? Truly, I know nothing."

A few late sparrows chirped and flapped their wings in a nearby tree, then quieted. Now everyone was silent.

ໜ໐໕

Terri and Lisa found a table next to the window at a downtown Starbucks with a good view of a busy street sale nearby. They raised their coffee mugs to each other in a mock salute. They had talked a great deal but not about the subject that was uppermost in their minds.

Lisa looked rested and relaxed. It was her special day, her Thursday the day of the week she set aside for research, though sacrificed all too often when a patient in need called. She turned to last night's conversation. "Whatever you want to find out, dear, your Dad's not making it easy. You needn't tell me, of course, but if I can help..."

"Of course, I want to tell you, I have to. I need to."

Outside, shoppers flocked to a new sale rack, others lined up at the counter with their bargains, crowding a man sweeping the sidewalk. It was another good day. Through the open doors, mild, fresh air flooded the room, and the bright January sun caressed the bare branches of the trees arching over the sidewalk.

Terri continued, her voice strained. "It's so hard. For years—all my life—we've lived with this problem. Still, I had no idea how hard it would be to break through."

"But Terri, what *is* it?" Lisa's brow knotted in exasperation. Her daughter had arrived unexpectedly on a mysterious mission she vaguely suggested but didn't explain. "*What on earth is it?*"

"I'll tell you in the car." Terri's voice became normal again. "Just avoid the interstate, so we can talk properly."

They drove slowly along city streets. Terri finally spoke. "When I was little, you and Dad would quarrel over someone named Francesca. Was her full name Francesca Mancini?"

Dead silence. The car slowed. A brake screeched as a car behind them swung past, the driver cursing.

"Yes. Why do you ask?"

Terri picked a sheet of paper out of her handbag, her own translation of the article in *Il Tempo*. She began to read.

"Fêting a Fascist. Gregor Matthäus. Once a German officer, now an artist celebrated in our land ..."

Lisa pulled over to the curb and listened while Terri read.

"Signed: Francesca Mancini."

She paused, looking at her mother. "I discovered it in the basement reading room of the Museum of Modern Art."

Lisa drove on and they drifted into a quiet street leading to a city park and stopped in front of a pleasant brick house with white window frames and green fake shutters.

"Mom, tell me who she really is. Why should she be important to us?"

For several interminable seconds, heavy silence filled the car. Lisa finally replied, but in a colorless voice.

"It's dead and buried. Don't pick scabs off old wounds."
She squared her shoulders and faced her daughter, resolute. It
seemed the time had come to speak. Her voice was still lifeless. "We
shouldn't have kept it from you." Then, after a deep breath, her words
exploded from her mouth. "She was your father's first wife."
A thunderbolt! From her earliest childhood, Terri secretly felt deep
trouble lurking in her parents' past. But this? Now it was out in the
open.

Not a hidden love affair, as she had suspected since her teens, but
much more than that. An earlier *marriage!* In three whole decades
she had not been told? The sudden revelation that this Francesca, the
intruder who had shadowed her childhood, was an unspoken 'other'
in their small family, shocked but intrigued her. Were there children
of that marriage? A half- brother? A half- sister?

Lisa spoke once more, breaking into her thoughts. "For a man to
have a first wife is not unusal, of course. But from our wedding to your
birth to this day, he could never speak of her beyond the barest facts,
and he insisted on keeping them from you. Something important has
been troubling him about her—still does—and he refuses to share it.
If it was dreadful, I should know. If not, what's wrong with the man
to carry on like this half his life?"

"Now you know why I'm here, Mom."

Lisa started the car. A curtain had stirred in the window of the
pleasant little house in front of which they had parked. Someone
seemed worried; it was time to move on.

They resumed their drive through quiet streets. Lisa continued her
monologue, her face averted as she stared ahead, the street unraveling
in front of them.

"Your dad may have been close to Communists after the war, and
this Francesca—he'd met her in Italy—got him into it. Pure conjec-
ture, of course. But, those *were* the McCarthy years. The way I see it,
dear, whatever happened between your dad and that woman took
place when he was investigated at the university by that McCarthy-
like committee."

Terri froze. One revelation after another. "Dad was investigated?"

"He was, but that's all I know. He won't talk about it."

"You never pursued it, Mom?"

"Your aunt Katya told me not to. Those were bad times."

Terri's headache was back again—the ache that had come before she'd discovered the article. Now the dread extended to the pit of her stomach.

"But we have to find out what happened. That's the point of my trip."

"But, sweetheart, where can we start? I thought an official government record would give me an answer. I got hold of a copy—you can see it, too. But it won't help us, sweetheart. Your dad and Francesca—none of that appears in it. Katya told me those parts were probably left out because of international complications. This Francesca may have had influential friends in Italy. Who knows? Nobody, *but nobody* would tell me."

Terri's mind raced ahead. The idea of McCarthy-like 'hearings' sent her off in a new direction. But she stopped. Would seeing her father, embracing him, seeking to understand him, keep her from exposing the truth, cleanly and completely? She couldn't say, but she knew that at the very least she had to face him directly. He had suffered long enough because of Francesca. But she would have to rely on more than vague hunches. One clue had come from a newspaper more than fifty years ago. A second clue might emerge from a source closer by.

She had no choice. She'd have to return to archives, but this time it was especially painful. She was about to track her father.

Chapter 20
Confrontation

Her mother's car enclosed Terri in a claustrophobic capsule. Early-morning traffic swarmed the freeway, and with her attention focused inward, she almost rammed a slow-moving sedan ahead. The dreary winter day gloomed gray around her, and yesterday's conversations with her mother buzzed in her head. Her breath came short, and uneasiness mounted as she approached downtown. She hoped to repeat her recent achievement in New York, finding traces of her father's hidden life in an old newspaper file. At last, the massive *Seattle Post-Intelligencer* building came in sight, with its imposing rooftop globe. A car pulled out of a convenient parking place just as she arrived. A stroke of luck? A good sign?

She pulled into the parking space, then just sat still, with her hands gripping the wheel, wishing for spring and relief from the gloom of the winter weather. A strong inhibition kept her from entering the building. The next step would be crucial, perhaps irreversible, in her campaign to unmask her father.

She bent over the steering wheel, her forehead propped on her left hand. What would she expose? A sexual scandal? A breach of professional ethics? Her father a Communist? She expelled a long sigh, opened the door, and got out, one reluctant leg then the other. With her purse tucked under her arm, she walked toward the door, paused, then continued in another direction. The small public garden, neatly kept as if waiting for summer flowers, invited her. She opened the little iron gate and sat on a damp bench. For half an hour she mused, oblivious of the cold and drizzle. What would she find in those files? Something about Matthäus? Not likely. About an Italian woman named Francesca? Possibly. And what of Jacob Becher himself?

She rose, closed the little gate with care like the good citizen she was, and at last approached the building's entrance. Thoughts of her mother came to mind, her life-long guardian, a strong, protective wall. Through all the uncertainty of their lives, Lisa had kept her safe. But from what?

Her hand closed on the shiny brass door handle, and the heavy hardwood door swung open. The search was about to begin. But a brisk young woman at the information desk told her she'd come to the wrong place. Back copies had not been kept on the premises for a long time. The young woman saw her disappointed face.

"If they're important papers, they're probably kept on microfilm," she said helpfully, "but we don't keep them here. You could try the collections at the university and the public library."

A reprieve, but brief. She drove straight to the public library, her old friend. She recalled her school years, lugging stacks of books to and from the Circulation Desk.

The microfilm room at the library reassured her with its familiar, worn vinyl floor and fluorescent lighting, its musty library smell. But at each stage her ambivalence returned. Dread of exposing her father in some unspeakable transgression stuck in her throat like a physical lump. She forced herself to read the material that slid past her eyes and knew that, in the end, she'd have to confront him face-to-face.

Progress was slow. She focused on 1946 as a starting point, when Francesca Mancini had published her article attacking Gregor Matthäus. She refocused the microfilm reader and turned the knob, but not until she reached 1947-48 did she begin to come upon truly relevant material. Her anxiety mounted as news stories inundated her about a state representative named Albert F. Canwell and his hearings to root out communist influence at the University of Washington. She focused intensely on the material. She'd heard of the Red scare and of the state committee set up to expose Communists, but until now it had been mere history, not meriting her attention. So far, the names she was hunting—Gregor Matthäus, Francesca Mancini, and her own Jacob Becher—did not appear. But now, she approached July when several dispatches listed them with sinister intimations. She sat up, her mind and muscles taut with expectation.

"*Mrs. Francesca Mancini-Becher,*" she read, "*wife of Dr. Jacob Becher, an instructor in the Department of History at the University of Washington ...*"

Terri gulped for air and glanced over her shoulder, almost expecting someone to be standing there. "*... being sought by the FBI as a Communist alien fugitive ... Mrs. Becher is employed by the university* *as a teacher of Italian...*" She looked at the date: *July 24, 1948.*

She froze for a moment. Yes, she'd discovered what she had so hoped she wouldn't find, but more was needed to explain that tangled past. Where to turn? Jacob would simply deny all allegations. Decades had taught her to expect his escapes. Suddenly, she knew what to do.

She replaced the microfilms with care in their cartons and carried them to the desk. Gingerly, she walked out of the building, as if her pain could show.

৪০০৪

It was distant, but she knew the way to Ballard, to Katya Rombeck's, her father's friend from *back then,* her own 'Aunt Katya.' Terri clutched the note with the address in her hand while she drove. She had just called Katya, hearing her voice first ring with delighted surprise, then fall silent at her question about Francesca. When Katya spoke again, her words were neutral.

"This is a wonderful surprise, Terri! I'd be delighted to see you. "

"I'm already on my way, Aunt Katya."

"Great. I'll be waiting. Remember, dear, you used to get off the bus at the corner." But her tone had resonated with shock, and Terri's dread returned.

She never forgot how they first met. She was six years old. Yes, it must have been 1970, and they'd just arrived in Seattle. The image returned with utter clarity: the small woman with rich brown hair peppered with touches of gray, braided and wound around her head. So appealing, and yet burdened, reserved. When her father opened his arms for an embrace, she saw again his stricken face when Katya stepped aside. Why?

Who was she? Her dad's curt answer was far from satisfying. "An old friend."

But she'd liked her at once when she returned to the living room, where the grown-ups sat making hesitant conversation, with the wonderful news that she'd caught a monarch butterfly.

"May I present our daughter, Terri," her dad had announced with pleasure.

Aunt Katya's voice echoed in her mind. "Ah! She resembles both of you. I can see a friendship around the corner."

And then something odd happened that now drew her to Ballard. When her mom asked simply where the two had met, her dad had responded with a grimace and shake of his head, seeming to ask for her forbearance and complicity. Why was that question difficult, why should it be a surprise to her mother? Why, as usual, had Dad kept it hidden? Her father, the psychoanalyst—like the cobbler, the grown Terri thought wistfully, whose children went without shoes—why would he invite an old friend and avoid telling his family who she was? That mystery became the occasion for yet another explosion.

Katya's answer rang in her mind. "We were friends, long ago. A long time back." And she'd hugged her, shook hands with her mom, waved politely at her dad, and left.

Lisa remarked when the front door clicked shut, "She seems to be a fine woman, Jacob, but what is she to you?"

Terri could not recall his response, but Lisa's reaction reverberated across all the years. Her mother all but shouted, "For heaven's sake, man, come clean!" And when he mumbled something about 'Francesca,' Lisa shouted even louder, "What *about* Francesca? Was she with you in Seattle? And you brought us *here*—me and Terri! Are you out of your mind?"

Terri had looked from her father to her mother, from mother to father, and saw only bitterness and anger. Her life, her safety, her support had collapsed around her, and she ran to her room, convulsed with tears. She threw herself sobbing on the bed, pulling up the comforter to hide her head. Wrapped in a smothering cloud, she mourned until, an hour later, she rose with dread to confront the remainder of the day.

Despite Jacob's discomfort, Lisa had built a tenuous friendship with Katya. "Aunt Katya" had become like a second mother to Terri, providing her with care and guidance, warmth and wisdom. Soon, she'd see the person whose voice she's just heard on the phone and in her mind, speaking across the years.

Terri found the small house on the hill. She knocked and waited. A dog barked nearby. The door opened and there stood Aunt Katya, wise counsel of her teens, who had steered her through problems at school. Her intense eyes were dark pools. Relaxed after her work as a small publisher of poetry, she wore blue jeans and a light brown sweater over a man's shirt, looking years younger than her real age of seventy-six.

Terri stood in silence, the present effaced by the past: so many welcomes, Katya's warm smile, the hours spent sitting at her feet. But Terri had always known that her father disapproved of their easy connection. She instinctively understood his jealousy of her close relationship with her 'second mother.' She'd take the bus to the corner, Katya would open her door, and Terri would be engulfed by music from Aunt Katya's hi-fi—resounding trumpets and singing violins. There would be tea and conversation. The funky room in the funny little house out in Ballard had been a haven.

But when she innocently told her father that Katya had suggested she start college at the University of Washington, he exploded, frightening her with his shouting.

"Why does she keep crawling out of the woodwork? Damn it to hell! She'd better stay out of my life! She has no right to haunt a man like this! And now my daughter!"

"But Daddy," she had the courage to say, "she didn't haunt, she just advised. I happened to run into her at the public library downtown and we talked about college and she gave me her opinion. What's the matter with you?"

But he was undeterred. "I don't like others to interfere. Why does Katya keep on popping up in our lives?"

ಐಖ

And here she was, that wise counselor. Terri smiled and held out her arms, her seventeen-year-old self once more. "Aunt Katya!"

They embraced. "Let me look at you, Terri." Katya closed the door behind them. "We haven't seen each other for such a long time."

"I've been in New York…" There was no need to go on. Where she'd been no longer mattered.

Katya led her into her living room. It was still the same as when Terri was seventeen, filled with mementos and heavy furniture; a Victorian lamp with a dark green shade and a large picture over the mantelpiece … and now she was over thirty. For the first time, she focused on the painting, suddenly gripped, at last realizing what it was.

"Yes, dear, it's a Matthäus, of course. Isn't it powerful? Those exploding shells! My friend Francesca gave it to me many years ago."

Neither spoke. Finally, Terri pleaded. "Aunt Katya, please, tell me about Francesca."

"I can't tell you, Terri. It's not my place. Jacob ... your father, must tell you. The main fact you know, of course. She was Jacob's wife ... his beautiful wife." She caught herself. "Please, Terri. I don't mean any disrespect for your mother, a wonderful person, too. But I loved, I love Francesca." She stopped, her eyes fixed on the painting. "I asked you to come here, because I wanted to see you after all this time. But I can't tell you what you want to know."

Terri looked stricken. She'd expected this meeting to clear up the mystery. Katya rose. "A cup of coffee?"

The young woman did not answer, and when she raised her eyes to meet the older woman's, she was unable to conceal her distress. "You *must* tell me something!" She tried to speak boldly, forcefully, but her despair rang through and troubled the calm surface of her speech. "There are things, Katya, that you should be able to tell me, things that shed light on some part of it, if not all. It can't *all* be a secret."

Again, neither of them spoke. Except for the weak bulb under the green shade, the room was dark. Spooky. She'd always thought so in her teens.

"The newspaper story from that distant past must have been a shock." Katya reflected for a moment before asking, "But what made you think of me?"

"When I was a kid, you were unmentionable at home, and I had to visit you behind Dad's back, remember? Why shouldn't I think you would know about this mess? I remember your first visit. I was six. Then, after you left, it was like a thunderstorm."

Katya stared, her pupils dilating, saying nothing for a while. "Mind if I smoke?"

"Of course not."

"I was Jacob's old friend." The match flared and lit Katya's face from below. "When he brought Francesca from Italy, I could love them both. We and some other friends saw a lot of each other."

"Katya, there was some kind of ..." She searched for the word, "... crisis. What was it? It had to do with Communists. Am I right? It must have!"

Katya cut in firmly. "Let's visit a little and talk about your work. What is it like to work at the *Times*? I loved your piece on Matthäus. Beautifully done. What a coincidence—that man, of all people! I should have called or written you at the time."

"Please, Aunt Katya!" Terri persisted. "Don't wall me off like this! Please! Dad won't speak to me about it. Where can I turn?"

"I'm not sure you should turn anywhere, child." Katya spoke slowly, pulling on her cigarette, returning to the subject with obvious reluctance. "Some things should remain buried. It's been so many years. Why dig it up?"

Terri smiled ruefully. "You sound like my friend Jeremy. But I say to you what I said to him: There's *something* there, though it's almost impossible to put it into words. It's like a heavy weight inside me ... and it's inside Mother, too." Her tone became bitter. "It's us women folk who're left holding the bag."

"No one asked you to hold it, child. The big folks have quietly agreed to close up shop and roll down the shutters." Katya's face told her she knew, too, that was no answer.

"Can you at least tell me where else I can go? You love her; you say you love me. Why can't you tell me more?"

"Please, let it go! A man's dignity and his loyalty—" She stopped. Clearly, she'd gone almost too far. Both of them rose. Katya reached up to embrace her, but she did not speak.

Dejected, Terri unlocked her mother's car. Katya waved goodbye from the steps.

ಬೋಗ

Stymied, Terri already saw herself at the end of the road. She could think of no further steps. Even so, she returned to the library to see if she could detect just one more clue in a newspaper. The morning passed with continual focusing, refocusing, turning the microfilm reader's knob, stopping now and then to rest her eyes. Abruptly, it flashed before her, the name Francesca Mancini. She straightened. This was new! Francesca's lawyer had been thrown out of the hearing room. The context was unclear, but his name gave her faint hope.

His name was James Ahern, an old lawyer, semi-retired but still maintaining an office.

A straw in the wind? There was only one attorney by that name in the phone book. She called the number and a man's voice came over the wire: "James Ahern here."

ﬆ

Sparse gray hair neatly trimmed, old-fashioned yet elegant in a dark gray suit and blue bow tie, he opened wide his office windows to let in the sunlight. They sat facing each other.

"Ms. Becher! What a pleasant surprise! I was once your dad's lawyer, as you know, but he hasn't consulted me in years.... Yes, a long time ago... fifty years. I was in my thirties, around thirty-five, I think. But I still love this job, Ms. Becher... can't be without my office and my old clients." He shook his head as if coming out of a dream, looked down at his well-creased trouser leg and his highly polished black shoes, then raised his eyes to her. "Did he send you? Is he OK?"

She answered with a smile. "No to the first question, yes to the second.

The lawyer's back stiffened, alert, like a sly animal on guard. "He didn't send you?"

"As I said, Dad knows nothing about this visit."

"Well then ... what gives me the pleasure, Ms. Becher?"

"I'm hoping you can help me. Recently, by the merest chance, I discovered that Dad was married before, to an Italian woman. She left under odd circumstances."

The old lawyer's gaze lay heavily on her. She needed to talk fast to get it all in. "I never knew about that former marriage, Mr. Ahern. It was quite a shock. I gather you handled some of the legal complications: the investigation, maybe. But I need your help to find out more. I *must* know more, for my sanity's sake! And Dad won't tell me anything."

He straightened his bow tie, lying slightly askew, and cleared his throat. "I don't know what you do for a living, Ms Becher, but you look like a professional to me. So, you must know what is common knowledge—confidentiality between lawyers and clients. Even though your father is now likely to have another attorney, you must know that I'm not at liberty—"

Terri was desperate. "Please, sir! There must be some well known facts that you can lead me to without exposing ..." She felt foolish, at a loss to explain to this stranger why it was so vital for her to know. And why against her father's wishes? "It's important to me," she said lamely. She looked up, feeling hopeless. "There were those anti-communist hearings I read about, but my mother already told me there's nothing about my father in any official report. I can still check it out, but my mother is a professional herself, quite thorough. I do hope you can help."

Ahern held up his hand like a policeman at an intersection. "No, dear lady!" His manner and cutting tone sent ripples of anger down her spine. "There's nothing I can do for you. Absolutely nothing."

A clock struck three times in the silence. The old lawyer's voice sounded doubly loud. "Not every story can be wrapped up neatly. To use that worn phrase, why not let sleeping dogs lie? It's been decades, Ms. Becher."

"Excuse me!" She was shouting and hated herself for her shrill voice. "What do you know of my life? Of my mother's life? We've had to watch my father suffer for years without being able to help him. We just want him to open up so we can love him."

It must have been too hard, too personal for this old lawyer. Seemingly desperate to get her out of his office, he began to fumble in his Rolodex. "There's a man who might help you, a man who's not under the same obligation to stay silent. He knows about the situation. Ah! Here it is!" He pulled out a card with a name and phone number. "His name is Mike Simonetti, a retired real estate man, who dabbles in politics. You'll like him, I think. You can give him my name, and he can decide for himself whether to talk to you or not."

She scribbled the information with a trembling hand.

All the way home, steering through traffic, she relived the visit, thinking of all these people surrounding her father, knowing. What could it be? What was there about her father and his first wife that made everyone refuse to divulge what happened between them? Her father must be in disgrace. What *could* he have done? She was his daughter, loved him and felt inevitably part of him. She would make his burden hers as well.

Later that night she shut herself in. No half-expected phone call from Jeremy. She was a shade disappointed that he didn't persist. Misery and anger fed on themselves. This man Simonetti; she'd never heard of him. But she had to meet him now. She'd go from place to place, from witness to witness, until she had solved the enigma of her father's past.

ജ✧ര

She had no inkling that Mike Simonetti had been her father's severest judge. But when he rose to greet her, a man of eighty with a shock of white hair but still in sweater and overalls, a wave of fear and attraction struck her and left her disconcerted. She met his eyes—clear blue to deep blue. He smiled faintly.

"So you're his daughter. Well, well. What brings you here, Ms Becher?"

"My name is Terri."

"Mine's Mike ... as you know. What do you want? Why did Ahern send you? He had no business."

"Don't blame him." Fear and attraction became impatience. "I need to talk to you about—Jacob and Francesca. He thought you might help. I insisted, Mike."

He relented. "Francesca," he said slowly, "I haven't heard from her in years."

Terri looked around the spacious living room. Its disordered elegance corresponded to his informal appearance. The modern furniture was in good taste, though papers and audiotapes were strewn about in happy disorder. On a glass table, next to a large television, she could see an elaborate sound system in a well-crafted homemade case. Next to it were piles of file folders neatly stacked. She saw no computer, but an array of comfortable chairs around a large circular coffee table.

Mike apologized in an offhand way. "Sorry about the disorder. I live alone. Have lived alone all my life."

Why tell me? She hoped to be offered a chair, but Mike remained standing in the middle of the room, and for a while they went on talking on their feet.

He faced her sternly as he kept them standing—so sternly that she felt she was being put through a third degree.

"What makes you think, Terri, that I'll tell you anything about Jacob and Francesca that you don't already know?"

Terri eyed a chair. "I know nothing." After a moment she added, "My mother doesn't either, Mike, beyond knowing that Francesca was his wife once upon a time."

"Then let me rephrase the question. What in hell makes you think, my dear woman, that I'll spill the beans your dad has kept from spilling for half a century?" Then, at last, his eyes a shade gentler, he asked, "Why do you want to know? Now? After all this time?"

The inevitable question, and she still couldn't answer it rationally. Again, she tried her appeal. "Don't you see? Can't you feel how not knowing eats away at you? Mother has always known about that marriage, also how he felt about that woman, but neither of us knows what she, Francesca, did to Dad—"

Mike grunted, but said nothing.

She continued, "—what really broke it up, what it was that sent Francesca off into the wilderness."

"Wilderness my foot," said Mike, finally sitting down and pointing to a chair for her. "A cushy job, I understand, and she deserved it."

"What? Where?"

There was a long pause.

"How about a drink?" He remembered that, like it or not, he was a host. But Terri made it easy for him; she declined.

"That communism stuff. Was *that* the scandal?"

"Jacob and Francesca." Mike rolled the two names over his tongue as if they were playthings. He smiled, and, alluding to Dante's tortured couple, "Or, Paolo and Francesca—but who, after that day, would have linked Jacob's name with hers?"

"What day? What happened?" Terri was bewildered. "I found a newspaper article in the *P.I.* for July '48. They were looking for one Francesca Mancini-Becher."

Mike's face became grave. He did not react to her report of a news story but spoke soberly. "I didn't mean to joke, Terri. It's very serious. But nobody can tell the man's daughter but the man himself. Go to him. Let me know how things turn out."

And with that, she was dismissed.

࿇

'The man himself.' Go to him. It was now or never. She heard Jacob settling down in his study later that evening, ready to write. She walked in uninvited and sat, beginning on an affectionate note. "You're late getting to your work this evening. What happened?"

"Nothing special, darling. Someone came in just before supper and pushed things back a bit. I'm still seeing patients, you know."

"Great you're still doing it, Dad."

She asked him about his practice, just as she used to when they were close. For the first few minutes she relished the pleasant illusion of reliving times when, still in high school, she'd find her father in his study and listened to him telling her about his work. How she admired him in those days! Her father's voice went on in the same way even now, and Terri realized how strong the bonds had been—and still were—that tied her to him and how fully in most ways he had repaid her with his affection. She shuddered, for suddenly it was no longer the same. His secrets, his unacknowledged secrets: Francesca Mancini and his break with her. How to begin? What kind of crisis had sent that woman away and had made marriage with her mother and her own existence possible? She thought of Matthäus, the painter, her favorite subject. She'd begin with him.

"Listen, Dad. I think you can tell me more about Gregor Matthäus. It's really important to me. I've been doing a lot of research and found a few leads, which I think you can explain. I need you to talk to me."

His spine stiffened visibly, and his voice became tight. "What I've told you many times, Terri, is the truth as far as it goes. He was talked about in Florence, as a favorite of culture-vulture GIs, when I was stationed up north. I admired his work and bought a water color or two, like the one in the dining room."

"And the others?"

"I sold them when I got home and needed money."

Terri was relentless. "Why not that picture? What was so special about it?"

He swung around to face her directly, his eyes clear but defiant, his expression determined. "My dear, there is more, much more, concerning Gregor Matthäus and my life back then. Those times were traumatic, and I needed help in working through that. That's the reason I was first analyzed myself and then became a psychoanalyst—a

big jump from the history professor I once was. Analysis helped, but
there are still things left unsolved … dark corners. All these years, I've
been avoiding the subject, ducking and weaving, even lying."

"Yes, Dad, Mother and I are fully aware of that."

He nodded and continued as if he hadn't heard. "It never occurred
to me that the best course of action would be to refuse to talk about
it if you questioned me. It's simple, Terri. Revealing those past events
would release such poison into our lives that you and Lisa might be
destroyed by it. I've barely survived that poison. I can't allow my family to undergo such pain." He stood now, with a half smile, but no less
determined.

She, too, rose from her chair, facing him. "I'm a grown woman now.
I can handle the truth."

"I have nothing further to say. As far as you and Lisa are concerned,
that past is dead and buried."

She exploded. "Dead and buried! Dead and buried? It's alive, Dad,
the whole thing, a secret acid. It's been eating away at all of us all my
life."

He shook his head and glanced toward the door, signaling her time
was up.

She ignored the hint. "Yesterday, Dad, I was at the public library. I
found a newspaper article from 1948, stating that a woman identified
as your wife was being sought as a communist fugitive. That was a real
jolt. You see, I'd also come across another newspaper article in New
York—an article by the same woman in *Il Tempo* from 1946, attacking
Matthäus for his politics. It fits, Dad …"

Jacob sat again and crossed his legs, clasping his hands tight around
his knee.

For a brief moment, she thought of Katya, of Ahern, of Mike
Simonetti, and considered appealing to them once more. But she
knew better. Why implicate them? Instead, she turned directly to her
father, just the two of them, face-to-face.

She spoke more gently now. "Dad, the author of that piece in Italy
seems to be the same woman the *Post-Intelligencer* called your wife."

She let the words stand for a moment as if waiting for them to
mature. "The name wasn't unfamiliar to me. Until a short time ago, it
was just an echo of what I overheard in my childhood." This time she

waited for three beats. Then, locking eyes with him, she pronounced the name: "Francesca Mancini." And in a louder voice: "What happened? What did she do to you? Sooner or later, you *will* tell me."

"I'm sorry, Terri, as I said, I have nothing—"

She did not wait for him to finish his sentence. The door slammed behind her.

ಐಐ

"Great to hear your voice!" She hugged the receiver between her shoulder and her cheek, reveling in Jeremy's warm baritone, which transported her from the privacy of her bedroom in Seattle to the warm Caribbean. Three-thirty in the morning: She'd had to catch him before he left for work at eight o'clock island time.

"Even greater to hear yours, Terri! I was getting worried."

"It's been hairy, Jeremy. I've spent the time tracking down this story about dad and his first wife, talking to people who knew them back then. I still don't know what it was. It does have something to do with the Red Scare. But no one will say anything except tell me to talk to Dad."

"And I'm guessing he won't talk to you."

"Only to deny everything."

Jeremy, across the huge continent between them, remained silent.

"He's got to come through, Jeremy. He's better than that."

She could tell that Jeremy wanted to shout at her, to say something he'd said before: *Leave him alone, Terri!* But perhaps he was reluctant to replicate the gulf in miles with a greater inward distance. Instead, he said, with just a trace of a sigh, "I wish I could take you away from all this."

"Thank you," she answered without irony. "That helps."

"I love you."

"Me you." She gently placed the phone in its cradle.

She turned off the light and lay down once more, her hands folded under her head, watching the darkness recede as the early morning sky flooded through the open window.

Chapter 21
"That Time of Year"
(July 23, 1948-July 23, 1998)

She gave up for a time, returning to New York, burying herself for the rest of the year in routine work for the *New York Times*. The united chorus pleading that she *let sleeping dogs lie* wore her down. A little more than a year had passed since her vigorous but failed effort to lift the veil of secrecy protecting her father. While she'd searched, she knew that her career crept along and her love affair threatened to come to a standstill. So, she resolved—for now—to leave those distant events under unbroken seal and to forget about 1948.

Jeremy had been most persuasive. "Let's give ourselves a little breathing space, Terri. For God's sake, I haven't seen your old man in a long time, and though his secrecy drives you nuts and so bugs me too, we need to free ourselves to think about *our* future, yours and mine, not your dad's past." His voice faded, dream-like.

"All right, love." Yet she lacked conviction. Still, they got along well in their separate places and thanks to frequent meetings. A good part of the time, Terri didn't think about the unsolved puzzle between them like a block of ice, ignored yet not melting: her insistence on penetrating her father's secret and Jeremy's desire to let sleeping dogs lie. But July 1998, the fiftieth anniversary of those distant events, brought them back to mind.

They seldom fought. But with the anniversary came a quarrel. Terri had just arrived on Tortola from New York and had sunk down on a chair on the patio of Jeremy's beach cottage. The trip had been difficult, the day was hot, and when Jeremy explained that the expected dinner with his family was postponed, her mood became thunderous. "Damn it, Jeremy! In two years, I've spent hardly any time with your family. I've barely *met* them. Seems to me something's going on there, too. You never talk about them; all I know is that your dad owns all those boats, sends you to negotiate with millionaires and ... has some kind of hold over you."

Jeremy's mood darkened to match hers. "Look, Terri, I try not to consider your dad and his problems any of my business, so just stay out of *my* father's affairs."

His emphasis and accent were the strongest she'd heard from him during the years they'd been lovers.

He went on, making his point sharper, "There's no mystery in *my* life, though; no scandal you don't know about. No 'phantom wife.'"

She didn't comment further and, though seething, left it at that. She glanced at the large print visible through the open door.

It was new. It was a Matthäus.

"Jeremy!" She felt a rush of pleasure, leaving irritation far behind. "Where ... ? How did you find this print? It's a Matthäus!"

He grinned, answering her shift of mood, knowing he'd pleased her. "Well, you know, his name's getting around, and maybe one Teresa Becher started something back then. Now there's a Web site for him and I just ordered it."

She rose and kissed him. "Oh, Jeremy, you really *are* something!"

It wasn't a good moment for bad news, but it had to be done. She had to tell him she'd decided to answer Lisa's plea and visit her parents in Seattle next week. "I don't know what's going on, but Mom sounded distraught. It's probably something with Dad."

Jeremy grumbled, "You're like a dog with a bone. You can bury it for a while, but you never forget it."

"You're right, Jeremy. I never forget where it's buried."

She didn't ask him to come with her, determined that this was to be her show.

☙ℭ₰

The clock on his office wall showed 11:00, and Jacob Becher eyed his telephone. He was not sure why he had just called to ask Lisa and Terri to lunch. It was a pleasure to see Terri at home, and without Jeremy whom he still found difficult, despite his efforts to rid himself of his instinctual resentment that another man had possessed his daughter. The lunch... yes, that might bring him some relief. He had a queasy feeling of estrangement from Lisa, and hoped Terri's presence might bring them together again.

His state of mind was nothing new. Queasiness overcame him at this season, just before the anniversary of his betrayal and especially now on the fiftieth. He needed Lisa, condoning a trauma he had never explained, her silence amounting to a tacit agreement to share his anguish without knowing why. He was unsure how Terri would feel about it. He remembered the tense hour in his study, but he counted on their old closeness during her teen years—those discussions in his office after his working day was done—to enlist her, too.

Mother and daughter had not yet arrived when Jacob entered Cutter's Bayhouse, a popular place in downtown Seattle with a view of the Sound. It would fill up after twelve, but now there were still empty tables. He didn't have long to wait.

The two women appeared, Lisa in a bright yellow summer dress with a green scarf, Terri nautical in navy blue and white, her light brown hair loose around her face.

She greeted him with a laugh, holding out her hand. "Hi, Dad, and thank you! What a great idea!"

Lisa smiled, too, and for a moment, it seemed they could forget the dark and rainy July day that matched the clouds encroaching from the past. They were seated at once, and Terri exclaimed with pleasure that their table overlooked the bay. Without asking, Jacob ordered a bottle of Chardonnay.

"Gorgeous!" Lisa exclaimed as she looked out on the shimmering surface below. They were silent, admiring the scene. Darting small boats churned the dark water that sparkled here and there in beams of sunlight breaking through the clouds. Larger boats and ships lay at anchor and the cranes of the harbor rose like arms of praying mantises in the middle distance. "It reminds me a little of the Caribbean," she continued, "Though the water is almost black. I wonder how Jeremy is doing."

"He's doing fine, I think."

Terri's words were guarded, hesitating. Jacob guessed she didn't want them to know too much about her love life. An invisible barrier still separated him from Jeremy.

"I visited him only last week, and he sends you his love." Terri glanced at Lisa. "I forgot to tell you. He's now entirely into his music—he's soon doing a short tour on the mainland."

Jacob, silent, fixed his eyes on the water. A flock of gulls flew screaming past the window.

Lisa's tone was bright. "It's lucky we were both free. We were about to go shopping when you called. Terri's looking for a new raincoat, and Seattle's certainly the place to get it." Mother and daughter laughed.

He, on the contrary, felt increasingly grave as his eyes found Lisa's. As expected, her face lengthened in response. He knew her well enough to see her mood change, turning dark like the weather outside. Their silent stare, complicit, with Terri as outside witness, lasted several moments. They dropped their eyes, and Jacob raised his glass to them both, but his mind framed a very different image. The Sound changed into a sun-drenched piazza in Florence.

Terri's voice startled him. "Mom? Dad? What's going on?"

"It's that time of year." Lisa's voice was low. "For years, decades, I've lived through 'that time of year' with you, Jacob. It begins in mid-July and stretches into August, and I've hardly ever asked for details. I've been your partner, your accomplice in this charade. But now ..." She glanced at their daughter, seemed to draw strength from her, and turned back to hold her husband's gaze.

His daughter broke the spell. "*What* time of year? This isn't *real*! You're acting out ... what? A Humphrey Bogart movie?"

The waitress bustled over to take their orders, but the moment she left, the unspoken confrontation went on. Jacob, startled, felt the anguish return. A busboy stooped over them to fill their water glasses, and the interruption saved him from answering. He again reached for his wine, caught in his memory, and Lisa's voice came from far away.

"This is a good time to talk. Finally, after all these years."

Terri glanced at her mother with visible pride. "Dad! Remember our talk last year? You never answered and, in the end, I didn't push you." She lowered her eyes to her lap. Then, her chin came up, and her eyes met his with a challenge. "But what *was* the scandal? That's all Mom and I want to know... so we can hold our heads high."

This was the second time she had spoken to him this way. It was still new to them both. Their food arrived at last, allowing some distraction as they inhaled the aroma of their shrimp and fish. He was almost certain the worst was over. He first glanced at Terri, then looked past her at Lisa and smiled at her in the old irresistible way.

"To talk about *what*?"

He caught her. She faltered, as he knew she would. "*You* know." Her voice grew faint and she dropped her eyes. No one had touched the food.

"I've told you, Lisa, many times." He saw that Terri was watching him as he played with the stem of his glass. Then he turned away from them, focusing instead on the bay, desperate to escape.

But Lisa once more gained strength from her daughter and returned with her professional voice. "Let me remind you, then: Francesca, Matthäus, so many loose ends. How do they fit together? How do they affect Terri and me? They *do* affect us, you know. You must come out of hiding, Jacob, for *Terri's* sake, if not for mine."

"I'm not in hiding." Jacob repeated the old myth, bankrupt now, but he found nothing better.

Terri's face was red with anger and frustration. "Dad!"

Lisa went on, ignoring this outburst. "This time I won't let you slip away, Jacob. Ever since our marriage, ever since Terri was born, I knew about Francesca, but not why she left you. You've gained an enormous benefit at our expense. If that Francesca had come and gone out of your life, as I thought when I married you, that's one thing, and you owed me no explanation. But the way you carried on…" and her voice became louder, bolder, "you used us, yes, used us, to find exoneration." That was strong. Even Terri, though proud of her mother, was startled at this display of strength. "Terri and I are *still* wondering. Francesca *still* continues to affect our lives. Perhaps for some people such things may not seem important. In our case, with all your deliberate obfuscation, they're *vital.*" Lisa leaned forward, seemingly oblivious to their daughter's presence. "You love that woman to this day, Jacob Becher. Come out with it and stop this… this crap! What happened?" She picked up her glass, her hand shaking, and took a long sip of wine.

None of them noticed the silence around them, the staring eyes, the forks loaded with food, suspended in space.

Terri stared at him in silence, her jaw set, leaving the battleground to her parents.

He met Lisa's eyes, then veered away again, seeing a possible escape in the increasingly busy surroundings. The nearby tables were already occupied. The place was filling up fast. He groaned inwardly at the nightmare this luncheon had become, so different from his expectation when he'd asked mother and daughter to join him. He questioned his judgment, and again felt overwhelmed by unbearable shame. His shoulders drooped, and he covered his face with his hands.

Lisa moved as if to touch him, to comfort him, as she'd done in former years, but perhaps fortified by Terri, who sat stiff and silent beside her, she restrained herself.

Then Jacob decided to act. Once more he felt he was on trial: His wife and daughter were judge and jury.

His crime? He had been careful not to injure them in a lifetime of regret. Why had Terri chosen to write a book on Gregor Matthäus, of all painters in the world? And why had the gods of perversity goaded her to delve into his own past? Once before, he had cowered and uttered that fateful "yes" that had destroyed two lives, Francesca's and his own. He would not repeat such cowardice. Instead, he shouted, banging his fist on the table, and the shocked faces of the lunch crowd turned toward him.

"Damn your prying into matters that don't concern you! I told you a year ago, Terri, all I have to say on the subject. Take me or leave me!" He rose abruptly, red-faced, glowering at his daughter first, then at his wife. The food remained untouched, congealed. "Good-bye!" He left quickly, navigating around tables of gaping watchers without a single mishap. He paused briefly to pay the bill and was gone. Not one backward glance.

The two women sat stunned and silent. Finally, Lisa spoke. "I was afraid something like this would happen. I'm sorry it had to be today."

"It could have happened any day, Mom. He felt betrayed by us, trying to force him to reveal the past that he's worked so hard to conceal all these years."

Lisa shook her head. "A past we'll never know, I fear. It's 'that time of year,' as he always told me, the anniversary of a hellish experience. He was expecting our support, and instead we interrogated him."

Terri pulled herself upright. "It's not 'that time of year' for me, Mom, whatever that means. I must go … to be free of Dad's past." She stood, and Lisa followed her into the busy street where the car was parked. It seemed to Terri that her sleuthing was at an end. She had failed.

When they reached the house, Terri climbed the stairs to her room, still hers after twenty years, opened her suitcase, and threw in her clothes willy-nilly.

Lisa watched her. "Terri, surely you don't have to rush off. After all, this problem is not exactly new!"

Terri didn't reply, and when Lisa saw her daughter's face, locked in stubborn resignation, she turned away. Terri heard her steps in the bedroom next door.

She called Mike Simonetti. Despite the initial coldness, she'd sensed a growing understanding between them. "I'm sorry, Mike, I'd looked forward to getting together."

"What happened? Something between you and Jacob?" He seemed to know this was another act in the drama of her father's history.

"Something's come up, Mike. I'll be in touch from the East."

Next she called Katya, and when Lisa heard her speak the name, she entered Terri's room again. "May I have a word with her?"

"No, Mom, she's not answering. I'll leave a message, have her call you." She then phoned the airline, changed her return ticket for flights to Atlanta and San Juan, Puerto Rico at an enormous cost. It was then she discovered that the next available connection left at 7:30 the next morning. How to survive the night?

"I wish you wouldn't go," Lisa said, "but at least you can get out."

Terri touched her mother's cheek. "I hate to leave like this, Mom, but Dad will be OK, same as always, and you can be in touch anytime. But I have only three more days of vacation and I know how I want to spend them. Mom, it's just that after all this effort, finding all of Dad's former friends, trying to pry the truth out of them and being told that Dad is the only one who can tell me, then I get stonewalled. I've got to break out of this before the poison chokes me. I wish I would take you from it, too. What could be the cause of this shadow over our lives? What could be so terrible?"

Lisa merely shook her head. "I've resigned myself, Terri. I'd hoped maybe you ... but it seems he's going to keep that secret locked up forever."

As Terri trudged downstairs at dawn, lugging her suitcase, she peered through her parents' half-open bedroom door. Jacob had come home during the night and was fast asleep. Terri felt relieved not to face a farewell scene.

Her departure seemed decisive. She glanced at the bedroom window when she and Lisa pulled out of the driveway and saw his pale face, distorted by the pane. They spoke very little on their way to the airport, afraid that one or the other would burst into tears. They stood at the curb under the sign that proclaimed DEPARTURES and hugged each other with dry eyes.

ଽଠ୪

Terri called her lover by phone from San Juan. Tired from the long flight, she hoped for his reassuring voice, but only an answering machine replied. Fear flashed through her. Was he away on a trip? Then she remembered their talk the night before last and his plans for this evening. He'd be back before long. She recorded her message. *"Hi, Jeremy! I'm not expected, but pretty sure I'll be welcome. There's one late flight to Tortola. It leaves here at nine, and I'm in a rush."* She ended exuberantly. *"I can't wait to see you. I love you!"* A freer declaration than she'd made in months.

She'd been in the air for nine hours. It was half past eight when she dragged her luggage up and down escalators from gate to gate. After the sleepless night, she felt leaden with fatigue. The jet engines, after criss-crossing the huge continent, still roared in her head. Her bags, light by normal standards, seemed ever heavier.

Had she done the right thing?

But now, on the short flight to the island, everything changed. As the plane rose above land and sea, her life rose weightlessly into the southern sky of the gathering night. Something also lifted her spirits into the air where the small plane was soaring, humming, humming. She felt vibrant again, alive, filled with energy and desire to be with Jeremy in a fresh communion.

Ever her father's daughter, she began to fidget and worry. Shouldn't she have warned Jeremy before leaving Seattle after all? Surprises like this often turn sour. But when the little plane landed, all her worries were over: She walked directly into Jeremy's arms. They kissed fiercely.

Jeremy found no words. He simply opened his arms. Whatever it was that had brought her to him so unexpectedly, it could only be their good fortune. As they drove to the beach and his small cottage, he basked in the warmth of her arm around his shoulders. She would not let him go, kissing him again with fervor when they stopped in front of his cabin.

He stroked her hair, kissed her forehead and her eyes and then, taking her in his arms, he quoted from a half-remembered poem, "Do not move; don't ever move, with the sunlight in your hair."

When at last they pulled apart and got out of the car, he asked the reason for his good fortune, her unexpected arrival.

"Wait till we're inside and can talk sensibly."

But even when they collapsed on the sofa facing the picture window with its view of the ocean, she was not yet ready to explain herself in full. Instead, she again seized his hand, her head on his shoulder.

"Actually, darling, explaining is a big order. I'll wait with details. For now, you're all I have. Mother is still Mother and I love her, but that's all. My dad had a hysterical episode... He isn't the same father anymore."

He needed to ask, *What kind of episode?* But he restrained himself as she turned to him fiercely, calling his name. They undressed right there on the sofa, trembling with expectation. Jeremy turned off the light, but Terri reached out and turned it on again, speaking almost inaudibly, "Let's keep it on a little. It's all sea out there. Nobody can see us. And I want to see you, to feel us. "

"A miracle," he said gently. "I don't care what brought you here. You're here. That's enough."

৪৩෪

They sat on the sofa, each with a shot of tequila in hand. Jeremy passed his other hand over his thick hair as he often did when he was uncomfortable or had something important to say. But Terri spoke first.

"Do you remember the time after we met? I remember you so clearly, standing by that wheel, gesturing with your microphone in one hand, and steering with the other. You stood there big and magnificent—like a sea god. I loved you then ... right away."

He ignored her compliment.

"It's been such an incredible journey. And now we're here."

They put down the glasses and turned toward each other to reaffirm their love.

ༀ

Jeremy cradled Terri's hand against his chest. They lay next to each other, two pairs of eyes scanning the ceiling. "We're caught, Jeremy, by what we are." She kissed his shoulder, responding to the gentle pressure of his hand. "I mean, our parents, our lives, the world. All those 'isms' ... racism, communism, capitalism, what have you. But," she pushed herself up to look down on his face and outline his lips with one finger, "don't give up on us, Jeremy. We'll make it! Just you wait!"

Embracing the Past
(1998-1999)

Chapter 22
Florentine Pilgrimage

July 1998: Another fiftieth anniversary, another generation. This year was an important anniversary: fifty years after the trauma that shook the University of Washington. She looked back on the previous two years since that birthday celebration on Virgin Gorda, knowing it had taken that long to gather the necessary strength, from her communion with Jeremy and the passion they shared, and from her own maturing. She stood, viewing the sparkling seascape through Jeremy's picture window, and called Aunt Katya in Seattle.

"I'm sorry I had to cancel our time together. I was looking forward to it, but something came up ..."

Katya didn't ask what it was.

Terri delayed briefly with small talk, then returned to her earlier request. "I need your help. It's about Gregor Matthäus. When I started my biography of him, I never dreamed it would get mixed up with my family."

Met with silence at the other end, she cried out: "Aunt Katya! I need your help! Please!"

She heard an intake of breath. Katya's voice sounded unexpectedly sharp: "What do you want?"

She became equally sharp. "Just a little help after a long friendship." She paused. "I've got to speak with Francesca Mancini wherever she is. She has the key to Matthäus ... and to my life."

"Francesca has thrown that key away, long ago. This is an expensive call, girl. I have nothing to tell you." Katya hung up.

Terri dialed again, surprised, knowing her, when her friend picked up after all. Her voice this time was gentler.

"I'm sorry. I don't mean to be rude, but this is a difficult subject, and Gregor Matthäus is at the heart of it. Give me a night to think things over."

Terri counted the morning hours until it would be decent to call
the West Coast. At noon on the island she picked up the phone again.
It would be eight in the morning for Katya in Seattle when, she hoped,
her old friend would be awake and ready to talk.

Her friend was more than ready. "Terri, my dear, you really know
most of the story, but the ending doesn't belong to either of us. It belongs to Francesca Mancini. She's living in retirement in Italy. She was
born there, of course. She knows all about Matthäus and both hated
and admired him. The first you know. The second probably not."

"Is there any hope of seeing her, Katya?"

"Patience! That never was one of your virtues, Terri. Francesca will
see you, and, by the way, it was your work that convinced her. She
was impressed by your article on Matthäus. I finally persuaded her to
see you."

"What's she like?"

"Sharp as a needle, child. She's a lawyer, first a prosecuting attorney,
going after Fascists and after that, for most of her life, in defense, fighting for political prisoners and other mavericks, both men and women.
I visit her every so often at her place—a modest house—about an
hour outside Florence. She's lovely ... and ready to help."

"Then why won't Dad—"

Katya cut her off. "There's good reason why your father won't speak
of her and won't like this visit."

Terri was pleased but worried. What she'd suspected, hoped and
yet feared, might come true. The quest for Matthäus was becoming a
quest for herself—for her and for her family.

She wrote to a still-mysterious Francesca, giving her own phone
number in New York.

ᘉᘓ

Back in her cluttered apartment, Terri waited with increasing impatience, assailed by doubts and uncertainty. An interminable two
weeks later, Francesca Mancini's letter arrived, a thin letter on thin
paper, formally inviting Terri for a visit.

"It will be very pleasant to meet you, Miss Becher. I liked your article on Gregor very much. Do call me if you can come."

Impatient, Terri telephoned at once. She was pleasantly surprised
to hear that the voice at the other end was warm and pleasant.

"Teresa Becher? So good of you to call me. Dr. Rombeck told me about you. Do I understand that you're planning to turn your fine essay on Gregor Matthäus into a full biography?"

The voice sounded British with a faint Italian inflection, and she pronounced Terri's last name with a soft 'ch,' the German way. "Let me repeat my invitation. If you can get away, by all means, visit me. That way we'll have more leisure to discuss Matthäus. Here, you'll have better access to his art-works. I greatly admired him, you know."

Terri was captivated by her voice.

Giddy with the prospect of success, she was hardly conscious of her movements as she gathered her purse and umbrella on this rainy day to rush to the subway. So much to be done—a leave of absence from the *Times*? How would she finance such an expensive trip coming right after all the money that had flown like a river in her flight from Seattle into Jeremy's arms? She'd not ask her parents for a loan, not with such twisted and powerful emotions involved. Besides, she'd been financially independent for years. A research leave perhaps—art institutes or museums helping with an innovative project? She might have to take a leave without pay, but she hoped such a sacrifice wouldn't be necessary. Did she know anyone with contacts in Italy? Mike Simonetti, perhaps? She e-mailed an elaborate letter, telling him what happened and asking him for help or advice. She got his reply within minutes:

"Friend Terri, you're a real person and I'm happy to know you. A breakthrough had to come, and Francesca will be pleased." The ending surprised her. "Godspeed. He will protect you. Mike." She knew he couldn't help or he would have done so. But she had his respect.

That night she was eager to tell Jeremy about Francesca Mancini's encouraging answer when he phoned. "I need this for my work, or I'll be stymied."

"That's not your only reason for going there," he answered over the wire. "You and I know it and your friend Katya does too."

"Of course, that whole business with Communism has to do with Dad. I wish I could make sense of it…" They hung up, but Terri called back five minutes later. Her words tumbled over each other: "Jeremy! Why don't you cancel one of your gigs or have someone else take your place and go with me to Italy! I badly need someone to share this with. I'm worried I'll mess it up with all that family stuff getting in the way. And," she added with a smile in her voice, "we could have a ball on this trip if we can swing it. Let's put our shekels together. I know it'll work! Do you think it's possible? Please try! So much depends on it."

Her tone of urgency reached him. "I hear you! Let's see what we can do about that money problem. Actually, I've always wanted to see Italy myself."

"I knew you'd come through! Thanks, Jeremy! Thanks a million!"

They would return to the island when it was all over, and she'd prepare him a triumphal feast in gratitude.

ഇൻ

Francesca still held the receiver in her hand, though the call had ended minutes ago. Jacopo's daughter had arrived in Florence. The young American voice at the other end took her back decades into a past that dogged her still, no matter how successful she thought she'd been in leaving it behind her on that long boat ride in 1948.

Writing about Matthäus? What should she tell that young woman? Katya had not called or written since their phone conversation last week agreeing they should encourage this meeting with Teresa, and Francesca had no further clues. Did Jacopo approve of his daughter's decision to see her? How much did Katya know of what went on between father and daughter? Was it perhaps a ruse, another way to approach her? His last attempt back in the sixties, she recalled, had also been about Matthäus. But she soon dismissed the thought. Katya had not mentioned any such possibility in recommending Jacopo's daughter so strongly. She knew her friend's fondness for Jacopo's second wife and her daughter, and also knew Katya did not bestow her affection lightly.

Besides, the young woman at the other end had sounded highly professional. She'd never mentioned her father, and Francesca was not so blinded by that old anger, or so suspicious of the person she had once loved, to allow herself to believe deep down that he would use his daughter to reach her. Teresa Becher, as she had introduced herself in her letter ('Teresa' spelled the Italian way), had cited only one person, their 'mutual friend, Dr. Katherine Rombeck,' as the individual who had suggested she get in touch with Signora Mancini. She would

bury her misgivings and adopt her friend Katya's confidence in this
young woman's integrity.

She replaced the receiver, still preoccupied, half-hearing its click
into the cradle. The sun slanted through the window of the pleasant
nook off her living room and lit up the large picture that covered
most of the wall in front of her desk, an overpowering watercolor by
Matthäus of Florence at the end of the war. It suited both her mood
and this new challenge—an isolated Ponte Vecchio blocked at each
end by piles of rubble, facing the bombed-out rows of houses on the
southern side of the Arno, all rendered in gray and bloody orange.
She'd bought it years ago in a fit of nostalgia. Florence after the fighting had stopped: denuded and partially crushed. And through it, in
her fantasy, Olga-Francesca met Jacopo once again, her brother and
friend.

The early-afternoon light was still bright enough to do some gardening. As she changed into her overalls, she stared at her reflection
in the bedroom mirror. What would Jacopo's daughter see? An old
woman, yes, but wiry, tall, square-shouldered. The black eyes were
still lively, defiant even, framed by a wealth of white hair. She nodded.
She liked what she saw.

Gardening was easy today. Last week she had spent many daylight
hours pruning trees and hedges and cutting the brambles that had tak-
en over in the spring. In past years, a gardener had done these chores
for her, but since her retirement two years ago, she had taken over
most of the work herself—even some of the heavier work—to prove
to herself that the old 'operative' was still strong in body as well as in
mind. Such strenuous gardening was more than an empty challenge.
She inhaled the perfumes of cut grass, of flowers, of upturned soil,
and a feeling of warmth came over her. As she trimmed the hedgerow
in front of her small house with special care, she prepared a suitable
entryway for young Teresa Becher.

ಬಲ

It was quite different from what she expected.

Teresa telephoned the next morning from her hotel in Florence, an-
nouncing her arrival. Her voice, bright and youthful as it had sounded
from New York, had a catch in it.

"Signora Mancini ... do you mind if I bring someone along for this interview?" And after another slight hesitation, "A friend. He's helping me with my project."

Francesca was stunned with disappointment. She hadn't expected the young woman to bring anyone else, least of all a man. Teresa seemed to look upon this meeting as a businesslike occasion. Instead, Francesca had looked forward to an intimate family event. In the hidden center of her being, where her marriage had endured through half a century of angry refusal, she had hoped to welcome Jacopo's daughter, at last. Unreasonably, she blamed her husband for allowing this intrusion, somehow feeling that Jacopo had failed her again.

The taxi pulled up before the wide opening between hedgerows. A slender young woman climbed out, and Francesca recognized Jacopo's build, the oval face and light brown hair, but she was taken aback by the bright blue eyes that met hers even from a distance. These were not eyes she knew, not Jacopo's eyes. Her anger had cooled, but there could be no cordial greeting.

Teresa stopped and waved. Turning slightly, she extended her arm with an inviting gesture to the tall man who extricated himself with some trouble from the small cab. Though she had been alerted a few hours before, Francesca felt a stab of disappointment.

The man turned after paying the driver and, as he passed through the gate, Francesca saw he was black. For a moment, she was swept by the old European prejudice against former colonials encroaching on the motherland. Despite her record as a crusading attorney for racial and political justice, there had always been impulses she had never fully acknowledged. But while she suppressed her awareness of the man's blackness, her anger at Jacopo and his daughter lingered. What could this role be in Terri's project? Fears and suspicions rose to possess her, born of years of insecurity.

"Welcome to Italy, welcome to Florence," she intoned, her face impassive, going through the ritual of introductions. "I'm Francesca Mancini, and this"—her lips thinned in the semblance of a smile—"I imagine, is Miss Teresa Becher." She turned to the man. "And you are ... ?"

Terri answered quickly, "This is my friend, Jeremy Taylor."

Francesca took his outstretched hand. Cool and correct, Signora Francesca Mancini, in every respect the distinguished retired jurist, was not, despite her words, a kind, welcoming hostess. Before inviting them to sit down, she led them to her cozy nook to admire Matthäus's painting on the wall above the antique desk, with the afternoon sun streaming in from the left. "If you truly wish to understand Gregor Matthäus, you must first understand his work." Pointedly, she lectured on the obvious while she gestured toward the painting. "The Ponte Vecchio. That's what it looked like just after the Allies arrived on that hot August day in 1944." She canted her head toward the sofa and chairs. "Do sit down." Her eyes flicked over the black man repeatedly, then she turned away, knowing she was being rude.

Despite her continuing disappointment, she forced them to engage in the usual small talk about their flight, their plans, and their accommodations in Florence. She kept up the polite veneer for the sake of her friend Katya, who had promoted this meeting with so much affection. She sensed that Teresa realized her mistake in bringing an uninvited companion. True, her unexpected visitor was a personable man in his thirties, whose manner gave her confidence. She noticed his unusual accent despite the long years that separated her from her brief English-speaking past. He soon explained it and engaged her interest by telling her about his home in the Caribbean. But though she might have gladly received him at any other time, she found it impossible at this meeting, which she had hoped would lead to an intimate reunion.

Why had he come along? Yes, by now it seemed likely that these two people had come for a formal interview, and yet she couldn't imagine that this man really was Terri's professional assistant. A business manager? No. A lover, more likely. That must be the real reason for this invasion. Yet, her sharp disappointment lingered.

When she finally allowed herself to look more clearly at Jacopo's daughter, she liked what she saw. The young woman wore a neat navy-blue blouse and beige skirt. She wore no make-up, an omission that only added to her charm. Now Teresa placed a new-looking leather briefcase on her knees and reached into her shoulder bag, extracting a notebook and a pen. Yes, the scribal tools were all there. She had come for a professional interview.

The man—Jeremy, wasn't it? Jeremy Taylor?—watched Teresa's every move. His intimate glances, though carefully concealed, told Francesca that they were indeed lovers.

"What can I tell you about Gregor Matthäus?" Signora Mancini began, realizing her duty. "As I said on the telephone, I admired the artist in him. That large watercolor I showed you when you came in is very precious to me. It catches the essence of that moment in history."

Terri felt the opportunity to create a bond with this woman, but instead, the conversation crossed at once into dangerous territory. "Yes, and with war in general, like the Matthäus in our house, *War and Peace*. It must have obsessed him." When she raised her eyes—her blue dipping into Francesca's black—Terri realized she had touched a raw nerve. The older woman's strong reaction reminded her of her father.

"In your house!" Francesca exclaimed, her face registering shock. "Even now!" She's been forced to abandon the painting to Jacob when she escaped from certain arrest. She had missed it.

Terri heard the outrage in Francesca's voice, but unlike Jacob's, it was instantly controlled. She masked her emotion quickly in an even voice.

"It's odd that you should mention it. I've seen that picture before … here, in Italy, before I came to America."

Terri sensed great depths beneath the surface of those words. She was afraid of trespassing further and withdrew. "Can you tell me a little more about Matthäus? I thought about getting in touch with you a couple of years ago when I ran across your newspaper article about him."

Francesca's forehead creased, then she sighed. "Oh, that article… It certainly caused a lot of trouble."

Another sore spot, another open wound! Terri felt as if she were walking barefoot on broken glass. But, concerned about the course of the conversation, their hostess bailed them out. "Your essay in the *New York Times* about Gregor Matthäus, Miss Bech—"

"Please call me Teresa. Actually I'm called Terri by my friends." She went on, avoiding Francesca's piercing glance. "I didn't know how to reach you for comments at the time, and I was busy on the job. But I didn't realize it would be so easy, that you and Dr. Rombeck—"

"Know each other?" Francesca interrupted the sentence with a laugh, her stiff posture relaxing. "We've been friends for many years. And that's how I found out about your fine essay on Matthäus. It's really excellent."

"Did you think so?" Terri grinned like a schoolgirl, unable to disguise her pleasure.

"Something cool?"

All three started as Anna, Francesca's housekeeper, matronly in a black dress, interrupted the interview, asking whether anyone wanted refreshments.

Francesca, the meticulous hostess, elaborated on Anna's offer. "A glass of chilled white wine, perhaps? Apple cider? An orangeade?"

They accepted a glass of orangeade, and Anna withdrew to fill their requests.

For Francesca, this was a welcome interruption, because she was not yet ready for the inevitable moment when her connection with Teresa's father would be brought up—a dread that had also colored her previous response. But she decided to take the initiative.

"You know that I was once married to your father."

"Yes." That was all Teresa managed to say.

The young man, Jeremy, spoke up, apparently to relieve his lover's discomfort. "There's surely something more to be known than just that you and Dr. Becher were once married."

Momentarily, anger welled up again inside Francesca, her tone oozing sarcasm. "Oh? And what might that be?" Her manner proclaimed her thought: *Who is this man to question me?*

It was not that he was a man that angered her, or even that he was black. He was interfering. Who was he—not even a Becher—to mix into a family matter, to intrude into that closed and locked chamber that Jacopo's daughter had so thoughtlessly violated? Until now she'd been confident she could manage the situation. She'd been trained to do just that by decades of dealing with defendants' intimate lives without allowing herself to be touched. She was a successful defense attorney for men and women accused of political crimes, a profession she'd always considered an extension of her service in the Resistance.

And although she often recognized herself in her clients, especially the women, she never allowed them to come close to her. Teresa and her escort were coming too close, and she could not endure it. "Forgive me, Ms. Mancini, but I object to your tone." The place was suddenly very quiet. "I'm concerned about Terri. But I guess you think of me as an intruder. I'm curious to know… would you consider me an intruder if—"

"—you were white?" she coolly completed the sentence. Francesca spoke like a lawyer, the image of her long-dead father. "Of course, I would. I've defended many people like you. With all my heart and soul." She realized she had turned on this man with excessive vehemence, and she couldn't let this meeting with Jacopo's daughter get out of hand. So she relented and ended her sentence with a courteous smile while Jeremy withdrew, frowning, and casually put his arm on the back of the sofa behind Teresa.

Anna appeared at this moment serving their drinks, her dark eyes resting, worried, on her friend and employer. But Francesca went on seemingly unperturbed. "To learn more about Matthäus's life, it might be more helpful if you looked up a German art dealer named Egon Scheffel. He was Gregor's lover for more than ten years until Gregor's death. He still lives in Florence, quite an old man now—old like the rest of us."

Francesca thought about Scheffel. They had become friends in recent years, though she still felt resentful that he had tried to use Jacob as an intermediary, decades earlier.

"I have his address." She walked over to her elegant desk in the alcove to jot it down. "You know," she said in a conversational tone, more warmly than at any time since their arrival as she handed Teresa the slip with the address, "you're really taking on a complicated job with this book project of yours. Matthäus was so many different things—he had so many unexpected sides. A fine painter, a warm person, community-minded, yet… He first came to us to seek cover about a year before the Allies took the city. Survival had become more and more precarious for him with his way of life."

Teresa leaned toward her. "I've been wondering about that for some time. How did he manage? Who protected him?"

She answered proudly. "We did, mostly. We hid him when he took off his German uniform and went underground early in '44." She watched Teresa. Time stood still as the young woman took her slip of paper with the address and carefully put it into her briefcase. The two people were getting up to leave. As if trying to catch a fleeting moment before it was too late, Teresa stopped and laid a light hand on her sleeve, as if beseeching her. "Oh ... one more question." Stammering a bit, seemingly intimidated by her intense gaze, "Ah ... have you written anything more about Matthäus by any chance? If so, I'd love to see it, Signora Mancini."

She felt as if a shadow had passed over her face. There had been enough trouble and tragedy as a result of the first essay. The Canwell Committee and Gerald Dougherty had found her name because of her first editorial about Gregor, and that piece of writing had almost destroyed her. Now, the daughter of the man who betrayed her to that same committee wondered if she had written any more incriminating material. "No! Never!" She was emphatic.

Teresa clearly longed to dissolve the space between them, and Francesca sensed they might both feel the same, straining to speak the word that would let them cross the bridge that could connect them. But the moment passed for them both.

"A taxi?" she asked politely. "I apologize, but I don't like to drive at dusk if I can help it."

"We'll walk to the station." Teresa declared. "We've got strong legs and good shoes. The weather is lovely."

They reached the door.

"Yes," said Francesca. "It's less than an hour on foot. A cool, sunny day." Seized by sudden doubts and regrets, she belatedly tried to make amends. She wanted to end it pleasantly after all.

"Good-bye. Thank you for your visit. I lead such a solitary life."

But that was not enough. She felt she had only a few words left and very few moments to say them. "If you have a moment, Teresa, let me know about your visit to Egon Scheffel. I do hope he'll help."

Francesca's two visitors ambled down the country road while their hostess, standing very still in the door, watched their receding silhouettes.

It had not been a discovery. It had simply been an interview that failed.

ഇന്റ

Jeremy held Terri's hand as, two days later, the cab wound its way through Florence's chaotic downtown streets on their way to Egon Scheffel. "No matter how much I love you, this is the last time. Perhaps this art dealer is different. At least I understand he's gay. These Europeans put me on edge."

"I'm not sure Francesca reacted to your race, Jeremy. Mostly, it was my thoughtlessness. It was wrong of me to bring you without telling her. She expected a more intimate meeting."

He shrugged, unconvinced. "An old revolutionary like her. She should be ashamed."

"I don't know yet how revolutionary she actually was. But you're right. Something was wrong."

"They're all alike."

Scheffel, however, was different. He greeted them cordially in elegant English touched only lightly by a German intonation and led them into a spacious salon. Three walls were hung with large canvases and delicate prints by Gregor Matthäus. They sank on silk-covered, green lounge chairs, astonished at the radiance of the display. A large mirror across from them on the fourth wall reflected an abundance of light from a sparkling chandelier. Even in his eighties, Egon Scheffel loved flamboyant surroundings, dazzling illumination.

The old man looked at them expectantly. "Fräulein Becher, Herr Taylor. You come recommended by my dear friend, the distinguished Signora Mancini. That's a high recommendation. What can I do for you?"

Terri explained quickly about her project and past work on Matthäus, including a deft reference to the *New York Times*. "Now I'm on a full-scale biography and there's much to tell, don't you think?"

"Inde-e-ed!" Scheffel's single, long-drawn word conveyed layers of cordial meaning.

A maid served drinks. Their host raised a glass and peered at the amber liquid. "I love good scotch." He turned to Terri. "I remember having it with your father many years ago. The meeting was memorable, though it led nowhere."

"A meeting with Father? What about?" Terri leaned forward, her gaze intense.

"Ah, an old story, Fräulein Becher. I'd thought your father, as Francesca Mancini's husband, might intervene ... for Gregor. But it seemed those ties had been severed."

"Intervene?" Terri was determined not to let this go.

"As I said, it never happened. Nothing came of our meeting but the memory of good scotch."

Jeremy's chuckle echoed Egon's mischievous smile. He clearly felt more at ease than in Francesca's salon two days before. "Well, Herr Scheffel, that's why we're here, to find out all we can about your friend, this remarkable painter." He gestured at the walls hung with treasures.

The old man straightened to face them as they sat next to each other on the comfortable chairs. "What do you want to know? You've spoken with Signora Mancini, surely? For many years that wretched article—you know about that, yes?"

Terri nodded. "Yes. The article in *Il Tempo*."

"Precisely. How shall I put it? The consequences of that wretched article entangled her in a network of conflict. Gregor was such a fine person! A great artist, yes, everyone agrees, and he wasn't—he was never—what people said he was."

"What DID people say he was?" Terri was again taking notes, her glass of scotch untouched.

Silence. Then Scheffel spoke at last. "A spy. He was supposed to have been a spy. It was a witch hunt because he loved men."

The silence became oppressive. Terri stopped writing and glanced at their host. He looked like someone who had grown inward. Tall and broad-shouldered in his younger years, he had collapsed into himself. But for all his grandfatherly appearance, he seemed lively, almost impish, as he held his glass delicately poised above his gently protruding stomach. The smile he turned on them was less mocking than benign.

"And he was not just a homosexual."

Terri smiled to herself as he pronounced the word with awkward precision.

"He was also a German. And you know what?" He paused with a wink. "We Germans lost the war."

They waited some more before he announced, "Gregor Matthäus was a great artist. He was also a wonderful man."

Before he could say anything further, Terri said, "I know that article well. I read it in *Il Tempo* a few years ago. Was there nothing to it?"

Egon drained his glass. "It was a sad and bad article. It turned a man's natural search for protection into treachery and subversion. He was saved by so many, not all of them in one camp." Egon spoke at great length about his many efforts to erase the effect of that article. "It was scurrilous," he continued. "But Gregor never lost faith in his friends—they lost faith in him even though he never did them any harm."

Terri began to protest. "But Signora Mancini—"

Scheffel raised his hand. "As I said, all kinds of people worked at great risk to protect him: partisans, churches, even some Germans in high places, and especially well-heeled patrons who loved his work. But it wasn't his fault that he was later taken up by Neo-Fascists and portrayed as a victim of the Communists."

As they looked on, their host's face became visibly transformed, anguished and pleading. "Gregor's friends deserted him. Even before he became very ill in the early seventies, he felt lonely and betrayed." Scheffel suddenly burst out with a passionate and eloquent appeal. "Please, Fräulein Becher, for the sake of your father, who admired him, be kind to Gregor Matthäus. Restore his good name. He was exploited and isolated in the end."

"But how can you count Signora Mancini among your friends?" Jeremy asked logically. "If, as you say, she started it all?"

Egon answered, brows drawn together. "We talked about it many times. She knew Gregor and loved him at one time and still loves his art. It's up to her to explain and excuse, maybe, what she did to him."

Terri intervened to ask him to talk at last about Matthäus the painter, his work, his style, his place in the art world. "Please! So all our time won't be swallowed up by this controversy."

Egon Scheffel nodded enthusiastically, and they continued for a whole hour talking about Gregor Matthäus's life: how it felt to be an onlooker who cared for him, to watch an artist grow, how he turned from his splendid watercolors to those magnificent oils that ensured his reputation.

"It all got undermined by politics, though, didn't it?" Jeremy returned to the original topic.

Egon shrugged and gave him a wry smile. "You're right, unfortunately. Now I depend on the two of you to correct that mistake."

They left with cordial farewells.

ဆဟ

"I must see Signora Mancini once more." Terri spoke firmly, tossing her purse on the bed when they got back to their hotel room. "Our last meeting was a waste, a failure. I should have told her much sooner about your coming along, perhaps on my first call from New York. It was inexcusably stupid—not that I brought you, darling," she inserted quickly, "but that I didn't tell her in time. Our talk with Scheffel opened up a lot about Matthäus, but it's obviously incomplete. And all of it leaves me still empty-handed as far as the family matter is concerned. That's a good half of the reason we came here."

"Oh? And here I thought it was mostly the book... !" He grinned. "Well, go if you must." Jeremy moved the purse to the night table and stretched out on the bed, head propped on two pillows, legs dangling from the side, "But you have to go alone. I won't go through that again."

Her voice was grave. "Of course, you don't have to. I was so glad when you spoke up. Having you there was a tremendous support for me—meeting my father's first wife who'd been a ghost for most of my life. I'm truly grateful. But, no, you don't have to go through that again."

She sat at the mahogany desk eyeing the telephone. "As you said, for an old dissident, which she surely was, even a slight hesitation should be out of the question."

"I probably exaggerate."

"No, you don't. I saw it, too. It was just muddled by my stupid error. But still, I can't let it go at that. I must see her. It's about my life."

"Sure. I know, love. Go ahead."

Relieved, she picked up the phone.

Chapter 23
Two Women

"She's coming back alone. I knew she would." Francesca turned to Anna with a triumphant smile. "She seems a likeable and competent young woman, don't you think?"

Francesca's housekeeper politely agreed. "She seemed so, but I only caught a glimpse of her when I served the orangeade. She was sitting on the sofa with that dark gentleman's arm behind her. That was unexpected, wasn't it? It all seemed so tense that I'm surprised you're looking forward to seeing her again."

Francesca didn't explain. "She'll be here in a little over an hour if she takes a taxi from the station."

The prediction proved nearly accurate. Precisely one hour and twenty minutes later, at four in the afternoon, Terri rang the doorbell.

They sat together in the sunny living room. Terri made herself comfortable on the sofa where she had sat before with her back to the window; Francesca sat facing her, the low coffee table between them. At first, they avoided difficult subjects. Francesca asked about her absent companion, apparently feeling the need to explain and even apologize. "I was just so surprised when you both arrived. I had hoped to see you alone, Teresa."

"Call me Terri, please! *I* apologize. I should have asked earlier. It was very rude of me. I know how you might feel not knowing him …the fine person he is…"

Her hostess' narrowed eyes, the slight crease in her forehead and that appraising look told Terri that Francesca had caught her diffident tone and knew she was alluding obliquely to Jeremy's race. Her own temporizing while speaking to a potential adversary reminded her of her father, and she guessed that Francesca had made the same association. Her hostess's vehement reply confirmed her surmise.

"Oh no, it wasn't that! I've known and defended people of many races. He just seemed… like such a stranger. I was merely, I must admit, a little disappointed. I had hoped we'd first get acquainted *à deux*. But I'm glad I met him and ... here we are."

Terri straightened. Her life was on the line, the success or failure of her personal mission. The first thing to do, she now knew, was to be wholly clear in talking to this woman whose black eyes under the crown of white hair penetrated hers, but with some warmth. Terri had to say what she had to say and remain herself.

"Signora Mancini," she began, and was struck by the loudness of her voice. For a second, once more, they marched in review before her inner eye: Aunt Katya, Jim Ahern, the lawyer, her new friend Mike Simonetti. The thought of them gave her strength. "I hope you will understand the admission I'm about to make, my 'confession' really ... I wasn't truthful about Jeremy."

"You don't need to, my dear ..." Francesca began, as expected, but Terri was a child no longer.

"I do need to, Signora Mancini. I needed him with me. He is my fiancé, and this meeting, *cara signora*, with my father's former wife who'd been shrouded in secrecy for most of my life—I needed his support."

The air was heavy with silence.

"Please understand," she pleaded. "I had no idea what you would be like. I knew you were an important and successful attorney, but that was all. At the time I knew nothing about your marriage with my father, but I did know I could count on Jeremy if things went terribly wrong."

The older woman raised her hand without words, her nod indicating she had accepted the explanation. She understood but was not over that initial disappointment. She changed the subject. "How was your time with Egon Scheffel? More than good scotch and great paintings?"

"I learned a lot. Thank you for the introduction."

The conversation stalled, and Terri, turning her head, followed Francesca's glance toward the alcove. The old lady's strategy was clear: the canvas of the embattled Ponte Vecchio would serve as a means of moving into safer territory—reminiscences about a war that had ended long before Terri was born. Francesca's voice was only a murmur as she gazed at the painting. "That war. Hard for a woman."

"I believe it."

Terri leaned against the back of the sofa, and Francesca went on speaking in a low voice about her clandestine work during the Second World War, sidestepping the awkward subjects—Matthäus, her father, Communism.

"At first I helped rescue soldiers in the field—Allied pilots who had jumped from burning planes and were hiding in the woods—that sort of thing. Also spy missions in German headquarters where I lowered their suspicions because I was so well liked."

Francesca watched Teresa shift in her seat, jittery, impatient. The young woman clearly wanted to talk about more treacherous subjects, about Matthäus and Jacopo. She drew herself erect. "My name was Olga. That was my code name. There was one moment..." She broke off. The exploding shell! How could she explain it to Teresa? Had Jacopo told his daughter about this at all? By her blank face, Francesca was sure he had not, and she had again wandered onto dangerous ground.

She was saved by Anna, who asked whether her guest cared to stay for dinner. "My Anna always cooks plentifully, so there's sure to be enough."

"That's very kind, Signora, but I mustn't stay so long. A cup of tea would be lovely, though." They chatted about neutral topics until the tea was served. Then the young woman plunged further into forbidden territory. "Yes, we learned a lot about Gregor Matthäus, but Egon Scheffel left so much out. What was his role, Signora Mancini? I must talk to you about it. His story is full of contradictions."

"How?" she was tense now. An imaginative leap sent her back fifty years to an investigator's office in Seattle. What was his name? Dougherty? She remembered a round face with a perpetual smile. She balanced her teacup on one knee and reached for a canapé.

Jacopo's daughter pursued her quest, innocent but relentless. "Forgive my indiscretion, but Herr Scheffel seemed to suggest that your article set off a lot of bad rumors about Gregor Matthäus— tragic, he said. But at the same time he insisted that you two were very special friends."

Crash!

Francesca leaped to her feet. She had knocked the cup of tea to the floor.

"Signora Mancini!" Teresa put down her cup and rose to help, but Anna was already there, muttering soothing words as she picked up the delicate white shards and sponged the damp spot on the rug. For a moment, Francesca was crestfallen. Family china ... another loss. Then she sat again and gestured for Teresa to do the same.

"You asked about the paradox, just before that crash? The truth is, Scheffel and I liked each other and still do. And I loved, still love and admire ... Gregor."

She could not repress a sigh and went on, resolutely ignoring the broken cup. "My article, like my feelings, merely registered Gregor Matthäus's role; it didn't create it. But I had also been Gregor's friend and tried to support him for quite some time, always aware of his genius, loving him for his enormous potential. Until ..." She paused to catch her breath.

Teresa folded her hands and waited. The afternoon sun behind her cast mobile shadows of tree branches on the white living room wall. The young woman raised her cup, holding it to her nose to inhale the strong sweet fragrance, while a wisp of steam curled about her face.

The pause lasted nearly half a minute, and Francesca kept her waiting still. She drew a sharp breath, feeling a sudden surge of energy. She opened her mouth several times but could find no words. When she finally did, her voice came out unexpectedly harsh. "It happened later in Seattle when I was your father's wife." She turned her head aside, hoping that Teresa would somehow catch her meaning without further explanation, would stop the interrogation. The sun traveled lower, and Jacopo's daughter fixed her eyes on the wet spot on the rug.

"Signora Mancini, I need to know what happened." The girl spoke deliberately, insistently, sitting straight-backed on the sofa, her head held high. "It's been everybody's secret long enough—only Mother and I were left out.""

Francesca could not speak, for the word 'betrayal' would surely force itself through her lips again as it had almost done a moment before. Matthäus had, after all, betrayed her and her friends twice: first, by cozying up to the enemy and, secondly, by having precipitated, personally and directly, the betrayal of 1948. Jacopo had not been alone in that.

She went on in a hoarse voice, elaborating, explaining, "Gregor lived under a cloud, a homosexual man, a deserter, hiding from the Germans and the Fascists. When he first emerged from hiding in parks and houses reduced to rubble by artillery exchanges, he came out as a free man who didn't have to hide. He moved among us as an admired artist and friend. That was before he became estranged from us and turned to the other side." She paused, enduring Terri's intense scrutiny. She exhaled a long gust of air. "Or so we thought. But now I've come to believe that Gregor was used. Scheffel is right about that. I never really thought so before, but when you get old, you see things more clearly. The anti-communist front encouraged him to think he was a victim—our victim, supposedly—but, you see, he never came forward to protest that they misused him for their purposes."

Like Terri, she sat very still, and they looked at each other, knowing they were approaching a crisis. The room, crowded with furniture, seemed to shrink and enclose them, almost like a confessional.

Francesca half closed her eyes. There had been an earlier occasion when she came close to accepting the artist's innocence. She had last seen Gregor Matthäus at an exhibition of ten years of his work in a private Florentine gallery.

Yes ... autumn ... 1974, I think. It feels like our old days together back in the late summer of 1945. Men and women ambling from picture to picture, leaning in to examine them or huddled in groups holding small cups of coffee or glasses of wine, talking in subdued voices. Along the high walls, under the vaulted, decorated ceilings, Gregor has hung row upon row of beautiful canvases. It's been so long since I've seen an exhibition of his work.

There he is! Standing with his back to me, he seems unchanged. Still slender, still wearing the denim jacket with its upturned collar. One corner of the green ascot—surely not the same ascot?—sticking out at the back of his neck as he assesses the best position for one overwhelmingly large print in his grandest style: huge, with the face of an angry god.

"Is that really a print?" I turn to my companion, an older artist and admirer of Matthäus. "It's so big."

Emilio laughs. "Of course it's a print. I assure you, Francesca." He tosses his gray mane with a quick movement of his head and looks at me, eyebrows raised, lips quirked upward.

Gregor must have heard us and turns to face us. I gasp. I haven't seen him for such a long time, and the change is shocking, far deeper than I could have imagined. His face is drained of color; his lips thin and compressed. Only the golden flick of his eyes remains alive.

"Gregor!" I am startled by the urgency in my voice.

He holds out his arms. "Francesca! Olga! Where have you been? It's been forever!"

True. I've avoided him all those many years since my return from America. And yet, somehow, it seems all right now, almost as if we could start all over and forget all the bitterness, the turmoil and the pain.

I turn to introduce Emilio, only to find that he has left discreetly for the other side of the room.

"I'll show you around." Gregor takes my arm ever so gently. "It's good to see you."

We walk slowly from one print to another, from one drawing to another, from one of the early watercolors to his splendid oils, stopping while he explains, gesturing with both hands and now taking my arm again. Egon Scheffel arrives, every inch the manager, in a tailored dark suit and a handsome paisley tie. He rubs his hands, elated as he surveys the wealth of art around the room. Yet he glances at Gregor and his face betrays concern.

"Francesca Mancini! How good of you to come."

Suddenly, as if on cue, Gregor Matthäus wheels around to face me, placing both hands on my shoulders.

"Why did you do it, Francesca? Couldn't you believe in me? Couldn't you believe?"

"Dear Gregor, how could I believe? You were in all the great houses—on the other side—and there were those strange happenings, disappearances—you know."

The light in his eyes seems to grow fainter, and I falter to a stop.

His hands on my shoulders grip me hard. "I want you to see. All of you! I haven't much time." Egon Scheffel moves nearer, his brow furrowed with worry.

"Why talk about it now, Gregor? I was in the prosecutor's office in those early years and we didn't prosecute, did we? I got back from America, a fugitive because of your word. At least that's what I was told when I returned to Italy. And yet, I... we... didn't prosecute."

"It wasn't me personally, Francesca. It was done in my name."

"How?" I lean toward him, eager to hear his explanation, his confession.

He releases me and turns to Egon, supporting himself on his friend as he extends his arm "I sold a great many paintings like these"—his lifted arm describes a circle—"to men and women of substance who often had connections with foreign intelligence—in England, in America, in many places. These people told me I was known to be a fugitive, that the East German police wanted me... all kinds of things. And they got me into politics I knew nothing about. But I never mentioned your name, Francesca, my friend Olga, my support..."

I meet his eyes, red with fatigue, his face pleading.

"I'm only a painter, my dear. Not a lawyer, not a politician, only a painter."

Opaque to be sure, these words, his last, to me. He shakes his head and turns back to Egon, who supports him as they move toward the door. Three months later, Gregor Matthäus is dead.

৪৩০৪৪

Francesca feared her reverie might have lasted for minutes, but a glance at her listener reassured her. The young woman's expression had not changed. "I mourned him, Teresa. He was a great loss, and I deplore the years of hostility. Still, odd things happened at the time. I still believe I was right when I wrote the article, but I also believe he recovered his senses."

She rose from her chair and paced. After a few moments, she stopped and looked steadily at Teresa. She felt like a very old woman, resisting the temptation to revisit a destructive past. She tried once more to explain the tangled moral situation.

"Gregor was friendly with the other side," she reiterated, "but I also think he was used, set up to entrap us, even in the States, where all they knew of him was that he was someone rumored to be 'hunted' by Communists."

Jacopo's daughter scribbled diligently.

For a few moments, Francesca felt calmer, but the anger came over her again. "At a crucial moment they used his name in the States to condemn some of us for hounding him—an act of subversion, they said. My article, how did they find that? How did they know about him over there in America? He is practically unknown there even now. I have no idea. Gregor seems to have worried a lot about being hounded, and he singled me out because of the article. Yes, of course, he was used, but, as I said, at some point he could have done more to help." She interrupted herself, her voice rough yet solemn to her ear. "Perhaps he didn't mean to direct his fire at us—hobnobbing with former fascists, gossiping about 'commie sympathizers' to those who were connected with American Intelligence—but I was unable to escape its effect. Nor were many of my friends. Some of them, close to me, were destroyed in the end."

There! She had almost said it. But she would let it drop. Fifty years, after all. Jacopo's lovely daughter. Her father had never been forthright, never open, not in the best of times, and his daughter had dissembled, too, about Jeremy, though she'd had the courage to 'confess.'

Francesca could sense the anger welling up inside her again—anger suppressed for five decades, choosing this encounter to erupt. Yes, like lava inside a volcano it came, slowly building, relentlessly rising. She looked at the young woman in front of her in the declining sunlight, her eyes now framed by dark shadows.

"I have two stories," she told Teresa Becher, daughter of her husband—he was still hers; she had no other. "They're both about me and your father, but one is also about Gregor. No, Teresa, Terri, don't take notes!"

Terri put down her pen.

Francesca felt her face stiffen. "Jacopo and I almost died together. When we met near the end of the war, I was a courier with important documents, and your father had to drive me in his jeep close to the German lines not far north of here. The Germans spotted the jeep and began shelling. One struck so near that we both ran for it, into the woods. The next shell almost killed us. We clung together. It was, in effect, our marriage." Francesca did not explain further, nor did she continue. She heard a slight noise, an intake of breath, and she knew that Teresa would want to find out more about this, at least to give vent to her feelings, to a natural response, but she quashed it all with the authority of her eyes and her raised hand.

The young woman on the sofa across from her was another woman's daughter, and yet she felt at this moment that Teresa belonged also to her and that she must rescue her from the pain she was about to inflict. She could never truly be hers—the gulf between them was too wide—but she could treat her gently, and allow her to keep her father, and then let her go. Still, much as she fought with herself against the temptation, she could not prevent herself from speaking to her of her father's disgrace, and perhaps her own. She might have been able to suppress the urge to inflict pain—pain on the father by inflicting it on his child—if Terri had not interrupted.

"Signora Mancini." Her voice was tight, anxious. "Please! What was the other story? I've waited since I was a child."

Francesca said it straight out. Her voice was flat.

"Your father betrayed me at the hearing."

"What?" Teresa's voice registered total shock and her stricken face showed clearly that she had received an intolerable blow. "My father—a betrayer? It can't be! How? How is that possible?"

"He testified I had been a Communist. He did so at the Un-American Committee 'trials' in Seattle in 1948."

"Were you?" Teresa asked softly. She rose from the sofa.

Francesca confronted that tensely drawn face, that slender body. *We're almost the same height.* She replied to Teresa's near-whisper. "No, not then or since. All they knew was that I had attacked Matthäus. But they asked about my past. My distant past—my student days in the Movement and so forth. No one knew about that except Jacopo—from intimate talk in the lovers' night."

Her voice broke when she heard the daughter's cry. It was brief, a sharp sound hovering in the evening's stillness like an echo.

She thought of Jacopo, the man with whom she had shared both grave and bed. Had they evened the score? She had struck out at him in anger, and his daughter's cry cut through the churning images in her mind. It was done. Quick like a murder. Once again, it was too late for regrets. This time, too, it was irrevocable—for her now.

But, unlike Jacob, she still had a moment's reprieve. Seeing the pale young woman in the waning sunset, her eyes brimming with suppressed emotion, Francesca was able to cross the room and take her in her arms. For a short time, the two women stood close together. Teresa's body shook briefly, but she was tearless. Nor could Francesca embellish that moment with tears. The young woman in her arms might have been her daughter, but she was not.

She pulled away, stroked Terri's hair, saying with affection, teasingly almost, "Hang tough," that old American wartime slang returning to her from half a century ago. "Hang tough!" she repeated, seriously this time. "We must live with it." And she spoke to her as if she, too, were her mother—mother to her husband's daughter.

The recognition of her loss flashed through Francesca, and she knew at last what this radical break in her life had cost. Could she have acted otherwise? There had been no crossroads in that past that she could recognize, no paths back to the beginnings: the vermouth and the laughter in the sunlit piazza, union with Jacopo in the train in North Dakota, the friends left behind. Had she swept too clean? Too injudicious in tossing out one future in exchange for another? Did she hover too long over the injury done to her? The future that had stretched before her then was as bleak as the future that enveloped her now. But a glimmer of light remained, a sudden fierce desire to prolong the embrace with Terri.

It would not be over. Somehow, she'd see to that. Nothing ever ends except human breath in its time. The love that had come to her at this crucial moment would remain as long as she shared this world with Jacopo's Teresa. But for now she must let her go.

Terri sensed a change. The arms that held her, she now understood, belonged to that ghostly woman whose presence had cast a shadow over her life. Still, she sensed in that vibrant old body a strength beyond knowing that had kept a failed love alive for half a century. Unlike Lisa, her mother, unlike herself, the person she had discovered endured like granite, able to love without forgiving, knowing above all that Jacob's betrayal could never be forgiven in its destruction of the lives around him. Yet at last, at the end of her quest for truth, Terri also knew that however great his love for his family might have been, her father had to live part of his life underground, away from her and her mother, in a space wholly inside himself. Francesca's embrace and the insight they had shared during the long and difficult afternoon led Terri to see her father's lifelong inferno as she had never done. She was his daughter after all; therefore she had to share in his loss. But she had also gained the chance to recover some part of the love, her shadow-mother's love, that he had forfeited by his own action.

The two women dropped their arms and Terri reached for her coat.

As Francesca watched her slowly walk away down the road, she knew she might not see her husband's daughter again. A moment's regret made her want to call out. Then, slowly, she turned inside.

Teresa will remain her own person, too. This much she now knew about their kinship. Bereft yet hopeful, she wished her well.

ঙ০ঙ৪

It was late when Terri returned to the hotel. She had walked to the station and sat on a lonely bench beside the road watching a few late birds scavenging in the early twilight.

Jeremy saw she was drained of emotion when she entered their room. His gesture to embrace her froze when he noticed her pallor. At her nod, he touched her face and left her, knowing she would need to work things out for herself.

Part Four

Homecoming

"It's a long way back—beyond childhood."

Chapter 24
Coming Together

"Without Jeremy," Terri mumbled. There was nothing she could do or say even to herself to justify including him at this time. She admired him for discreetly leaving her to her musing. He must have sensed that she needed her privacy to work through the feelings and implications of that second meeting with Francesca, something he could only distantly understand. She loved him, wanted him, but she could no longer include him in this part of her life. That long, torturous afternoon with Francesca had matured her in a way she had never thought possible. She felt vulnerable at the thought of her father as a betrayer: vulnerable as a human being, as a woman, and as a daughter.

Earlier, she had reacted to her father's secrecy, his refusal to live openly, his exclusion of her mother and herself from his vital core, and she had fled to Jeremy in her pain. She'd flown to him all the way across the continent, but now that she knew the truth, he could do nothing to console her. She had to go home, had to see her father. She needed to confront him, more than at any time since she began her sleuthing, to attack him for his hysteria, for the transgression she now knew to be real—or perhaps to console him for it.

Jeremy returned to the hotel room an hour later.

"Please forgive me, Jeremy. I must shorten our trip." When she saw his face fall, she quickly amended, "Let's stay another day in Florence but not go on to Rome. I have to go home and talk to Jacob. Perhaps I can see him ..."

And when he continued to look crestfallen, "I'll change my ticket, but you don't have to. As for me," she repeated, "I MUST talk to Jacob NOW."

She had never called her father by his first name or thought of him that way before, as a man in his own right, no longer her origin, an intimate part of herself. She could at last see him as he was: desperately human, a failed human being.

"I have to make this call, Jeremy, just this once. When this is settled we'll go on with our lives." She looked at him with her clear eyes.

"OK," he said, his voice still heavy with disappointment. "I'll meet you back in New York. Just promise me that we'll come back here together." He pulled her to him and kissed her. "I'll miss you."

She hugged him close. "I'll miss you."

Her hand reached for the phone as it had when she called Francesca. This time it was to Seattle. Her mother answered.

"It's Terri, Mom. Let me speak to Dad."

They spoke briefly. Both parents would come, but what she had to say was for Jacob alone. They would meet in New York.

༄ഗ

Jacob strode into the lobby of the Gramercy Park Hotel, looking fit despite his eighty-three years. Terri, his Terri, stood waiting, her face and body in profile. How elegant, how beautiful she was! He felt stunned.

She must have recognized his step, for she turned. "Thanks for meeting me here," she said in place of a greeting. "It's a long way from Seattle."

"I came to you," he answered in a low voice. "How many times did you come to me ... to us? I can't even count them."

They said nothing more until they sat opposite each other at a table in the bar. For a moment her attention seemed to drift as she looked out at the park on the other side of the street.

If he thought her mind had wandered, he was mistaken.

"I saw Francesca," she said simply, facing him again, "I know."

Something moved inside him as if a key had turned in a lock and he was open to her and vulnerable.

"Terri, my dear," his voice pleaded. "I came to meet you to preserve our friendship—those years when I told you about the history I once taught and the responsibility that knowledge brings. I let you share what I learned in the war so you could work to prevent another." It seemed strange to him as it surely did to her to speak in this way of their past bonding.

Terri curbed her feelings. Too much had happened between them. "Yes, Dad, we were close at one time."

"I don't ask to be forgiven ... by any of you three—you and Francesca and your mom. You've all been victims of my failure, my betrayal."

He saw her face harden. "I never thought it possible that my father was a betrayer."

"No, *no*, NO!" He spoke loud enough for people to turn. "Or rather, YES! I betrayed the person I loved. But, it wasn't deliberate. It crept up on me unawares."

Another silence. But when she opened her mouth to speak, he cut across her unspoken words.

"You now know the end, Terri. I must tell you the beginning. It goes back, far back. Much farther back than Francesca, even the war, even America ..."

She waited, then he spoke again: "Germany. Jews. Everyone knows about the Holocaust. I can't claim the usual exemption. Our whole family got away in time."

"So?" said his expectant judge, his daughter.

Their drinks arrived. They raised their heads as the waitress left. Their eyes locked.

His hand lay on the table. Terri ignored it.

"There have been times in my life, Terri, times when things happened. I can't really explain, except that they covered me with shame. This happened just before Crystal Night and my brief imprisonment. I was stopped in the street by a uniformed SS man. He looked at me in a peculiar way, then grabbed me. Without asking for identification, he shoved me into the back seat of a small sedan parked at the curb.

"My head hit the window on the other side, and the SS man got in beside me. Another man who wore a plain jacket and tie sat behind the wheel.

"'A mistake!' I shouted in a high-pitched voice. The man beside me barked, 'Shut up!!'

"No one else heard us, of course.

"We sped through the familiar streets, and I saw cars and buses and clumps of people and boys on bicycles—normal, every-day, as if nothing had happened, and yet something terrible, something frightening had happened to *me*, and I had no idea what it was about.

"We stopped in front of a large building. '*Raus!* Get out!' I was dragged out of the car and hustled through the entrance. It looked like a post office, but it was really a police station or something like that. The SS man grabbed my upper arm and hustled me to a small room. He slammed the door behind us." Jacob massaged his biceps. "I feel that grip on my arm even now. I still hear him as he whirled to face me. It was more than a shout, more like a scream. 'Now, tell me about Gustav!'"

Jacob took in a breath and looked at Terri, seeking her response. She met his eyes. "We know how it went from there, don't we, Dad?"

"Not quite. It was all about a duplicating machine."

"A what, Dad?"

"A copying machine. 'Sir,' I beseeched the man. 'Believe me! I don't know any Gustav.'

"My head snapped to one side and I felt a stinging blow on my left cheek, then another from that bony, flat hand on the right side. It was then that I feared for my life.

"'Sir,' I said submissively, hating myself, 'believe me. I don't know any Gustav.'

"'Liar!' he screamed. 'Then tell me the name of the man you protect! That whole gang of commies! We know you have a duplicating machine.'

"He had struck pay dirt, Terri. I remembered. Three years before, when I was active in my Youth Movement Group—the one I told you about—our leader who, I guess, was a Communist, asked me to hide a duplicating machine in our basement. That was long ago, and it had been out of the house for at least two years. I'd been scared and asked them to move it some place else." He looked up with a sad smile. "Sounds familiar, doesn't it?"

Terri bit her lips, and Jacob continued, "I shook my head at the man. 'No! No! Not me!' At that point, his partner in civvies appeared. 'Let me talk to him.' He was very smooth. 'Tell us what you know' or words to that effect, 'and you can go about your business.'

"'But sir!' Again I tried to assure him that I knew nothing, that I was the wrong person. 'Nothing about the duplicating machine? We've been swamped by pamphlets with underground messages.' He finally asked for my *Kennkarte*, the new identification. He looked at it and his eyes widened. With an oath, he hurried out of the room. I could hear yelling.

"The door opened and the uniformed man appeared again. I tried to hide my trembling. Did their memories reach back to the time that machine was in my family's basement? Fortunately, I was not put to the test. He shouted at me, 'Get out of here, you commie!'

"It was like a miracle, but they let me go. I ran. If they had touched me once more, I would have spilled everything I knew from two years before. Who knows? Maybe that machine was the same one they were looking for, which had simply been moved someplace else." Jacob took a sip from his glass. He looked at her and sighed.

"So, Terri, things like this have haunted me all my life. I've had nightmare versions of that arrest, that interrogation, even in the war, even as an officer in the Army."

"Why didn't you confide in Mom and me? Don't you think we would have understood?"

"I never felt safe ... there always seemed to be powerful forces outside my knowledge and control."

Again they were silent together. Glasses clinked. Voices sounded all around them. Her drink remained untouched.

He resumed. "I felt, I still feel about it just as you do. Betrayal is inexcusable. Still, when it was not said out loud, I hoped it could ... it could be made not to have happened."

"But it *did* happen, Dad. And you hurt *a lot* of people."

"I know, Terri, I know. But I never intended to."

"Don't." Terri raised her hand as if to push his words away. "You can't use that as an excuse."

Jacob looked at the table. "That day in Seattle, I was back in pre-war Germany. Don't you see? I had been warmed up by a 'good cop'—Dougherty—and I ... I caved. That time, that fatal time, they won."

Terri didn't speak. His hand again lay on the table.

"Why did I say that 'yes'—that simple syllable, that single sound that ruined my life, hers, yours, and your mother's? Simply, I saw those men at the hearing as the same men who had beaten me and had almost thrown me into prison or worse, the men of my nightmares and waking dread." He paused.

"I was a coward."

Terri stirred, but said nothing. The room and all the people seemed frozen around them.

"There. I said it. It's what everyone has always thought, what I've always known."

At last, he met her gaze frankly, openly.

"Mine has been a life of betrayal and being betrayed ... confronting power, running away from power ... the power others exercise over you followed by your surrender. That was my greatest sin. I've never forgiven myself for almost destroying Francesca—"

"—and Mom and me." Terri leaned forward. "Do you still love Francesca?"

Drunken laughter erupted behind them. Jacob's face remained an impassive mask, but his trembling voice betrayed his emotion. "Terri, I love you and your mother, but you met Francesca. You spent time with her. You must know I could never forget her."

Tears filled Terri's eyes, tears of compassion and tears of deep hurt—for herself, her mother, and their links to this man who had exposed his soul to her. She had heard what, deep inside, she already knew. Her father had been honest at last, and his honesty had reached far back, beyond her childhood.

She heard his small voice, almost childlike. "Do you understand now?"

What could she say?

"Jeremy's waiting for us, Dad, and Mom is too. Let's all get together tomorrow." She took his hand.

To the Reader

Characters
The five principal characters—Jacob and his great love Francesca
as well as Lisa, his second wife, Terri his daughter and her Jeremy—all
exist in the open range of my imagination, together with most of the
other figures in my book like Katya and Ahern or Mike Simonetti.
Only those who were actually involved in the hearings have been
taken directly from life (See footnote in Chapter 9), and even among
them, the private investigator Gerald Dougherty is a product of
fiction.

As source and core of the mystery, however, the painter Gregor
Matthäus casts his shadow from the wings. This brilliant artist and his
role in the plot is completely imagined. Still, some of the paintings
that appear in the book may be reminiscent of the work of Eduard
Bargheer, whose art I have always admired.

The following books and documents are listed for the convenience
of the reader:

The War in Italy and its Aftermath:

Botjer, George F. *The Sideshow War. The Italian Campaign 1943-
1945.* Texas A&M military history series #49, 1996. This book includes
various pertinent discussions of the role of the partisans (the Committee
of National Liberation or CLN) in relation to the Communists and
Socialists as part of an overall anti-monarchical coalition opposed to the
German occupation. It also includes a close description of the battles
surrounding the Allied capture of Florence and the campaign against the
so-called Gothic Line, which ran between Florence and Bologna.

Keegan, John. *The Second World War.* Penguin Books, 1989. In an
exhaustive history of the Second World War in both European and
Pacific theaters, this British military historian devotes twenty-five
succinct pages (pp. 344-369) to the Italian war and its ramifications in
the Balkans, which explain, among others, the struggle of the partisans
in Northeast Italy and the Yugoslav border.

Lamb, Richard. *War in Italy 1943-1945. A Brutal Story.* New York:
St. Martin's Press, 1994. An Italian-speaking officer who served in the
British Eighth Army tells the history of the campaign from the fall of

Mussolini in September 1943 until the end of the war in May 1945, on the basis of documents newly available in Italian archives.

About the struggles within the partisan movement between Communists and non-Communists he has this to say, quoting from a newspaper account in Bern, Switzerland of 20 December 1943: "Today it can be stated that all Italian partisans are under a single powerful and well-organized leadership. Since 1 November all activities have been directed by the National Committee of Liberation [CLN]....The situation was especially difficult, as the Communists organized the first partisan groups in the beginning...This resulted in clashes and it soon appeared as if the partisan groups intended to fight each other rather than the enemy. The CLN succeeded in intervening and after much argument was able to place the Communists under the command of a Supreme Commander." (p.205).

Merrill, Charles. *The Journey. Massacre of the Innocents*. Cambridge, MA: Kenet Media, 1996. A richly documented memoir, which contains a vivid account of the Italian war from the landing in Salerno to Florence, the Gothic Line, and beyond, with a few succinct details, including the theft of important German documents by an Italian patriot. (pp. 33-50).

Morante, Elsa. *History: A Novel*. (translated from the Italian by William Weaver). New York: Alfred A. Knopf, 1977. A novel that gives a vivid account, from a left wing point of view, of the agony of living in Italy during this crucial time. It will illuminate for the reader the brutal atmosphere that prevailed in Italy before, during, and after the military campaign.

Puzzo, Dante. *The Partisans and the War in Italy*. Studies in Modern European History. New York: Peter Lang, 1992. Puzzo's conclusion explains the dramatic situation, which underlies the tensions in this story. "The partisan threat to the established order in Italy would have been far greater if partisan unity had been less a matter of military necessity and more one of ideological commitment." The coalition consisted of Communist, Actionist, and conservative forces represented by the Christian Democrats (the pro-Catholic party). Puzzo also noted that "of the three European resistance movements, Tito's Yugoslavs, the Greek ELAS, and the Italian partisans, it was only the Italians who relinquished their arms and disbanded, seeking to gain through the electoral process what they were reluctant to essay by armed strength." (pp. 95-97).

Maria de Blasio Wilhelm, *The Other Italy. The Italian Resistance in World War II.* New York: W. W. Norton, 1988. Perhaps the most useful book about the partisan movement, which I want to share with my readers. Helpfully, this book includes, among others, a perceptive and informative chapter on "Women of the Resistance." "There were also many women who fought alongside the partisans. Of these 35,000 women, 5,000 were imprisoned. 650 were executed or died in combat, and 17 were awarded gold medals for valor. For the first time in Italian history, large numbers of women were partners with men, fighting together as equals for a common cause." (p.119)

The Cold War in Seattle and the University of Washington

The following books, articles, Web sites, etc. form the basis of a historical record, where even some of the places and buildings correspond to reality, while the work as a whole is a product of my imagination.

Official documents:

Second Report: Un-American Activities in Washington State, 1948: Report of the Joint Fact Finding Committee on Un-American Activities. Established by the Thirteenth Legislature under House Concurrent Resolution No. 10. Rep Albert F. Canwell, Chairman. See also footnote on page 87.

Communism and Academic Freedom: The Record of the Tenure Cases at the University of Washington, including the findings of the Committee on Tenure and Academic Freedom and the President's Recommendations. Seattle: University of Washington Press, 1949.

Important Sources:

The Cold War and Red Scare in Washington State, edited by Michael Reese, including forty-six documents under the Web site http/www.washington.edu. An extremely useful curriculum project for Washington schools.

Gilmore, Susan, "Fear Walked the Streets: The Cold War and Albert Canwell, *The Seattle Times Magazine (Sunday, August 2, 1998)*, pp.12-22. This edition of the Sunday Magazine of the *Seattle Times* commemorates the fiftieth anniversary of the hearings. In addition to Susan Gilmore's informative essay, the edition contains many useful photographic mementos.

Jenkins, Mark F. *All Powers Necessary and Convenient*. Seattle: University of Washington Press, 2000. This is the publication in book form of a play performed to good success as part of the fiftieth anniversary in July, 1998. Using the correct names of the people involved in these hearings, it represents one of the most moving portraits of this painful moment in history.

"McCarthyism in the Pacific Northwest," Commemorative issue of the *Pacific Northwest Quarterly*, edited by John M. Findley. 89 (Winter 1997-98): 3-32.

Rader, Melvin. *False Witness.* Seattle: University of Washington Press, 1969. One of the intended victims, Professor Melvin Rader (named Professor Richards in this story), who was an active liberal but no Communist, was persecuted by the Committee with false evidence. His book is a forceful exposé of the Committee's methods.

Sanders, Jane. *Cold War on the Campus: Academic Freedom at the University of Washington, 1946-64.* Seattle: University of Washington Press, 1979. A full scholarly study of the changing picture of academic freedom at the university before, during and after the hearings. This book has been an essential tool in developing the historical base of this novel.

Wick, Nancy. "Seeing Red," *Columns, University of Washington Alumni Magazine,* 17 (December 1997) #4, 16-21. One response in a collection of responses to the hearings, many of which were supportive of the committee, others of the accused professors.

In addition to these sources, I found considerable material in the Manuscript and Archives Division of the University of Washington Libraries (Karyl Winn, Curator).

Until her untimely death, Professor Lore Metzger, my late partner, strongly supported this project to turn fact into fiction through her erudite suggestions and keen insights.

About the Author

Ralph Freedman, who grew up in Nazi Germany, emigrated at nineteen to England and ultimately the United States. He served in the US Army during World War II, in Tunisia, Sicily and Italy, afterwards graduating from the University of Washington and earning a doctorate at Yale. He taught 12 years at the University of Iowa, 22 at Princeton and for two post-retirement years at Emory University. He wrote and published a novel (*Divided*, 1948), criticism (*The Lyrical Novel*, 1953), biographies of Hesse (1978), Rilke (1996), and many essays. His works have been translated into German, French, Italian, Spanish, Korean, and Japanese. A Chinese version is in press. He loves hiking, travel and good talk.